GW00494116

THE REMAINS OF
SHERLOCK HOLMES

THE REMAINS OF SHERLOCK HOLMES

by

Paul W. Nash

Strawberry Books

MMXI

ISBN 978 1 872333 54 0

Dr Paul W. Nash hereby asserts his moral rights
as the author of this book

Printed in the UK by MPG Biddles Ltd, King's Lynn

Designed and typeset in Baskerville
by Armand Dill

Published by Strawberry Books
19 Fosseway Drive, Moreton-in-the-Marsh,
Gloucestershire GL56 0DU
books@strawberrypress.co.uk

First edition, first impression

Author's Note and Dedication

You will read opposite that 'Dr Paul W. Nash hereby asserts his moral rights as the author of this book'. However, I am more than happy to acknowledge that the characters of Sherlock Holmes, Dr John Watson, Mrs Hudson, Professor Moriarty, Lestrade and Gregson are the original creations of Sir Arthur Conan Doyle (1859–1930). I have, I hope, used them in the spirit, and without distressing the spirit, of their creator.

I would like to thank the editor of *Ellery Queen Mystery Magazine* (Dell Magazines, New York, NY) for first publishing 'The adventure of the scarlet thorn' in February 2010 . A version of 'The mystery of Dorian Gray' was published as a pamphlet by Strawberry Books in 2005. Special thanks are due to the late Dennis Felstead, my partner's father, who kindly posed for the image of Holmes in old age used on the jacket of this edition, which is dedicated to the memory of:

SIR ARTHUR CONAN DOYLE (1859–1930)

and

DENNIS ALFRED FELSTEAD (1917–2009)

Contents

Editor's Note

When the premises of Lloyd's Bank Ltd at 16 Charing Cross, London, were damaged by bombing in 1941 it was believed that all Dr John H. Watson's unpublished case-notes had been destroyed, along with the commonplace-books and papers of Sherlock Holmes. Watson had deposited his case-notes there around 1920, when the building was owned by Cox and Company, regimental agents, and added Holmes's papers following the reported death of the detective in 1929. However, in late March 1930, an iron deedbox, painted black and with the initials 'J. H. W.' in white on the lid, was deposited in the vaults of the London and Westminster Bank (now part of the National Westminster Bank) in Marylebone High Street, under the strict condition that it should not be opened for eighty years. When, on 1 April 2010, the Manager of the Marylebone branch opened the box, it was found to be stuffed with manuscripts, well preserved and easily legible. This material was quickly identified as a series of unpublished memoirs of the cases of Sherlock Holmes, fully-formed and complete, written in Watson's characteristic neat hand between around 1890 and 1930. A short note attached to the inside of the lid of the box recorded that the stories had been kept from the public at the request of their subject, but that it was the author's intention that they should one day be published, if it was felt they were of sufficient interest.

The seven stories which follow have been selected from among the fifty-six previously unknown cases uncovered in 2010. They have been placed in chronological order, and lightly edited to remove occasional inconsistencies and mis-spellings. A few footnotes have been added where it was felt these might be helpful. Apart from these modest interventions, the text is presented precisely as it was written by John H. Watson.

P. W. N.

I

The Adventure of the Surrey Giant

IN THE SPRING OF THE YEAR 1882 I had been lodging with Sherlock Holmes for little more than a year, and had already assisted in a number of his cases. At this period his practice as a consulting detective was not so busy as it became by the middle of that decade, and my friend's name was hardly known to the public. Holmes was busy enough that spring, however, and I find among my notes records of several important adventures from this period. The story of the Third Boot and the death of the Wimbledon Seer are both worthy of publication,[1] but perhaps the most interesting problem of the period was the appearance and apparent crimes of a giant in the secluded town of Wartonholm in Surrey. In truth I had intended to publish the details shortly after the case was concluded, and had gone so far as to include an incomplete version of the story, along with two others, in a small volume of memoirs which I arranged to have printed in 1883. But the book was lost in circumstances connected with the case I have called 'The Adventure of Nightingale Hall' and the story has never yet been told in print.[2] It was a grotesque business, and I cannot remember one which came to our attention in a more sudden or unexpected manner. In March and April of that year Holmes had busied himself with the Freeman forgery case, and one morning he received a telegram at breakfast which made him sit bolt upright in his chair.

1. Both stories mentioned were among those found in the vaults of the National Westminster Bank in 2010.
2. The Nightingale Hall story was not among those found in 2010. For details of the lost 'memoirs' of Dr Watson see *The Private Library* (Spring 2006, pp. 9–13).

'What is it?' I asked.

'This Freeman business,' he replied. 'Lestrade has blundered and the man is ready to fly. I must go at once.'

'Can I be of help?'

Holmes nodded. 'Can you be ready in five minutes? Capital!' He sprang from his chair.

'Shall I bring my revolver?'

'I should say not, Watson. Our man is as crooked a devil as I have come across, but he is probably the greatest coward in London. We have only to bar his path, and he will be caught.'

'Why then does Lestrade need your help?'

'Because no policeman has yet laid eyes upon the forger, while I have met him twice, in the person of an unscrupulous bookseller, and can identify him to Lestrade.'

We dressed hurriedly and ran out into the street, where Holmes hailed a cab.

'To the East India Docks,' he said to the cabman, 'and here's a guinea if we arrive before ten o'clock!' The man whipped up his horse and we sped away along Baker Street. 'That is the hour the *Patagonia* is due to depart,' said Holmes when we were under way. 'Lestrade's telegram begged me to meet him at the Docks, where we must prevent one particular passenger from ...'

His words were cut short, however, by a most singular occurrence. As we raced towards the southern end of Baker Street an unusually small man in a black bowler and a long brown coat flung himself from the pavement directly into the path of our cab. It was all the driver could do to bring his horse up in time, and Holmes and I were dashed forward as he pulled on the brake and dragged at the reins. The horse stopped within two feet of the unfortunate man, who lay face down in the street before us, apparently insensible. I have seldom heard Holmes use strong language, unless in the character of a sailor or other common man, but he cursed then. We recovered ourselves and leapt from the hansom to see what might be done for the fellow. I felt his pulse, which was strong and rapid, and gently turned him over. He groaned and a little blood dripped from the corner of his mouth. His face was smeared with dirt from the road and his hat had rolled into the gutter, revealing his fair, wavy hair. Then his eyes blinked open and he came to himself.

'Sherlock Holmes?' he asked in a high, tremulous voice.

'I am Holmes,' said my friend severely.

'Are you injured?' I asked.

'No, no,' he replied, 'I must talk with you, sir. It is a matter of the gravest importance.'

Holmes turned to me. 'Is this man seriously hurt?' he asked. I shook my head. The blood on his cheek appeared to come from a small cut in his lower lip, caused no doubt by his collision with the road, but I could detect no other marks of injury. 'Then I must go,' said Holmes curtly.

'No, no,' begged the man.

'Watson here will look after you. I shall be back at Baker Street before eleven-thirty.'

The man raised a trembling hand, but Holmes was back in the cab before he could frame an appeal, and I caught a glimpse of my friend's pale face peering back at us from the window of the departing hansom. I helped the little man to his feet. He brushed down his soiled coat, wiped his face with a pale yellow handkerchief and retrieved his hat from where it had fallen. The small crowd of onlookers which had gathered on the pavement began to disperse.

'I am sorry,' he said, 'to have acted so precipitously. But there were no cabs available at Waterloo, and I have run all the way here to consult Mr Holmes. When I saw two men emerge from his address and climb into a cab I was horrified at the thought of missing him, and decided I must stop him at all costs. But now I have lost him!'

'Have no fear,' I replied. 'He will soon return. In the meantime, let us wait in comfort, and perhaps you will tell me of your problem while we wait. I have assisted Holmes in several of his recent cases.' We began to walk back along the street.

'Thank you, sir, but what I have to tell is of a most delicate character, and I can only confide it to Mr Holmes himself.'

'Very well. But perhaps you would favour me with your name.'

The little man mastered himself, paused, bowed and handed me a card upon which was printed the name Featherstone Molloy, and the address The Larches, Wartonholm, Surrey.[3]

I introduced myself, and soon we arrived at the door of number 221. Once in our rooms, I invited Molloy to sit and take some refreshment, but he declined and spent the next two hours pacing the carpet, stopping only to peer from the window every few minutes. My attempts to engage him in conversation were met with monosyllables. As the half hour approached, and passed, Molloy became increasingly agitated. It was nearly five-and-twenty past twelve when we heard the sound of a cab pulling up at the door, and Molloy rushed to the window.

'It is he!' he cried. It was all I could do to prevent him racing from the room to meet my friend at the door. Holmes trod the stairs with painful slowness and, when he entered the room, it was clear that all had not proceeded smoothly at the Docks. There was a dark swelling beneath his left eye, and his face was troubled.

3. The original *carte-de-visite* was pinned to the manuscript of this story, and is reproduced here.

'Did your man escape?' I asked.

'No, we have him. But he proved a rather harder opponent than expected. He fought like a tiger, knocked a constable unconscious and managed to throw the plates into the Dock before we mastered him. It will be a hard job to recover the package as the Dock is very deep there, and it will have sunk into the mud. But we have our man. Now, let me take a little tobacco and an easy-chair, and I shall be ready to listen to our new friend who took such extreme measures to meet me.'

Molloy was so tense now as to be almost paralysed and stood quite rigid before the window, while Holmes removed his street clothes and filled his pipe from the Persian slipper. At length he sat before the fire, smiled at Molloy and invited him to tell his story.

'What I have to say is of the greatest import and delicacy,' he said, casting a sideways glance at me.

'Doctor Watson has materially assisted me in several of my recent cases and you may speak before him as you would before me.'

'Very well. My name is Featherstone Molloy, and I am a man in hell. In short, Mr Holmes, my only cause of joy, my Sophia, has been taken from me, and the police seem to have abandoned their investigation. Please help me, sir. I am at my wits' end to know what to do. She was murdered, sir, murdered I say, and yet the police blame Craddock and say that nothing can be done.'

'Mr Molloy,' said Holmes in his most soothing voice. 'Pray pause a moment and begin your narrative again, telling it from the beginning and with as much detail as you can. Perhaps a glass of brandy would help you, after the rigours of the morning.' I poured Molloy a large brandy and he tossed it back. 'Now, take a seat and tell us everything.'

'Thank you, sir.' Molloy at last took the chair beside the fireplace, facing Holmes. 'I have lived at Wartonholm in Surrey, with my younger brother Benedict, for the past nine years. My father made his fortune in the 'sixties from an original invention, a species of cardboard faced with aluminium foil, which he called "Alucard".[4] After father's death, we bought The Larches and settled into village life. Wartonholm is an ancient place, very picturesque, with only twenty or so houses, among which ours is by far the largest. At first I spent most of my time here in town, attending to business, dining with friends, or at the Goliath Club.' At the mention of this institution Holmes raised his eyebrows but made no comment. 'As the years passed I came to enjoy the country life, until only the pleasures of the Club could tempt me to leave my rural home. Who would have thought that there too I could find love? Sophia Carter was the daughter of the local schoolmaster, and the most beautiful woman I had ever seen. It is strange to think that such a small town should beget such a pearl as she. I am not a young man, Mr Holmes, being nearly forty, and I had never thought to marry. But when I found Sophia my mind, and heart, were changed. She had had many suitors, but had spurned them all, and was herself not quite so young as she looked. I pressed my suit and, at length, became the happiest man alive when she consented to be my wife. If you had asked me the day before yesterday what the future held for me, I would have said nothing but joy and satisfaction. But that was before she was taken from me. I learned about it yesterday morning, when the police came to call.

'Sophia lived in her own cottage – she was very independent-minded – and it was here that she was murdered during the night. Her head ...' he paused, his mouth twitching with suppressed emotion. 'Her head was broken in, sir, with some heavy

---

4. This invention, Alucard, was renamed 'Alumincard' in 1898 when it was pointed out that the trade-name was a reversal of the title of Bram Stoker's novel *Dracula* (1897). This was probably a co-incidence, although it has been suggested that Stoker reversed the name of Molloy's invention to create his infamous vampire. The new name Alumincard did not catch on, and the firm which held the patent, then named Molloy and Bride, was declared Bankrupt in 1902.

object. The window of her bedroom was smashed in too, and the police believed at first that a burglar had broken in and killed her in panic. But then they found curious traces in the flower-bed beneath her window, and gathered stories from some of the locals that made them think again.

'In the village there are many legends, but perhaps the oldest and most curious is that of the giant Craddock. He is said to live out on the Downs, in a kind of earth, and to go hunting at night with a great club. Legend has it that there were originally two giants living there, Cardon and Cora. They were man and wife and had a son, called Craddock. The villagers were afraid of the giants, and one night got together a party of brave men to drive them out. They attacked the giants, and killed Cardon and Cora, but Craddock, who was just a child, escaped by digging himself an earth and hiding in it. It was said that he bore great malice towards the people of Wartonholm for the killing of his parents, and would sometimes come into the village at night and make havoc, smashing windows with his club and stealing animals for his food. Of course, I paid little attention to such stories. They were very ancient, and mothers used them to frighten disobedient children. There was nothing I could see of truth in the tale of Craddock.

'Then, about a year ago, one of the villagers said he had seen the giant. He was an old man, and given to drink, so no one believed him. But later others looked out of their windows at night and saw a tall figure in the moonlight, too tall to be a normal man. Other traces were found, and soon windows, high windows, were smashed and precious things taken from upstairs rooms. The villagers blamed Craddock, but I thought little of the stories, believing some local thief to be at work. I still cannot believe in the reality of this brutal giant. And yet, beneath the smashed window of my Sophia's bedroom, the police found a gigantic footprint.'

Holmes leaned forward in his chair. 'Did you see the footprint?' he asked.

'No, sir. But the police described it to me. It was nineteen inches long. What manner of man has feet nineteen inches long?'

'What manner of man, indeed? Was it the print of a shoe, or of a bare foot?'

'A bare foot. The police seem to believe that Craddock was responsible for my Sophia's death, and have abandoned the search for a human killer. They are out on the Downs now, looking for a giant, Mr Holmes, for a legend! I am at my wits' end! But last night I remembered how a friend at the Goliath Club, Dr Carroll of Kensington, told me you had cleared up a little problem for him last year, when the police had despaired of the case. So I found out your address, and took the first train here this morning. Can you, will you, help me?'

'I will look into the matter,' said Holmes gravely. 'There are several points of interest in your story, and I have hopes that we may cast a little light into the darkness. I have a good deal of work on hand at present, and this Freeman business is far from concluded, but I shall travel down to Wartonholm tomorrow and spend a day there. Is there a local inn where we can stay?'

'Yes, the Black Horse. But you would be most welcome to room at The Larches. We have several bedrooms for guests.'

'I thank you, but I would prefer to lodge at the inn. I fear I can only spare the time to stay one day at Wartonholm. After that I must return to London, but perhaps the good Doctor would agree to stay on in my stead and continue the investigation.'

Holmes glanced in my direction. It was the first time he had made any such suggestion, and I confess my breast swelled a little with pride. 'I should be pleased to do what I can,' I said.

Molloy looked disappointed and seemed on the point of raising some objection. But he thought better of it and said, somewhat dejectedly, 'If that is all you can manage, then I shall be most grateful for it. Thank you. Now I must rest. I have not slept for twenty-four hours and have been very full of my tale. Now it is told I am passing weary.'

He stood and I handed him his hat and coat. 'I shall stay at the Goliath Club tonight. The first train for Reigate, which is the nearest station to Wartonholm, is at eight tomorrow morning. Perhaps we could meet at Waterloo and share a compartment?'

'Certainly.'

'Thank you. I shall wire my brother and ask him to meet us at Reigate tomorrow morning.'

'Just one question before you go,' said Holmes. 'Who is in charge of the police investigation in Surrey?'

Molloy sighed. 'An Inspector Raven, sir. A most incomprehensible man, who speaks English in great volumes yet leaves me wondering what on earth he has said.'

Holmes scribbled the Inspector's name in his pocket-book and bade our client farewell.

When Molloy had departed Holmes rubbed his hands together and smiled to himself. 'This promises to be a most amusing case,' he said.

'Amusing? The murder of a young woman?'

'A tragedy, of course. But look at the circumstances, my boy! The legend of the giant, and the evidence of his great footprint!'

'But surely, you cannot give credence to such a story?'

'The police evidently take it seriously. But I cannot afford the time or mental energy to consider the matter further at present. I must give myself to this Freeman business so that I can leave for Reigate tomorrow with a clear head.'

The next morning we met Molloy at Waterloo as arranged, and shared a compartment for the journey to Reigate. Molloy's chin and lip were swollen and dark now with bruising, where he had thrown himself face-down in the street before our cab. He was morose and hardly said two words throughout the journey, though Holmes tried to draw him into conversation several times on such matters as Sullivan's recent taking of the bare-knuckle crown in Mississippi and the new electric lighting at the Savoy.

When we arrived at Reigate we found two men waiting for us outside the station. One was so similar in appearance to Featherstone Molloy, with the same pale, wavy hair and slight build, that he could only be our client's brother Benedict. The other man was introduced to us as Inspector Charles Raven of the Surrey Police. He was a ruddy-faced man of portly build and little taller than Molloy.

'Good morning, Mr Holmes,' said Raven. 'Mr Molloy here asked me to join the reception party, though I don't quite understand what a private person such as yourself can do in such a case, sir. I understand, however, that you have a certain reputation in certain matters and, therefore, I am willing to approach the question with a certain freeness.'

'You are most kind,' said Holmes.

A handsome coach and four was waiting for us, and as I approached I could not help but notice a brilliant crest incorporating ostrich feathers on the door, somewhat in the manner of the arms of the Prince of Wales. Benedict noticed my glances, and said proudly, 'Our new crest, sir, granted to us last month by the College of Arms.'

When we were about to climb into the coach I touched Holmes's arm and reminded him in an undertone that our client was stricken with grief, and questions to the Inspector had better not touch on such matters as the murdered girl's injuries. He snorted dismissively, as if to suggest that no such lack of tact could ever be ascribed to him, and on the journey from Reigate to Wartonholm he seemed disinclined to talk at all. Despite the comfort of the coach, the long journey passed slowly due to the downcast mood of the Molloys, Holmes's reticence and the Inspector's evident bashfulness.

We approached Wartonholm after more than an hour of bumping along country roads, through a landscape which would no doubt have been beautiful in the summer, but was bare and lifeless now. Just outside the village we passed a circus, encamped on the Downs, whose painted tents and scarlet pennants gave a sudden merriment to the scene. Holmes gazed keenly at the camp as we passed, and I fancied a faint smile came to his lips.

Featherstone instructed the coachman to stop at the Black Horse, and we alighted. Wartonholm was, as Molloy had suggested, a very pretty village, consisting of a cluster of stone houses and cottages, the inn itself, a combined Post Office and general store, a schoolhouse and a small church with a spire. Featherstone pointed out The Larches, an imposing villa set a little apart from the other houses, behind a high stone wall, and repeated his invitation to lodge there. Again Holmes declined.

'Perhaps then you would dine with us this evening,' said Featherstone.

'We should be honoured,' said Holmes, bowing slightly.

'Is there anything we can do to help?' asked Benedict.

'You and your brother would do well, I think, to return home and rest. Try not to brood upon this business. I will no doubt have some questions for you this evening, but, in the mean time, please be assured that I will give the case my full attention for the next few hours. Perhaps the Inspector would show me Miss Carter's cottage?'

Raven assented and, when we had said farewell to the brothers Molloy and left our luggage at the inn, he led us along the main street of Wartonholm and down a side road. Almost at the end stood a small, neat cottage with tall chimneys and bi-coloured brickwork. Above the door was a window which we could see even from the street had been smashed, and was now blocked with a sheet of cardboard. At the gate Holmes asked us to wait, and approached the cottage with his habitual slow care, examining the path, the verges and flowerbeds until he reached the front door. He took out his glass and scrutinised the doorstep, then beckoned us to join him.

'See here,' he said, indicating an empty bed beside the door. 'The ground is soft, and it has not rained for several days.' Sure enough, deeply impressed in the dark earth was a huge footprint, almost twice as large as any I had seen. It was pointed towards the cottage, directly beneath the broken window. Holmes measured it carefully with a tailor's tape, then indicated a second, partial footprint at the furthest extremity of the bed. 'No doubt this singular trail will lead us somewhere. Please follow me at a distance.' He walked to the corner of the building and disappeared round it. We followed, and watched as he examined and measured a series of footprints that extended all the way round the cottage, as if the giant had circled it, seeking ingress, before returning to the street where the trail was lost on the cobblestones. Once this itinerary was complete, we returned to the lawn behind the house where Holmes invited us to look more closely at the trail.

'Here is the left footprint of our giant,' he said, indicating an impression in the grass, 'and here the right. How far apart would you say they are, Watson?'

'About five feet,' I answered.

'Quite so. Now, clearly, a man's height may be deduced from the length of his stride, and we may presume the same rules can be applied to a giant, who is after all no more than a very large man. I am six feet high, and my stride is approximately two feet long. The calculation is a simple one. A man with a stride of five feet must be some fifteen feet in height.' The Inspector drew in his breath but said nothing. 'Have you ever heard of such a man?'

'Goliath of Gath stood six Hebrew cubits and a span,' said Raven slowly.

'How does that translate into feet and inches?'

'Nine feet, six inches, sir.'

'Bravo, Inspector! But still a little short of our fifteen feet, I fear. Do you have a description of this singular individual?'

'All witnesses agree that he is very tall, sir, very tall indeed.'

'How is he dressed?'

'In a long, dark coat or cloak, and a large hat or hood which covers much of his face.'

'What does he carry?'

'Some have seen him with a heavy stick or club.'

'How many witnesses do you have?'

'Five now, including Mrs Almond, the old woman who lives in the house opposite Sophia's cottage.'

'When did she see the giant?'

'Twice, sir, once walking down a certain road past her house, and then again a few days later, peering in at the window of a certain cottage.'

'This cottage?'

'Indeed.'

'And when was that?'

'The night before the murder.'

'I see.' Holmes's brows came together for a moment. 'Did the good lady happen to mention whether the giant was crouching, or bending, to look into Miss Carter's window?'

'Crouching or bending, sir?'

'Yes, yes. The window is some eleven feet from the ground, and we have already established that our giant must be fifteen feet tall. He must therefore have bent or crouched to look in at the window.'

'The lady said nothing about the matter sir, but I will take it upon myself to put to her a certain question …'

'That is very good of you, Inspector. Now, perhaps we might see the room where the unfortunate girl was killed? Thank you.'

We returned to the front of the cottage, where Raven opened the front door, which was not locked. Indeed, the lock had clearly been forced, and the jamb was shattered on the inside. 'Is this your work, Inspector?' asked Holmes.

'Yes, sir, I had to force the door.'

'Aside from the broken window, was there any evidence of burglary?'

'None. The house was locked up tight.'

We entered, Holmes leading the way with his glass in his hand. 'I see from your boot-prints in the hall that you were alone when you broke into the house, Inspector. Is it not usual to bring at least one constable with you on such an expedition?'

'It is. But there is no constable living in the village, while I have my home here. The Police Station is in the next town, so my house serves as a certain outpost of the Constabulary ...'

'How did you know that something was amiss?'

'It was Pedderborn, the naturalist. He lives in a certain house in the village, and was expecting Sophia to come to him that morning to undertake certain work of a secretarial character. When she failed to keep the appointment, he walked round to her cottage and knocked on the door. Receiving no answer, and seeing the window broken, he came at once to my house and roused me to action ...'

'What did you find when you entered the house?'

'All was quiet, just as it is now. I called out her name – Sophia – but there was no answer. I looked round downstairs, and everything seemed to be in order. Then I went upstairs and found ... a certain scene. The window had been smashed in and glass was spread across the sill and floor. The fire had burned out and the young lady lay upon the bed. She might have been sleeping, save that her head was a bloody mess.'

Raven seemed, I thought, unduly moved by this recollection. No London policeman would allow himself to show feeling for a murdered woman in this way. But, I reflected, it was probably most unusual for a rural Inspector to come across such a brutal crime and he must have known the victim at least by sight. Holmes's mind was evidently working along similar lines, for he next asked Raven how well he had known Miss Carter.

'Not well, sir. But I passed her in the street, of course, and we exchanged certain words of a friendly character ...'

We climbed the stairs and came to the bedroom. It was a dark, narrow room at the front of the house, with a bed against the wall opposite the window and a small fireplace beside the door. There was also a nightstand with a bowl and jug of water, and a small wardrobe at the far end. The bed had been stripped, but the pillow and under-sheet that remained were horribly stained with dried blood.

Holmes asked us to remain at the door as he crossed to the window and carefully removed the cardboard that covered the shattered panes, admitting the weak spring sunlight. It glinted on the fragments of glass that extended across the sill and over the rug which covered the floor. The window was about three feet by two, with two panes, one of which could be opened, and both of which had been smashed. Holmes began to conduct a close study of the bedroom, measuring the distance from the window to the bed, turning over the ashes in the grate and examining the logs, the washstand and the wardrobe.

'Thank you, Inspector. I have finished here,' he said. 'Where is Sophia's body now?'

'She is due to be removed to the Police Station at Laxton, the next town, sir, tomorrow morning, for examination by the Police surgeon. But at present she is in my dining room.'

'I see. When will she be buried?'

'The inquest will be on Friday, sir, and Sophia will probably be interred on Sunday. Although the weather has a certain cold-ness of character we cannot afford to leave a body unburied for more than a week …'

'Might we be permitted to see her?' asked Holmes. 'I should very much like Dr Watson to give his opinion.'

'I do not see any objection.'

We quitted the cottage and walked back to the main road of Wartonholm, where Raven took us to a middle-sized house facing directly onto the street. He unlocked the door and took us into his dining room, where a body was laid out on the table, covered with a sheet. Holmes drew it back.

The face and hair of Sophia Carter had evidently been washed, for there was little trace of blood there now. It was clear that she had been a very beautiful woman. Her hair was of a pale golden colour, tending almost to silver where the sunlight struck it, and her skin was pale and delicate, albeit with a slight puckering round the eyes and corners of the mouth, the first witnesses of relentless time. Her figure was slight, though she must have been at least as tall as her *fiancé*, and may have risen above him by an inch or two. The left temporal and much of the parietal bone of her skull had been smashed, though her face was unharmed and peaceful, her eyes closed. The wound had been carefully cleaned, but was still grisly enough. Holmes examined it closely, then asked my opinion.

'A single blow,' I said. 'To the side of the head, with a heavy, rounded object.'

'Like a club?' asked Raven.

'Indeed. I would say, from the appearance of her face and body, that she was struck as she slept and died instantly, without waking.'

'Her face must have been turned towards the window,' said Holmes, gently gripping her head and attempting to turn it to the left. *Rigor mortis* was too advanced, however, and he was obliged to leave her as she was, facing the ceiling of the room. The Inspector winced at this interference with the corpse, but said nothing. Holmes was intent upon the body, however, and did not notice. He bent even closer to the dead woman's head, and carefully drew her hair away from her left ear. 'Have you some tweezers in your bag, Doctor?' he asked. I produced the instrument and he gently inserted it into Sophia's ear and drew out a dark, pellet-like object, which he dropped into an envelope and put away in his pocket. 'Would the murderer have been marked with blood?' he asked.

'It was a blow of such force,' I replied, 'that blood and cerebral fluid must have splashed onto the killer's hand and clothes.'

'I also found droplets of blood on the wall,' remarked Raven.

'Quite so.' Holmes's eyes narrowed as he regarded the Inspector. 'And who do you believe killed your Sophia?'

'She was not *my* Sophia, sir!'

'Come, come, Inspector. I am not such a simpleton in matters of the heart. You held Miss Carter in very high regard. You have referred to her repeatedly by her forename, and, I believe, took upon yourself the duty of cleaning and beautifying her remains, once you had them under your roof. Aside from that, your emotions betray you in every word you say about her.'

'Well, sir, I cannot deny a certain feeling of a ... reverent character. Sophia was a lovely girl, and I could not help but feel a certain attachment. But I am a married man, sir, and entertained no thoughts of an improper character. Any emotions I had for the lady were of a discreet character ...'

'She did not know of your feelings, then?'

'I never once told her of them.'

'That is not quite the same thing. I repeat my question.'

'Sometimes there was a certain look in her eyes, a look of a kindly character, which led me to believe she had detected a certain sympathy on my part ...'

'I see. We will leave the matter there, then. But you must know that, in cleaning her face and hair you may have destroyed vital evidence.'

'I examined her very carefully first, sir. And I could not have left her like that, all plastered with filth!'

'Then I return to my first question. Who do you believe killed Sophia?'

'I do not know, sir, and that is the honest truth.'

'What of the giant?'

'I have heard stories of Craddock all my life, and am not ready to deny them yet. Someone made those footprints, and someone killed Sophia. For now the giant is my chief suspect, and I have men out on the Downs, looking for traces of him.'

'Does anyone live on the Downs, nearby.'

'There are several farms, and a band of gypsies sometimes camps there. My men have been instructed to question them closely if they come upon them.'

'I notice that Marshall's Circus is encamped nearby. Does that not strike you as interesting?'

'Perhaps, sir. Circus folk have a certain reputation for wild ways and dishonesty, if that is what you mean.'

'Then you do not know that Marshall is famous across the south of England for his beasts, for Vittoria the trapeze artist, for his dwarf-clowns and for Gregor, the Russian Giant.'

'I had not heard of the Russian Giant, sir,' said Raven, taking out his notebook. 'The circus arrived the very night of the murder, and certain inferences may be made ...'

'Indeed. Now, Dr Watson and I must return to the Black Horse and take some refreshment. It has been a long and tiring, but not entirely unrewarding, morning.'

After we had lunched, Holmes engaged the landlord of the inn in conversation. He was a man of middle age with the flattened nose of a professional pugilist. His name was John Sutter and he seemed almost as moved by Sophia Carter's murder as Raven had been. Holmes introduced himself as a friend of the Molloys, and quickly won the confidence of the landlord, who readily told us all he knew of the villagers. In addition to the Molloys, Raven and a number of maiden ladies, there was a Rector, several families of farm workers employed by Robert Bryce, the local Squire who lived in the Manor House at Laxton, a carpenter named Redmayne, a doctor named Robertson, and Ephraim Pedderborn, the naturalist.

'Is there no schoolmaster?' asked Holmes.

'Not now, sir. That was Sophia's father, Mr Carter, but he died a couple of years back. Now a schoolma'am comes over from Laxton to teach the children.'

'Thank you. May I ask, are any of the villagers, apart from the Molloys, unusually little?'

'Well, now you come to mention it, Josiah Redmayne, the carpenter, is a very small man. But he is a fine worker, sir, and none the worse for his little hands.'

'Thank you.'

That afternoon we visited the Rector and the Doctor, but found both to be elderly and infirm. They could tell us nothing helpful and, as Holmes remarked as we walked towards The Larches to keep our dinner appointment, the murderer of Sophia Carter must have been a young man, or an unusually strong woman, or possibly a giant, and we could therefore exclude anyone frail from our investigation.

Featherstone and Benedict Molloy greeted us warmly, and took pleasure in showing us their home. Each room was filled with fine works of art, books and furniture in the best modern taste, and it was clear the family was indeed a very wealthy one. The Molloys were evidently skilled sportsmen, for there were hunting trophies on the walls and a large cabinet filled with cups and prizes won on the sporting field. Once we were seated at their grand dining table, they questioned Holmes on the progress of the case.

'Do you have hopes?' said Featherstone.

'I have,' replied Holmes. 'But the case presents more difficulties than I had anticipated. Having seen the evidence, I am now convinced that the giant Craddock is no legend.'

'Surely not!' said Featherstone.

'There is no doubt in my mind.'

'And do you believe that Craddock killed my brother's *fiancée*?' asked Benedict.

'That is less clear, though the evidence against the giant is most persuasive.'

'But this is the worst possible news!' wailed Featherstone, wringing his hands. 'I had been told that you were a man of science, a logical man, a man who might see more than the absolutely stupid Raven sees.'

'I do not believe Inspector Raven to be stupid,' said Holmes gravely. 'He may be distracted, but I do not think he is entirely on the wrong trail.'

'I am very glad to hear it,' said Benedict. 'Sophia's killer must be found, be he man or monster.'

'Do you believe, then, that Craddock killed Sophia?' Holmes asked Benedict.

'Well – no, of course not. But if you say that Raven is on the right track, then his hunt on the Downs must turn up the killer, perhaps among the roving gypsies that infest the place.'

'I know,' said Holmes, turning to Featherstone, 'that you were profoundly attached to Miss Carter. I know too that she was a woman of independent mind, and means, and I wonder if I might ask you an impertinent question.' Featherstone looked uneasy, but assented. 'Do you, by any chance, have a key to Miss Carter's cottage?'

'I do. She gave it to me willingly. Indeed, she is – she was a most ... remarkable woman. Sophia was always very discreet, of course, but there were nights, I confess, when I went to her house after dark and did not return until the morning. I would not wish you to think less of Sophia for it. She was a noble soul, a great and kind soul, and wished to share herself with me in a manner which I consider quite beyond reproach. I tell you this because I know you have a high regard for the truth. But I should be extremely obliged if this information were not repeated outside these walls, for the sake of Sophia's name.'

'I believe there may be one further secret for me to keep. When were you to be married?'

'Next month.'

'And when was her confinement due?'

Featherstone covered his face with his hands. 'It is true!' he said. 'She was with child!'

Benedict let out a snort of disapproval, from which I understood that he had known nothing of Sophia's condition.

'We had hoped to save her reputation by pretending the child was born somewhat later than was the case,' cried Featherstone. 'It was only a matter of a few months, and no one would have known! She would have been my wife, and all would have been perfect. But now, you see, the murderer has robbed me not only of my bride, but also of my heir!'

'Indeed,' said Holmes soothingly. 'It would not have been the first time a bridal veil concealed such a secret. A little adjustment of birthdays and calendars would have made all well. I promise you Mr Molloy, that I will not repeat what I have learned here today, unless it is absolutely necessary to bring the murderer to heel. Do you happen to have the key to Miss Carter's cottage about you now? Good. May I see it?'

Featherstone mastered himself, and drew from the fob pocket of his waistcoat a small iron key.

'Have you ever lent it to anyone else, or lost it for a period?'

'No. It has always been here in my pocket, close to my heart.'

Holmes took the key, held it up to the light, examined it briefly with his lens, then did a most curious thing – he licked it, first on one side, then the other.

'What on earth ...?' said Benedict.

'Indulge me, please,' said Holmes, 'I have my own methods, as the Doctor will attest.' I nodded, though I had not the slightest idea what my friend was about. 'Does anyone else have a key to the cottage?'

'Why yes, Mrs Almond, the widow who lives in the house opposite. She and Sophia were good friends, and she gave Mrs Almond a key for safe keeping, in case she ever lost her own.'

'Pray tell me, Mr Holmes,' said Benedict. 'Will you be licking that key also?'

'If it is still in the possession of the good widow,' said Holmes lightly, 'no doubt I will.'

The remainder of the meal passed in near silence. Holmes was wrapped in thought, and the Molloys were too depressed, or shocked, by what had been revealed to engage in conversation. At length the meal came to an end and we made our farewells. I was tired and somewhat disheartened, and expected Holmes to suggest an early night. However, he seemed in an exalted mood and, as we walked away from The Larches, he turned to me and said 'I think a short walk would do us both good.'

31

'A walk? Where to?'

'Oh, out on the Downs a little way. If we hurry we can catch tonight's performance of Marshall's famous circus!'

We arrived at the brightly-lit camp twenty minutes later, and paid a shilling each to see the show. I confess I had not been to a circus since a lad, and found the antics of the clowns a good deal less amusing than most of my fellows in the tent. All the people of the village seemed to be there, and they laughed vigorously as the little dwarves, painted like pierrots and columbines, chased one another round the ring. More entertaining were the trained animals, the lions and the elephant, and the fine display of horse-riding by Vittoria, a young woman of great beauty who leapt upon and bestrode the animals in a manner that was almost indecent. Later she performed upon the trapeze too, drawing many gasps and sighs from the crowd. At last it was the turn of Gregor, the Russian Giant. A little play was acted for us, in which Gregor, in the costume of a Cossack prince, was wheeled into the arena standing in a cart, a captive of a troupe of hideous dwarves, also in Russian dress. His great height was exaggerated by the cart, and the smallness of his captors. After allowing himself to be tormented by the dwarves for some minutes, Gregor cast off the artificial chains that bound him, and took up a huge scimitar which he wielded in a great arc, sending the little men running in all directions. When they were gone the raucous music which had accompanied the play was replaced by a sombre, Russian march, to which Gregor stepped down from the cart and walked ponderously from the ring, waving the scimitar as he went.

After the show, while the people headed back to their houses and farms, Holmes and I sought out the circus folk in their caravans behind the main tent. Marshall himself, a tall figure in a scarlet cape who had presided over the show, was talking with Vittoria (now modestly covered with a cloak) beside one of the animal cages. Holmes introduced himself, and asked if he might be allowed a few words with Gregor. At first Marshall was unwilling, but when Holmes remarked that the police might take a keen interest in the presence of a giant in the vicinity, and might even arrest and remove to prison one of the circus's best attractions if not shown the folly of this course, Marshall quickly agreed. We were taken to a caravan set a little apart from the rest and of unusual height, standing a good four feet taller than the others. On the side was a painted board bearing Gregor's name and image that rose still higher above the roof of the tall caravan.

'How tall is Gregor?' asked Holmes.

'Eight feet, five and one third inches,' said Marshall in ringing tones. 'He is the second tallest living man in the world, since the death last year of Kasim the Magnificent, the Turkish Giant, who stood eight feet, five and two thirds inches from toe to crown.'

'Who then is the tallest man in the world?' I asked, wondering if we might gather yet another suspect for our murder.

Marshall lowered his voice a little. 'I shall not speak too loudly,' said he, 'lest Gregor hear me. He does not like to hear the name, for there is great rivalry among professional giants. His name is George Washington Carver and he is, as the name may suggest to you, an American gentleman just one and a half inches short of nine feet in height. But here we are, gentlemen, and I must beg you not to mention the name of Carver before Gregor, if you value your lives!'

The caravan was in darkness, and it appeared that Gregor was not at home. But Marshall rapped upon the great door, and we heard sounds of movement within.

'I will leave you now, gentlemen,' hissed the circus-owner. 'Remember my words.' He hurried off into the light and hubbub of the camp. Soon a flicker of light could be seen behind the windows of the caravan, then the door opened and we caught a glimpse of a huge body inside. A great, pale hand holding a candlestick emerged, and above it we could see the giant's face, fully twice as large, it seemed, as my own or Holmes's.

'What, have I visitors?' said Gregor in a deep, rich voice. It could hardly be said to sound Russian, however, and struck me rather as of Northern English origin.

'Good evening,' said Holmes, removing his hat. 'My name is Sherlock Holmes, and my friend, Dr Watson, and I are students of humanity in all its forms. We wish to pay our respects to so remarkable a performer.'

'Indeed? How very gratifying. Do come inside. As you will see, there is plenty of room for gentlemen of modest stature.'

He disappeared into the gloom of the caravan, and we climbed the steps after him. The door swung shut behind us, and Gregor lit several further candles until we could see the interior clearly. It was certainly spacious, with a huge bed running along one side, and a similarly large carved wooden chair piled with cushions at one end. Before this were a chair and table of normal size, the latter with a bottle and several brandy glasses upon it. Next to the great chair was a bookcase full of books, and the walls were covered with posters and bills for Gregor's appearances, and those of Marshall's circus, around the country. His Russian costume hung from the back of the door, like a second giant standing silent guard. A pair of enormous leather boots stood beside the bed, and I tried to calculate, without making my interest obvious, if the feet they were made to contain were large enough to have made the footprints we had seen. Gregor himself was now wearing an elegant dressing-gown and red leather slippers.

'Please take a seat, sir,' he said to Holmes. 'I hope you will forgive my informal appearance. I am not accustomed to company, and when I do have a visitor it is usually a single person, so that I have only one chair. Perhaps the Doctor would not mind sitting on the bed.'

'Not at all,' I said.

'Would you care for some brandy, or a cigar?' asked our host. We accepted the brandy gladly, for it was a chilly evening, and I took a cigar also, though Holmes preferred his pipe. In the light of the several candles we could see our host more clearly now. He was even more impressive at close quarters than he had been in the circus ring, and his face had a certain gravity, a beauty even, which had not been evident before. The lower jaw in particular was unusually square and well-formed, and his eyes were dark and sensitive. His hair, which had formerly been hidden by a helmet, was quite white, however, and hung to his massive shoulders, which were stooped, as if his frame could not bear their weight. In the ring this deformity had been hidden by his costume. He drank deeply from the brandy glass, which seemed a tiny bubble in his hand, and said, 'I suppose you gentlemen are interested in the recent murder in Warton-holm? You look surprised. Circus folk usually hear any news or gossip which is circulating in the towns they visit. And when I heard that a giant had been seen, and may have killed a young woman, I wondered how long it would be before the police came to visit.'

'I do not represent the police,' said Holmes. 'I am a consulting detective and follow my own course. But I may have some influence with the official forces. I will do my utmost to convince them to leave you alone.'

'Ha!' said the giant. 'You are convinced then that I am not your murderer?'

'Perfectly. You could not possibly be our man.' He paused. 'I suppose your life and work here are not so onerous, but it must be a great strain for you all the same.'

'You understand! So few do. Every time I perform it grows more difficult, more painful. But I have my compensations. There is my brandy, and my books, and sometimes other balms – and my good friends are here too, though there is one fewer this year.'

'One fewer?'

'Yes, Cricket the dwarf died last autumn. He was my greatest friend, and often sat in that very chair as we laughed, and smoked and talked of this and that. He was a great performer too, with his own special skills, unlike your servant – all I do is stand, and walk a little, and wave a wooden sword. Cricket was a man of talent, and we would perform together in the ring. But dwarves, like giants, have poor health and short lives.'

'I take it you are not, in fact, a Russian?' I asked, feeling the conversation had become rather melancholy.

Gregor gave a deep, sonorous laugh. 'No, sir, I was born in Lancashire. Mr Marshall takes liberties with my ancestry, in order to make a good show, and I am content to play the part of the Cossack in the ring to earn my bread. For all his shouting and noise he is a kind master and treats us as well as he may, man and beast alike.'

'Is this your last night at Wartonholm?' asked Holmes.

'No. Marshall will give the show again tomorrow and we leave the day after that for Laxton. I shall be with the troupe, unless I am in a prison cell.'

'I have every hope that you will still be a free man when the circus leaves. When will you pass this way again?'

'At this same time next year,' he said. 'We have our circuit, which lasts twelve months, so that the people of the towns we visit know when to expect us each year.'

'Admirable. But we have kept you from your bed for long enough, Mr Gregor. You must be weary after the labours of the day.'

'It is very pleasant to have visitors. I have wanted for intelligent company since Cricket died. But I will not deny that I am fatigued.'

'Good night, then, sir.'

We shook the giant's huge hand and departed. When we were a few yards from his caravan, I turned to Holmes and asked how he could be so certain Gregor was innocent of the crime.

'Clearly you are not as familiar with the pathology of gigantism as you are with other aspects of medicine.'

'I admit to ignorance on many matters,' I said, a little hurt.

'I know something of the subject, and will gladly pass on what knowledge I have.'

'Thank you.'

'Have you heard of kyphoscoliosis?'

'Curvature and fusion of the spine.'

'Precisely. It is a particular affliction of the gigantic, and the taller a man grows the worse the condition may become. Poor Gregor is in some pain, and can only walk a few yards. Indeed, it is likely he will not be capable of that much in a few years' time. Many giants are crippled by the condition, and spend their latter years in a bath chair.'

'How dreadful.'

'It is a sad fate for such a great soul. By the way, I think Mr Marshall has stretched the truth in rather more directions than Gregor's nationality. As the giant opened the door of his caravan I marked his height against the doorpost, then compared it with my own as I entered. It was the most inexact process, accurate, I should say, to little more than an inch. Nevertheless, I would estimate Gregor's actual height as no more than seven feet and nine inches – around eight inches less than is claimed for him by the theatrical Mr Marshall. His height is, of course, another reason why he cannot be our giant. A man of seven and three-quarter feet, or even eight and a half, could hardly look in at a window eleven feet from the ground, unless he were to stand on some other object. Hullo, I see the fair Vittoria and must beg a few words with her before we depart for our beds.'[5]

We were among the other caravans now, and Holmes slipped between two of them and was lost to sight. He was gone only for a minute or so, and when he returned had a familiar, satisfied

5. Vittoria (real name Mary Reece, 1858–1918) evidently remembered the visit of Sherlock Holmes to the circus that night, for she later consulted him in her own right when troubled by a ghostly visitor. This case was written up by Watson as the 'Adventure of Vittoria, the Circus Belle' and was among those discovered in the National Westminster Bank vault in 2010.

look upon his face, indicating that some private theory had been confirmed or some guess substantiated.

'What did she tell you?' I asked.

'What I expected her to tell me,' he replied. 'Now for the Black Horse and sleep. I must catch the London train at eight o'clock tomorrow.'

The following morning, after a very early breakfast, I bade farewell to Holmes, no wiser about the case. He had hired a trap at the inn for the journey to Reigate, and as he climbed in he said, 'Watson, I leave the case in your hands. You know something of my methods now, and I trust you to employ them and send a report to Baker Street at the end of each day. I recommend you particularly to look into the question of Mrs Almond's key – does she still have it? If so, see if you can acquire it and send it to me with your first report. Also, please try to dissuade the good Inspector from arresting Gregor – it would be a most unwise and unkind move. I shall be with you again in two or three days, when my London business is concluded and I hope we may clear this little matter up. Drive on.'

When he was gone I felt a mixture of pride and apprehension at the considerable responsibility Holmes had laid upon me. It was the first, but not the last, time he left me in charge of a case while he pursued, or feigned pursuit, of other matters, and I was determined to do my best in my task.

After some thought I decided my best course was to visit and question those villagers we had not so far interviewed. It was still too early to make house-calls, however, so I returned to the Black Horse to think the matter over. I made several pages of notes on the case, and attempted to draw up a list of suspects. It ran in this way,

1. The giant Craddock – highly unlikely.
2. The giant Gregor – Holmes believes impossible.
3. One of the gypsies from the Downs – possible.

4. Insp. Charles Raven – possible.
5. Josiah Redmayne – unknown.
6. Ephraim Pedderborn – unknown.

After a little thought, I added two further names.

7. Benedict Molloy – possible.
8. Featherstone Molloy – possible.

A few minutes of further reflection gave me another suspect.

9. John Sutter, Landlord of the Black Horse – possible.

This seemed to account for all the strong men I knew of in the vicinity, and made quite a long list. It appeared to me vital to attempt to discover what each of my 'possible' and 'unknown' gentlemen was about on the night of the murder, in addition to pursuing the particular tasks Holmes had given me. By this time it was nine o'clock, and I determined to begin visiting my suspects. Remembering Holmes's curious question to the land-lord of the Black Horse, I thought first of the diminutive Josiah Redmayne, and asked Sutter where I might find him.

Redmayne's workshop was on the main street of Warton-holm, and my knock was answered by what I took at first to be a young man. However, as soon as the figure spoke I realised it was a woman, though dressed most queerly. She wore a work-man's soiled overalls and her hair was stuffed up under a cloth cap. A lock had escaped, however, and I could not help noticing that it was a most attractive red-gold colour. The expression on her face was somewhat less than welcoming.

'I have come to see Mr Josiah Redmayne?' I said.

'My husband is not here,' she replied sullenly.

'Then perhaps you can help me. My name is Dr John Watson, and I am assisting the police in the investigation of the death of Miss Sophia Carter.'

'Oh, Miss Carter!' said the lady, and sniffed. She introduced herself as Eleanor Redmayne, and invited me into the workshop. I quickly perceived from the wood-shavings clinging to Mrs Redmayne's overalls, and the tools laid down upon the bench, that she had been working at her husband's trade.

'My dear lady,' said I, attempting to imitate Holmes's best manner when addressing the fair sex, 'I would be very glad to know where your husband is, and why you are working in his stead.'

'Josiah is in London, working at that damned Club!'

'What Club?'

'The Goliath Club. I wish to heaven we had never heard the name of that society of gentlemen, for they are always on at him to make this piece of furniture or that new door-frame for their premises, and they pay little and late, when they pay at all. He spends days on end working there, and sleeps in one of their rooms. He calls it a privilege to work for the Club, but I see no privilege in servitude to a band of misers. That is why I work at my husband's trade, sir – to keep the bailiffs from the door!'

'I see. Was Josiah in London last Sunday night?'

'The night Sophia was killed? No, Josiah was here with me. He travelled up to London on Tuesday and has been there ever since. I believe he will return tomorrow, if you would like to speak with him.'

'Thank you. I will not keep you from your work much longer. May I ask you please to tell me whether you knew Miss Carter?'

'Oh, yes, I knew her,' said Mrs Redmayne. 'And a more cunning little flirt you could never hope to meet. I daresay it is wrong to speak so of the dead, but I had no love for Miss Sophia Carter. You will not hear any *man* speak ill of her, for she had such winning ways with the gentlemen – but women saw right through her, Doctor, and had no time for her ways. I am sorry she is dead. But Wartonholm will be a happier place for wives now that she is.'

In my mind I added a tenth name to my list of suspects. Mrs Redmayne was evidently young and healthy, with the strength to work as a carpenter. Could she have wielded a club to strike down a rival? I thought it not impossible.

'Do you believe then that her engagement to Mr Molloy was a sham?'

'Perhaps. She may have loved him. But I am sure she adored his riches. Featherstone Molloy is the wealthiest man for miles around, richer even than Bryce, to whom she was also once engaged.'

'You mean Robert Bryce, of Laxton Manor?'

'I do. Now, if you will forgive me, I must to work. There is a new drawbar to be carved today, and the work will not do itself, nor indeed be done by my dear Josiah.' With a sigh she returned to the workbench and took up a spokeshave. I wished her good-day and took my leave.

As I departed I wondered whether an eleventh suspect might not be added to my growing list of names in the person of Robert Bryce, who had been thrown over by Miss Carter. In the street I noticed a commotion outside Inspector Raven's house and arrived there in time to witness the appearance of what could only have been Sophia's body, carefully wrapped in a sheet and laid upon a stretcher carried by two constables. Watched by several of the villagers, including John Sutter, it was placed in a waggon. Raven emerged from his house and locked the front door.

'Inspector,' I said. 'Might I have a moment of your time?'

'Certainly, sir,' said Raven. He unlocked the door again and, asking the constables to wait for him, ushered me into the house.

'Mr Holmes has returned to London, but he has left me in charge of the case. He asked me particularly to convey to you his belief that Gregor, the Russian Giant of Marshall's circus, has nothing to do with the crime.'

Raven smiled. 'I had come to the same conclusion, sir. You look surprised, Doctor, but we country policemen are not so simple as you city detectives may believe. While Gregor was performing last night, I took a certain liberty and entered his caravan. The lock was easily circumvented, and no one saw me. I found one of Gregor's slippers, and took certain measurements, which showed me that it was not he who had left those footprints at Sophia's cottage. His foot is barely three-quarters as large as that of our giant.'

'I congratulate you, Inspector.'

'A simple matter. But I must see to the removal of Miss Carter's … remains to Laxton, if you will excuse me.'

My next port of call was Ephraim Pedderborn, and I asked Raven to direct me to his house, which I was informed was on the outskirts of the village. It was a large and comfortable villa, not so extensive as The Larches, but fine enough to indicate that its occupant was no pauper. The door was opened by a man of late middle age with old-fashioned Dundreary whiskers, mottled with grey. His hair was rather long and unkempt. He greeted me kindly enough when he heard the nature of my business, and invited me into his study. Here the shelves, his desk and much of floor were piled with old books and the specimens that he had collected. There were butterflies in cases, the pelts of songbirds, the skulls of tigers and other creatures, and several stuffed animals, including a crocodile suspended in the air above Pedderborn's desk, in the manner of an antique *wunderkammer*. For all his years and unconventional appearance, the naturalist appeared strong and healthy, quite capable of the act which Holmes and I were investigating.

'Poor Sophia,' said Pedderborn. 'Such a sweet girl. She had not an unkind thought in her head.'

'You knew her well, sir?'

'Quite well, indeed. She worked for me from time to time, as a secretary. I have been trying to catalogue my curiosities, and she was of immense help to me. Sophia was a clever girl, and I don't know how I shall get on without her.'

'Can you account for yourself on the night of last Sunday?'

'Why, I was here, sir. I am usually here, when I am not out on the Downs collecting specimens. I had arranged with Sophia to come the next morning, and when she did not appear I walked round to her house. It was clear that all was not well, so I roused Raven.'

'Can anyone confirm that you were here?'

'My housekeeper was in bed, and she is, in any case, rather deaf. So I fear it will be hard for me to prove an *alibi*. But surely, sir, you do not suspect me? It was the giant who killed her, as everyone knows.'

'Craddock?'

'Some call him that. But he is no mere legend, you know. I have seen him with my own eyes, striding about the streets with a mighty club. Let me show you something ... I have it here.'

He crossed to a dusty glass cabinet and opened the doors. The shelves inside were piled with dirty bones, pieces of pottery and what looked like rough stones. He rummaged for a moment, and drew out, to my astonishment, a huge human skull.

'It is by far the most remarkable thing I have found on the Downs. I like to dig, you know, for bones and other evidence. The remains of the ancient peoples who dwelt here are to be found in great profusion. I often excavate their burial mounds, and examine the bones and treasures within. Usually I leave them as I found them. But this skeleton was too remarkable to re-bury.'

He put the skull down on top of a pile of books on his desk, and drew out several further bones – a scapula, a femur and part of a pelvis, all much larger than is usual. I examined the skull. It was very dirty, but complete and of remarkable size, almost twice as large as my own. The brow-ridges were unusually pronounced, and the lower jaw well-developed. I remembered Gregor's face, with its heavy, shapely jaw. This was clearly the skull of a giant, one at least as large as our circus friend.

'It proves that a race of giants once lived in these hills,' said Pedderborn.

'It proves that one giant died here,' said I. 'No more than that.' I felt Holmes would have been proud of this logical interpretation of the evidence. The orbits of the great skull were dark with soil, and in the gloom of the naturalist's room I could have fancied it was looking at me with a certain disapproval, just as Holmes might regard me if I failed in my responsibilities in this case.

'I shall prove it,' went on Pedderborn. 'When I find a second skeleton of the same dimensions. Or when Craddock is captured. I believe he is the last survivor of his ancient race, and can teach us much about man's forebears.'

'What motive could he have for killing Sophia?'

'One must not look for motives with primitives, Doctor. Craddock is a creature of the dim past, when man was little more than a great ape with a spear in his hand. Had he been surprised, or frightened, while hunting in the village, he would have lashed out with his club without a thought. It was mere survival instinct, not a rational act.'

'I see.'

'I mean to write a monograph on the subject, as soon as I have assembled my evidence. It will shake the world of natural science, sir, just as Darwin's works have done, and my name will stand alongside his for all eternity.'

I was beginning to detect a streak of madness in the naturalist's discourse, and felt his position as a suspect in the case grow ever more secure. His physical strength (developed no doubt during archaeological diggings), his doubtful reason, and his strong desire to blame the giant Craddock for the crime all pointed in this direction. Yet I could not imagine what his motive might be, unless perhaps he, too, had been enamoured of Sophia, and had killed her in a jealous rage.

'Did you approve of Sophia's betrothal to Mr Molloy?' I asked.

'What a curious question. I neither approved nor disapproved. Her engagement was merely a fact. I know Featherstone Molloy slightly, and have no objection to him. My only concern, and it was, I confess, a petty one, was that after her marriage she might no longer be willing to act as my secretary. Now that question is quite resolved, of course.'

We talked on for some time, and I attempted to draw him on his feelings for Miss Carter. He seemed, however, infinitely more interested in his own research and theories than in any matters of the heart or flesh, and returned again and again to his belief in a race of man's giant ancestors and the prospect of his fame once that hypothesis had been proven. At length I left him to his old bones, and made my way back to the Black Horse for lunch.

Afterwards I visited Mrs Almond in her small house facing Sophia's cottage. I found her frail, but still sharp-witted, and asked her to tell me what she knew of the giant. She seemed immensely frightened of the creature, but confirmed what Raven had told us of its appearance, crossing herself and calling upon the Good Lord to protect her all the while. Remembering Holmes's question to Raven, I asked whether the figure had appeared to be bending down when it looked in at Miss Carter's window.

'Why bless you, no,' she replied. 'The monster was looking in quite easy, his face level with the window, and his body quite straight and all, may the Good Lord protect us.'

'Then he must have been about eleven feet tall, since the window is that distance above the ground.'

'Oh yes, sir, I would say so.'

'I understand you have a key to Miss Carter's cottage.'

'Yes, sir, I have it here.' She crossed herself again, and took a ring bearing several small keys from the pocket of her pinafore.

'Have you ever lent the key to anyone?'

'Oh no. It has been safe here with me since she gave it to me three year ago.'

'My friend Mr Holmes would like to examine it. Would you mind lending it to me for that purpose?'

'Not at all, sir. I shall do what I can to help rid the village of this curse, tho' I think a priest would serve us better than a London detective.'

She showed me which key it was, and I removed it from the ring, for her fingers were stiff with arthritis and she could not achieve it herself. I thanked her, and slipped the key into my pocket. It seemed she could tell me nothing further, so, assuring her that Holmes would do what ever he could to solve the case, I returned again to the inn, where I spent the next two hours writing a detailed account of my actions and discoveries for Holmes. I sealed it into a packet with Mrs Almond's key, and took it to the Post Office in time to catch the last post.

That night I slept soundly, believing that I had made a good start on the investigation. The next day, however, I found myself at something of a loss. I had done all that I could think of, and spent the morning looking over my notes and wondering what Holmes would do next. My list of suspects had grown longer, and I had failed to remove any of the names during my previous day's work. After lunch I determined to investigate the local squire, Richard Bryce, and began to question Sutter on the matter. It quickly emerged that Bryce had been abroad for some months, however, touring Europe with his new bride. The circumstances of his absence from the country and recent marriage suggested that I could, at last, strike one name from my list of potential murderers.

Remembering what Mrs Redmayne had told me, I decided next to return to the carpenter's workshop, to interview her husband, if I could. When I knocked on his door, however, his unfortunate wife informed me that he had been detained at the Goliath Club, and would not be back in the village until the following evening. Finally, I decided to visit the Molloys and try to learn a little more of Featherstone's attachment to the murdered woman. Here too I was destined to be disappointed, however, for the maid informed me that both Featherstone and Benedict had departed for London that morning, on business, and were not expected back until the next day. As I left the house I met Inspector Raven coming up the path, and informed him that the Molloys were not at home.

'That is a shame,' said he. 'I had certain questions for those two gentlemen. I have just returned from Laxton, and was a little surprised not to see the brothers at Sophia's inquest this afternoon.'

'I had quite forgotten about that,' I replied. 'What did the coroner say?'

'What could he say, sir? His verdict was "murder by person or persons unknown". I wonder, sir, if you have come to certain conclusions yourself? I have certain theories, sir, but should be glad to know what you have determined.'

'I had better say nothing until I have spoken with Holmes,' I replied, trying to sound as confident and casual as possible to conceal my growing sense of failure in the case. 'But what have you found, Inspector? Is an arrest likely soon?'

'I have hopes, sir, but am not yet in a position to make my move.'

He would say no more, and I left his company feeling very dejected about the prospects of solving the case. Nevertheless, I was determined to do my best by Holmes and returned to the Black Horse to write a second, and much less weighty, report to send to him in London. However, I had barely begun this task when a telegram arrived for me. I was delighted to see that it came from Holmes. Its content was a little unexpected, however. It read 'Come London earliest tomorrow. Meet at Goliath Club, 23 Pall Mall, 10 a.m. Bring Raven. Holmes.'

And so it was that next morning I said farewell to Wartonholm. With my luggage, and Holmes's, which he had left in my charge, I boarded a trap in company with Inspector Raven, and set off for Reigate. We caught the second London train at eight-fifteen, and arrived at Waterloo with half an hour to spare. Throughout the journey Raven seemed in good spirits, whistling to himself and smiling as he gazed out across the Downs. For my part, I could see no light in the case, and we seemed to be speeding with every passing minute further from the clues and evidence that Holmes would need to solve the problem. We left our bags in charge of the porter, and walked from the terminus across Waterloo Bridge, along the Strand, past Charing Cross and so to Pall Mall.

The premises of the Goliath Club were impressive indeed, with a huge portico supported by Corinthian columns. There was no name to be seen on the building, only the street number and what I took to be the device of the Club, a large 'G' supported by the figure of a bearded giant. Very shortly Holmes drove up in a four-wheeler, in company with two uniformed policemen.

'My dear Watson,' he said. 'And Inspector Raven. Our party is complete. Come, the murderer waits within!'

'He is here, then?' I asked.

'I believe so.'

We entered by the huge double doors and found ourselves within a comfortable, oak-panelled lobby, where a uniformed servant sat behind a counter. To the right was a large door, and straight ahead a much smaller one, but curiously carved and gilded so that is shone like a burnished icon. The servant started up when he saw us, and asked our business.

'It is police business,' said Raven gravely.

'If you wish to see one of our members, gentlemen, you must wait in the Strangers' Room,' he replied, indicating the door to the right.

'I think not,' said Holmes. 'Our business cannot wait. Come.' He walked to the small, gilded door and regarded it.

'You cannot go in there, sir!' cried the servant. 'You are forbidden!'

'On what grounds?' asked Holmes.

'Why sir, on the grounds that you are not a member, and that you are … quite unsuitable!'

Holmes snorted, put out a hand and opened the door. 'You will observe as we enter,' he said, 'that this doorway is precisely five feet and one inch in height. Any man who can pass through it, without his shoes and without stooping, may become a member of the Goliath Club – provided, of course, he can afford the two-hundred guinea subscription. Beware, gentlemen. Even you, Inspector, must needs bow as you pass through this door.'

We lowered our heads and walked in single file into the extraordinary world of the Goliath Club. At first sight the large room beyond the door appeared unremarkable, though very lavishly appointed. There were mirrors and paintings in gilded frames, and elegant book-cases, armchairs and cabinets against the walls. But as I moved into the space a curious perception came upon me. I seemed to be growing, for everything in that room, every piece of furniture, every door and work of art, was perhaps a quarter-size smaller than is usual. The chairs were perfect miniatures, in which a child or small man might sit, but which would scarcely accommodate my own frame in comfort. It was like entering a doll house. Holmes glanced keenly around.

'You see, gentlemen,' he said, 'it is quite the most remarkable club in London, for everything is designed to make the wealthy small fellows who are its denizens perceive themselves great men.'

At that moment a servant entered carrying an empty silver tray. He was a dwarf, no larger than those we had seen cavorting at Marshall's circus. He stopped short, and looked up at this party of giants with fear and a certain incomprehension in his face. 'Can I help you, gentlemen?' he said at length.

'Thank you,' said Holmes sweetly. 'I am looking for Messrs Featherstone and Benedict Molloy.'

'I believe they are in the blue room, sir. Along the south corridor, turn left and the blue room is the second door on the left.'

Holmes nodded and we followed him in the direction indicated. We ducked through a doorway and passed into a long corridor, brilliantly lit by gaslight. Holmes stopped outside a door marked 'Library', and pushed it open. Inside there were no books, but a great many empty shelves, and work was evidently in progress, for one of the cases was in pieces on the floor. A bald, middle-aged man in overalls was planing a scantling, and looked up at Holmes. He too seemed astonished, and a little frightened, at our ungainly size in this shrunken world.

'My apologies,' said Holmes. 'I have the wrong room.' He let the door swing shut again. As we walked on he whispered to me, 'That, of course, was Josiah Redmayne, the slave of the Goliath Club.'

We moved into a second passage, decorated with small statues in wall-niches. We passed an open door, though which a typical club interior could be observed. Well-to-do gentlemen lounged in wing chairs or on sofas, reading newspapers, smoking and conversing in low tones. The trick of the eye was complete, and one could not have known from mere observation of the scene that none of its actors was more than five feet and one inch tall.

The next door was that we had been seeking. Holmes opened it quietly, and we followed him inside. Featherstone and Benedict Molloy were engaged in a game of billiards. Two other small fellows were playing at a second table, further down the room. Our entrance had the same stupefying effect on the tenants. They looked up from their games and stared at us with open mouths. Then Featherstone threw down his cue and rushed forward to meet us, followed by his brother.

'Mr Holmes, Dr Watson – I hardly expected to see you here. You are quite forbidden entry, of course, by the rules of the Club. But I am delighted to see you, never the less. You have news of the case?'

Holmes's face was grave. 'I have solved it,' he said.

'Thank you, sir, thank you! What ... who ... tell me what you have found, I beg you.'

'There is further pain for you, I am afraid.'

'Tell me. I must know!'

'Very well. But perhaps there is another who can tell the tale better than I.'

He turned to Benedict Molloy.

'What, sir?' said Benedict after a moment. 'Are you mad? What do I know of this?'

Holmes shook his head. 'It won't do – really it won't. There is no escape for you, Mr Molloy. I know everything.'

'You know nothing!' snapped Benedict.

Quite suddenly the little man ducked sideways, swerved past the constable who tried to catch him, and ran out into the corridor.

'Quickly,' cried Holmes. 'He must not get away!'

The policemen gave chase, followed closely by Holmes and myself, with the stout Raven puffing along in the rear. Our quarry fled towards the south corridor, and it was clear that he meant to escape from the building by the main entrance. At the little golden door, one of the constables caught up with Benedict, and threw himself at the fleeing figure with all the vigour of a rugby half-back. But Benedict was remarkably lithe, slipped from his grasp and burst through the door. We followed as best we could, but by the time I was back in the lobby there was no sign of the little man.

Then came a terrible noise from the street. There was a squeal of brakes, followed by a thump and a crunch, then a pandemonium of cries and screams. We rushed outside to find a crowd gathering round a body lying in the middle of the road. A hansom was pulled up a few yards away at an awkward angle. The driver jumped down. His face was dead white as he approached, and I heard him cry 'Gawd 'elp me, I've killed a child!'

We pushed through the crowd, and I knelt beside Benedict Molloy, as I had knelt beside his brother just a few days previously. It was clear that the hansom had passed right over him, and his injuries, both from the hooves of the horse and the wheels of the cab, were dreadful. There was nothing I could do. Holmes knelt beside me.

Benedict uttered a terrible moan, and opened his eyes.

'I loved her!' he said between gritted teeth.

'You loved her,' said Holmes. 'And yet you killed her.'

'I did not intend to hurt her,' hissed the dying man. 'I wanted to plead my case, show her the depth and truth of my love, and persuade her to come away with me. I thought I could convince her. So I copied *his* key, and crept into the house. When I saw her sleeping I was overcome with passion. She looked so pure and peaceful. There was a smile upon her lips. Then I saw her right hand, which lay beside her head upon the pillow. It held a pale yellow silk handkerchief. Oh, God ...' Benedict groaned again, and his body twisted with pain. He rose up a little towards us, baring his bloody teeth. 'It was *his* handkerchief, I recognised it – she had fallen asleep with *his* gage to her lips! I knew my cause was lost. But why should *he* have her? *He* had taken everything. So I deprived him of the greatest prize! My God, I am sorry for it now ... not for *him*, or for myself, but for Sophia's sake, even though she was filthy with *his* child!'

Raven had joined us now, and, between great gasps, he said 'Do you wish to make a certain statement regarding the death of a certain young lady in the village of Wartonholm during the night of Sunday last?' But his question was too long, and Benedict had passed to a place where no earthly inquiries could reach him.

Four days later Featherstone Molloy and Charles Raven dined with us at Baker Street. Molloy's face was still marked with livid bruises and he was clearly very shaken by his experiences. In little more than a week he had lost his intended bride, his unborn heir, and his closest relation. Raven was in good spirits, however, having already been credited by the papers with the solution of the most sensational crime he was ever likely to encounter as an Inspector in the Surrey police.

After dinner we sat and smoked for a while in Holmes's room, and I begged him to explain the case to me, for it was still as dark as night. He had declined to give any explanation until such time as we might have Molloy and Raven present, to prevent the necessity of repeating himself. I had been itching to know the details of my friend's investigation all through dinner, but had not thought it a suitable subject for the table. Now we had withdrawn, however, I could wait no longer.

'Very well, my dear fellow,' said Holmes. 'I have kept you waiting long enough. But first, there is something I must return to you, Mr Molloy.' He took from his pocket a pale yellow silk handkerchief and handed to Featherstone, who unfolded it and held it up. It had his monogram embroidered in one corner, and was spattered with dark brown stains.

'Thank you,' said Molloy. 'It is all I have of her now.'

'Your brother took it from her hand, of course, after he had done the deed, and kept it with him. I took it from his pocket as he lay in the street.'

Molloy re-folded the silken sheet with great care, and slipped it into his sleeve.

'I must confess,' continued Holmes, 'that when I accused Benedict, though I was convinced of his guilt, I had only the flimsiest of evidence, which would hardly have stood in court. But I hoped by showing my understanding of the crime to convince him that I knew all, and induce a confession. I am only sorry that I was so successful in this aim that he took rash action, and put himself beyond our questioning, or the reach of the law.

'But I must not tell this story back-to-front, and should begin with the preliminaries of my reasoning. At first I did not know what to make of this business, and the apparent presence of a giant in the case made it quite unique in my experience. But, when I saw the little room where Sophia had died, I began to understand. In the first place, it was immediately clear that any notion of a huge man breaking in the window and striking the girl with a club was impossible. Imagine it, Watson. You are lying asleep, and a giant smashes your window. What do you do? Why you wake, of course, you leap up in terror and attempt to flee. But the traces in that room indicated that Sophia had been struck down as she slept, and sight of her peaceful face later confirmed this. No giant was responsible, but a man had stolen quietly into her room and struck her a deadly blow.'

'But with what, Mr Holmes?' asked Raven 'We found no weapon.'

'That is simplicity itself. The murderer took up a heavy log from the basket by the fire, and struck her with that. It was the first and only weapon to hand. The fire was still alight, or smouldering at least, so he dropped the bloody log into the grate and thus destroyed his weapon. I had formed this theory before I had seen Miss Carter's body, but my examination provided further evidence. You may remember, Watson, that I removed something from the girl's left ear. Here it is.'

He took an envelope from his pocket and shook out its contents into the palm of his hand. We all craned forward to examine the small, dark pellet that lay there.

'It's a woodlouse,' I said.

'Quite so. A dead woodlouse. There were several others in the log-basket, and clinging to the logs themselves. This little body must have adhered to the murderer's club, and been dislodged by the fatal blow.'

'Good heavens.'

'Benedict was overcome by passion when he committed the crime, but at length he grew calm and saw the best way to cover up his actions and mislead the police. In addition to burning his weapon, he took a second log and used it to break in the window, thus creating evidence that an intruder had entered the room. It was well done. He opened one pane and leaned out, breaking the other from the outside to make the glass shatter inwards. Then he closed the open window, put his arm out through the broken pane, and smashed in the other side. He put this second log too upon the fire. I found fragments of glass, which had become embedded in the log, among the ashes.

'It was lucky for Benedict that Craddock had been haunting Wartonholm, and causing such fear among the villagers, smashing high windows and stealing precious objects. Benedict may not have known of the giant footprints, or of the recent sightings of Craddock, when he smashed the window. But, luckily for him, all this evidence served to draw suspicion towards the giant, and away from any human criminal. For a time I was not unwilling to see the giant blamed, for it gave the murderer a false sense of freedom, so that he might more readily make an error. You too, Inspector, took this attitude, I believe, and went so far as to announce a search of the Downs, knowing full well that the killer was nearer at hand.'

'You are quite right,' said Raven. 'Though I confess I was slow to see a certain gentleman as culpable ...'

'Having established, to my own satisfaction, that Craddock was a mere distraction in the case, I began to consider the actions of the true killer. Since the cottage had been locked up tight, the crime must have been committed by someone with a key, or else by an accomplished burglar. The latter was highly unlikely since nothing had been stolen, and the business had been covered up in a considered manner – the burning of the logs, the smashing of the window. A house-breaker who had killed in a panic would hardly have acted so. The next link in my chain was, therefore, to establish who had a key to Sophia's cottage. I quickly learned that there were only two people, apart from the girl herself – the widow Almond, and you, Mr Molloy. The widow was too feeble to have committed the crime. And though I have thrice been retained by a murderer to solve his own crime, in order to cover his actions and attempt to outwit me, in this case the indications were that you too, Mr Molloy, were perfectly innocent.'

'Thank you, Mr Holmes,' said Molloy, somewhat uneasily.

'The scene, Baker Street. The time, last Tuesday morning. I know something of the theatre, Mr Molloy, and it would have been a remarkable actor indeed who threw himself before our cab and poured out his soul as you did on that occasion, had you not been utterly in earnest. So, having eliminated Mr Molloy and Mrs Almond, the next point was to discover who might have had access to one of the three existing keys in order to make a copy. It was possible any of the keys might have been borrowed, or stolen, although Mrs Almond claimed not have let hers out of her possession, and it seemed unlikely that Sophia had been tricked into giving up her own key. Had it been stolen or lost, she would no doubt have asked Mrs Almond to return her key, and then changed her locks. And so, Mr Molloy, my eye came to rest upon you. Who could have laid their hands upon your key? Clearly the most likely person was someone within your own household. My eye moved from one brother to the other. On the evening we dined with you at The Larches I watched brother Benedict very closely. He showed clear signs both of an attachment to Miss Carter and a desire to divert me from my proper course. I will say little more of that evening, for matters were discussed which it would be better not to repeat. However, I ventured to test my theory by asking to see your copy of the cottage key. Perhaps you will remember your surprise when I licked it. Of course, I was not licking the key, but tasting it, and at least one other person in that room understood the significance of my act, as his reaction showed. On one side of the key I detected the unmistakable flavour of soap. Now it is a commonplace in the more sensational literature for a key to be copied by pressing the wards hard into a bar of soap, and then employing an unscrupulous smith to make a copy from the mould. The original key need only be in the hands of the criminal for a few seconds. Benedict evidently found a moment to extract it briefly from your waistcoat, perhaps while you were bathing or sleeping.'

'The former, most likely,' said Featherstone. 'For I always slept with the key under my pillow.'

'I also tested the widow Almond's key in the same manner, once the good Doctor had secured it for me. If it too showed signs of copying I knew I would have to widen my investigation. But happily there were no traces of soap, or any other signs of duplication. So I was persuaded that Benedict had made a copy of his brother's key. I considered his purpose and, when I had returned to town, undertook a little research into the history of the family. The brothers Molloy attended one of our best public schools, and I was able to trace their old House Master, now retired. He told me of the great rivalry that had existed at school between the brothers, with Featherstone always the victor, both on the sporting field and in the examination hall. You will have observed, Watson, the many cups and trophies at The Larches. Almost all were inscribed with the name of the elder brother, while Benedict was lucky to take a second place. Such rivalry is not unusual between brothers, and I reasoned that it may have extended beyond the halls of Eton, to business and, ultimately, to matters of the heart. Sophia Carter was a very beautiful and remarkable woman, and it was not unnatural that both Molloys should have fallen in love with her. I could only guess at what passed through Benedict's mind when he stole into her house that night, but his dying words served to confirm much that was supposition.

'Having drawn up my theory, however, I knew I was extremely short of evidence. Indeed, I had nothing concrete. The flavour of soap, and the ashes of a fire, could hardly be presented at the criminal court. I did not know then of the yellow handkerchief, which Benedict had abstracted from the cottage and which would have linked him to the crime. But *he* was aware of the danger of keeping that small piece of silk, which he could not bear to dispose of, for sentimental reasons. This awareness no doubt made him all the more anxious to escape, if only for long enough to dispose of the handkerchief, when I intimated my understanding of the case, precipitating the flight which ended so unfortunately beneath the wheels of a London cab. I think that explains everything, unless you gentlemen have any questions ...'

'I see now how you came to suspect Benedict,' I said. 'And understand all that followed. But there is still the little matter of the giant. Does Craddock really exist?'

'He does,' replied Holmes. 'But I should be very surprised if he is ever seen again at Wartonholm.'

'But what was he?' asked Raven.

'He was a legend, brought to life, then allowed to die again. I can say no more than that.'

'Well, I daresay you know a little more,' said Raven. 'But I imagine I shall have to be satisfied with a certain assurance on that matter, and ask for nothing more. I am very happy with the outcome, as a certain quite undeserved glory has attached to your humble servant, and I feel sure a certain call from Scotland Yard is only a few days away. It is to you, Mr Holmes, that any real credit must be given, however.'

'I shall keep my name out of the case, Inspector. You may continue to take the credit, with my blessing.'

'Well, thank you, Mr Holmes,' said Raven, as he rose to leave. 'That is very large of you, sir. My train departs in thirty minutes, and I must make my way to Waterloo.'

When he was gone, Holmes remarked 'I believe he will do well in his chosen profession, if only he can learn a certain concision in his use of language!'

We both laughed. 'But, surely,' I said, 'you can tell me something of the giant. Who made those footprints, and smashed those windows? If the murder of Sophia Carter was not planned, these things can hardly have been a confection to help cover the murderer's tracks.'

'You may remember our night at the circus, and our absorbing conversation with Gregor. What was most interesting to me, however, was his mention of a lost friend, the dwarf Cricket. I spoke to Vittoria, and confirmed what I had guessed. Cricket was a stilt-walker, Watson. He and Gregor performed together, the little man made up to the same height as the giant with tall stilts, strapped to his short legs. He wore a long robe, and only revealed the secret of his stature at the end of the act, after he and Gregor had performed a mock-fight. Marshall's Circus moves round the country on an annual circuit, and last time it was at Wartonholm was just a year ago. It was shortly after this that Craddock was first sighted in the streets. Someone saw Cricket at the circus, and conceived the idea of bringing the legendary giant to life by using stilts.'

'Extraordinary. But what was the motive?'

'Simple gain, Watson. Craddock was a thief, stealing from upstairs rooms after breaking the windows, and keeping the villagers in terror by his appearance. I knew there was something curious about our giant when we calculated his height from his stride. Despite his apparent fifteen feet, he had looked straight in at a window eleven feet from the ground without stooping. It was clear that here was a rather short giant, but with unusually long legs, and hence a long stride. A man or woman of average size could achieve an overall height of about eleven feet, and a stride of five feet, if they wore stilts roughly six feet high.'

'So, who was the giant?'

'Examine the evidence, Watson. Stilts are not too complex to manufacture. The footprints, however, were of huge bare feet. I believe the stilts bore carved terminals, which left that fearful spoor. Who might possess the skill to make such remarkable carvings?'

'Josiah Redmayne!'

'Or, perhaps more probably, his wife.'

'Then Craddock was a woman?'

'I think it not unlikely. Josiah has been engaged in ill-paid work for the Goliath Club for several years now, and his wife has been keeping his business alive. Eleanor Redmayne it was who felt the poverty of their situation most keenly, and was in a position to make both the carved stilts and the clothing necessary to perform the part of Craddock. She evidently has a good deal of determination and imagination, given her labours at a trade not normally considered suitable for members of her sex. If her house had been searched two weeks ago, I believe the police would have found the stilts, cloak and hat of the giant, and perhaps some of the stolen property too. But no doubt all that was disposed of when news of the murder, and of the popular belief that Craddock was responsible, went abroad.'

'She will not be punished for her crimes, then?'

'It is merely a theory of my own. I have no proof. Eleanor Redmayne may have been a thief, but, if so, she stole to meet a need. And, as I told the good Inspector, I think the villagers of Wartonholm will never again be troubled by Craddock.'

'I believe you admire the lady.'

'It was a brilliant plan, though one more creditable to her head and hands than to her conscience.'

'Are you really happy to let Raven take the credit for the solution of the case.'

'Well, Watson, that depends on you.'

'On me?'

'Yes. I see you have already made copious notes upon the case. Are you considering publishing the story?'

'Perhaps so,' I admitted.

'It has been an interesting case in many ways. I could have wished for a less sudden end to Mr Benedict Molloy. But, perhaps after all, it is for the best. He has saved the Nation the expense of a rope, and the family the pain of a trial. But I cannot rate the case among my successes. We learned secrets too, whose time is not due, most notably the condition of Sophia Carter at the time of her death. I think you will agree, Watson, that if you do publish this story you must alter or conceal some of the facts. Unless, of course, you place your notes on the Adventure of the Surrey Giant among those cases to be published after my death.'

I could see the force of his argument. 'By the way, Holmes,' I said, 'I forgot to ask about the outcome of the Freeman forgery case.'

'Oh, that was all cleared up,' he replied casually. 'Our man threw a package into the Dock, and we believed it contained the printing plates that would have condemned him. With great persistence, Lestrade and his men retrieved the parcel from the mud, only to find it contained a revolver and some old magazines which the forger had packed for his journey. The plates, I discovered, had been sent in a small crate to a confederate in America, and were quickly retrieved by the Washington police. They are now on their way back to London, and will seal the fate of Mr Victor Lynch.'

'I thought his name was Freeman.'

Holmes laughed. 'No, indeed. I should have told you a little more of the affair. I called it the Freeman case because Lynch's operations came to my attention when he forged an American document, *The Oath of a Freeman*. It was, I believe, the first item printed by the pilgrims on American soil, and no copy has survived, though its text is known. Lynch created a copy of the small broadside in suitable style, and tried to sell it for twelve thousand dollars, through an accomplice in Washington. Had he asked for less, he might have succeeded, but the price brought the closest scrutiny to bear upon the document. I may perhaps have mentioned that I spent part of the year 1880 in America. Among the many pleasures of that Continent was a visit to the Congressional Library, where the *Oath* was in safekeeping. I had heard of the controversy, and was able to spend some time examining the broadside. The paper used was quite unimpeachable – the flyleaf of a folio from the middle of the seventeenth century – but I was able, by an examination of type and ink, to show that the piece was a recent confection. It took me two years more to trace the hand responsible, and last month I turned the evidence over to Lestrade. The case against Lynch hinged upon his possession of the relief plate which he had made to print the *Oath*, and it was this, along with half a dozen plates for bank-notes, which we believed he had deposited in the Thames.

'Soon we will have those plates, and Lynch will face a jury at the criminal court. It was a bold, but foolish, stroke to re-create the *Oath*. Had Lynch stuck to his last and concentrated upon bank-notes and other common pieces, he might still be at work. It was *The Oath of a Freeman* that did for Victor Lynch. I doubt that anyone will ever again be so imprudent as to attempt to forge such a momentous and valuable piece'.[6]

6. Holmes was wrong, of course. The forger and murderer Mark Hofmann (b. 1954) followed in Lynch's footsteps in 1985, and was unmasked by a similarly astute investigator.

II

The Mystery of the Camden Rose

THE LATTER MONTHS OF THE YEAR 1882 found Sherlock Holmes at his lowest ebb. Despite his involvement with more than a dozen notable cases during the previous two years, he had yet to establish a reputation as the foremost consulting detective of this, or any other, nation. Weeks and sometimes months would crawl past without a single new problem to occupy his keen intellect. At such times he alternated between fierce activity – reading, writing, chemical research, and maintaining his curious collection of scraps and miscellanea – and profound lassitude. It was the latter phase I feared most, for when boredom and exhaustion overtook him, Holmes would seek relief in a bottle of morphine or cocaine. Despite my sermons on the dangers, he seemed unable, and at times unwilling, to resist the power of these drugs.

I could not devote much time to caring for my friend for, while his career had entered the doldrums, mine had a good following wind. I was working hard, too hard perhaps, as a junior in a Paddington practice, while continuing to lodge at Baker Street. At the same time I had been courting a young woman named Charlotte Carwitham, whom I had met at Covent Garden that summer, though I had, as yet, told Holmes nothing of the affair.

One cold Thursday evening in October I returned from attending a patient to find Holmes insensible upon the divan, an empty syringe dangling from his limp fingers. I felt his pulse and found it rapid and irregular. His arm was shaking violently. His eyes were closed, but I could see they were dancing in his skull from the ripples and twitches of the lids. I pulled him upright and attempted to force a little brandy between his lips. After a minute or so his eyes opened a crack, and a low sigh came from his lips.

'Is that you, Mycroft?' he asked in a tiny voice.

'It is I, Doctor Watson.'

'I am sure I heard Mycroft's voice. He has come to take my watch! He always coveted that watch.'

'Mycroft is not here,' I said. 'Only I am in the room.'

'You will rebuke me, I know, old friend. But seven-per-cent was no longer sufficient. My mind would not be quiet. I had to make it twelve-per-cent!'

'If you wish to serve your mind,' said I, with some feeling, 'you would do better to curb your mania for that damned drug!'

'You are no doubt right. But my mind is a racing mill, Watson, and if it has no grain to grind it will wear itself to nothing – only the cocaine can slip a little oil between those great millstones.'

'The cocaine will kill you, Holmes.'

'Then give me grain, give me work!'

'Call on Lestrade, for God's sake. He must inevitably have some small mystery on hand which is beyond his own powers.'

'I visited the good Lestrade this afternoon, and Bowyer and Gregson too. They had nothing for me, nothing but a few simple thefts among the theatre-folk, which a child could solve.'

He sighed again, and passed back into a semi-conscious state. I picked him up and carried him to his bed, praying all the while that there would soon be something to occupy that great mind. Over the next few weeks I watched him as closely as my practice and courtship of Miss Carwitham would allow. He repeated a cycle of intense activity, followed by a black reaction and a powerful injection of cocaine or morphine; depression and remorse ensued and, in this state, he would accuse himself of the gravest crimes against his own body and nature. Then he would return to energetic activity, only to fall almost at once into the same slough of boredom and exhaustion. When I had watched him pass through this cycle four times in as many weeks, I knew I could stand it no more. His skin was fish-belly white and his hands danced nervously, while his eyes were for ever glancing round, half in fear, half in anticipation of some intervention in the form of a new case. I knew I would have to act soon, to prevent my friend from falling into that physical and mental state from which he might never recover. I formulated a plan of action, hoping all the while that it would not be necessary to act upon it.

The end came in the form of a letter. There was all too little post in those days, besides circulars and my medical periodicals, so that when an envelope came addressed to Holmes in an unknown hand he lighted upon it with increasing glee. This particular envelope was a cheap one, addressed in blue ink in the hand, Holmes informed me, of a woman of between thirty and forty years of age. The content of the letter was startling. It read:

Dear Mr Holmes

I hope you will forgive this unsolicited approach, but I am at my wits' end. I need your help in the most personal and difficult matter. Every year, since I attained the age of twenty-one, I have received on my birthday a small square of card. It comes in an envelope with my name and address written with a type-writer. Each square bears a letter of the alphabet, drawn in ink with a pen. I have no idea who sends these letters to me, but I received another last Thursday. When placed in chronological sequence, these letters now spell out the sentence YOU WILL SOON DIE!

I realised some years ago that I was being sent a message by degrees, but even on my last birthday I did not understand its sinister nature. It was only with the arrival of the final E that I was able to read it all. And now I am very much afraid. Does the sender of this message mean to murder me? Or is it merely a reminder of that same mortality which affects us all? Please help me, if you are able.

I am forced by circumstances not to give you my address, and I beg that you, who have the power to discover much that is hidden, do not attempt to find me. For now I will communicate with you only by letter. Your reply, left at the tobacconist's in Camden High Street under my name, will swiftly reach me. I entreat you, as you are a gentleman, not to try to follow me or even catch a glimpse of me. My life may depend upon it.

Yours very sincerely

Miss Rose Welch-Hall

'Well,' said Holmes when I had read the letter. 'What do you make of it?'

'Curious and sinister, indeed,' I said. 'But is it serious? Surely, this is no more than a cruel joke, perhaps by some disappointed follower of the lady.'

'Perhaps so. But I read more into these carefully-chosen words. How did the lady come to know of my work? Why does she insist upon remaining unseen? Could it be that I would recognize her? And, if so, how would that affect my understanding of her case? There is certainly mystery here, Watson. If her story is true, what might induce someone to threaten the life of this young lady in such a protracted manner? It took the sender of these characters fifteen years to reach the conclusion of his message, assuming that the message is concluded. If he intends Miss Welch-Hall harm, why prolong the threat in this extraordinary manner, and why include in the message the word "soon"? If this is a threat of death, then the date of the intended execution must have some particular significance for the correspondent.

But all we have to go on is "soon". And then there is the little matter of her name.'

'Her name?'

'Yes. Do you notice nothing peculiar about it?'

'The double surname suggests a family of the better class, but, beyond that, it seems perfectly unremarkable.'

'It is an anagram.'

'Is it? Of what word?'

'The name of a young woman I once encountered, though I never saw her face. You will remember the story I told you last spring of Reginald Musgrave and the peculiar fate of his butler, Brunton. There was a woman in the case.'

'Rachel Howells, the servant girl who was Brunton's accomplice, and possibly his murderer. She fled after his death, and was never again heard of.'

'Quite so. I think there are three possibilities. Either the writer of this letter was christened Rose Welch-Hall, and the anagram is the most remarkable co-incidence. This is possible, but wonderfully unlikely. Secondly, I may have in my hand a communication from the absent Miss Howells, using here an *alias*. Thirdly, this letter may come from someone who intends, for reasons as yet obscure, to capture my attention and knows that an anagram of the name of Rachel Howells would be an excellent way to achieve this end. In this case, the sender must be a lady who knows Miss Howells, or at least knows something of her story and her connections with Musgrave and myself. It is a pretty puzzle.'

I was delighted to see his eyes sparkle, and a little colour rise into his sallow cheeks. He took out pen and paper and wrote the following note:

Dear Miss Welch-Hall

Thank you for your recent, undated letter. I shall be glad to look into your little problem, and should find it very helpful if I could see the squares of card you mention and, if possible, the typewritten envelopes in which they were delivered. If you cannot meet me in person, then perhaps you might send me these items, along with a more complete account of your history. I would ask you, when writing this, to consider any curious incidents in your early life, before you reached the age of twenty-one, and any ideas you might have about the sender of this singular message. Think, particularly, please, if there is anyone in your youth who might have come to wish you harm, even for the most trifling incident or misunderstanding, perhaps related to an affair of the heart.

In the meantime, I beg you to be extremely careful and look to your safety. If you have a brother, or a trusted male friend, please keep him close at hand.

Your servant

Sherlock Holmes

'I shall take it to Camden Town at once,' he said, folding the sheet and placing it in an envelope which he addressed to the lady. 'Will you come with me?'

I assented and we took a two-wheeler to Camden High Street, where we quickly found the little tobacconist's shop. Here Holmes deposited the letter with the owner, an elderly, bearded man who seemed quite used to such transactions. I half expected Holmes to suggest we lie in wait for the lady, and try to catch a sight of her. But he hurried me back to the cab, which he had asked to wait. When I taxed him on the point he looked a little affronted and said, 'The lady asked me to respect her *incognito*, and I intend to do just that'.

Holmes did not have to wait long for his reply. It came the next morning, in the form of a large manilla envelope stuffed with pieces of cardboard, each about two inches square and with a letter drawn upon it in black or blue-black ink. The envelope was addressed in the lady's neat writing, but bore no postage stamp and had evidently been delivered by hand. It contained also a letter from Miss Welch-Hall, which read in this way:

My Dear Mr Holmes

I am so grateful to you for agreeing to take my case. You cannot imagine the relief that your decision has brought to me. To know that you are taking my part in this business means a very great deal, I assure you.

I enclose the cardboard letters, just as they came to me on each of my birthdays for the past fifteen years. I regret to say that I discarded all the envelopes in which they were delivered, save the most recent. However, I hesitate to send this to you since it would, quite obviously, impart to you my address, which I must, for the moment at least, keep hidden. As to the cardboard letters, I thought it best not to trust such precious evidence to the postal service, so have delivered them by hand. Perhaps you would do me the great service of keeping them safe until the matter is resolved.

You ask for an account of my history and for any ideas I might have about the sender of the letters. There is not much to tell. I am the daughter of a wine-merchant of the city of York, who prospered for many years and retired with my mother and myself to Camden Town five years ago. My father passed away last year, but my mother survives and we live together still in a quiet street in that district. I have never married and your query concerning affairs of the heart can be quickly answered. I was for some short time engaged to a grocer in the locality named Henry Evans, but broke it off two years ago when I perceived that he was not quite the kind-hearted gentleman I had imagined him to be. It is quite unthinkable that he could be my mysterious correspondent, however, since I only met him when we moved to Camden, and the first square arrived some ten years previously, when we were still living at York.

My father had, at one time, an unpleasant business associate who appeared to take an excessive interest in me. His name was Bryce Feather, and he was, for a while, my father's partner. He evidently spoke to father about the possibility of proposing marriage to me, to cement the partnership, as it were, but neither I nor my dear papa were pleased by this prospect. In 1874 he disappeared and we heard later that Mr Feather had been wanted by the police for some thefts he was believed to have committed before he moved to York, and had fled to America to escape arrest. His ship was apparently lost at sea, and he was presumed drowned.

I fear there is little more I can say. My life has been, apart from these few incidents, extremely peaceful.

Yours very sincerely

Rose Welch-Hall

'How curious,' said Holmes, when he had read this letter over several times, and examined the squares of card with minute care. 'Firstly, we must agree that there can be no doubt about the message being quite complete. You see here, the final E has an exclamation-point drawn after it?' He held up the square of card in question and I nodded. 'But look, each of these cards is cut from a different stock, and most are quite plain and un-identifiable. However, two are cut from tobacco boxes, and one,' he held up the letter U, 'from what I suspect to be a packet of Fortnum and Mason's Indian tea. See, here is the Royal coat-of-arms and the warrant.' He held out the card to me, and I read, on its reverse, the name of Fortnum and Mason and the subscription 'grocers to her Majesty Queen Victoria, Empress of India'.

'You perceive the problem?' I shook my head. 'If we are to credit this story of an annual progress towards a complete mes-sage, this letter would have been sent to Miss Welch-Hall in the year 1871. But our noble Queen was not titled Empress of India until 1876. So this square must have been written in that year or later. Could Miss Welch-Hall have lost this piece and reconstructed it for my benefit, but omitted to tell me as much? It is possible. But it is much more likely, I think, that we have found a flaw in her artifice. And with such a flaw, the whole building begins to look extremely unsteady.'

I was obliged to agree. 'But if she is not telling you the whole truth, what can be her aim?' I asked.

'As usual, Watson, you cut to the marrow of the question. I must satisfy myself upon this point.' He took out pen and ink and wrote the following letter:

Dear Miss Welch-Hall

Thank you for your most informative letter and for the fascinating enclosures. Can you tell me, please, if these are all the cardboard letters, exactly as they came to you on each of your birthdays? It would help me very much to know.

Yours very sincerely

Sherlock Holmes

Rather than take the letter himself, Holmes summoned Wiggins,[1] and gave him sixpence to deliver the envelope to the tobacconist in Camden Town. When the boy had departed Holmes remarked, 'that sixpence was to allow him to take the omnibus. But, if I know Wiggins, he will run all the way and keep the sixpence for himself. In any case, the boy is wise enough to be completely reliable, and I can be as sure of a safe delivery as if I had taken the letter there myself.'

Sure enough, the reply came by post the next day.

Dear Mr Holmes

The letters I sent are all those I received. However, there was one, I forget which, that was accidentally lost – I recall that a maid took it out with the discarded envelope and burned it in the kitchen. That letter I remade for you so as not to lose the sense of the message.

Yours very sincerely

Rose Welch-Hall

Holmes read this reply with a look of perplexity upon his face. 'If she wished me to continue to believe her story,' he said, 'she has answered my question in the only way she possibly could have. And yet …'. He was clearly troubled, and sat for some time in silence, sending up clouds of blue smoke from his pipe. At length he smiled, knocked out the pipe, and said 'There is no purpose in our indulging this lady's whims any longer. I must meet her.' Again he took out pen and paper and wrote:

1. Daniel Wiggins (1873–1898?), a street-urchin and the leader of the Baker Street 'Irregulars' at this period. Later, in youth and manhood, he served Holmes several times, and accounts of two adventures in which he feature were found among Watson's papers in 2010. One involves his apparent death at the hands of another former member of the Irregulars, Frank Simpson, in 1898.

Dear Miss Welch-Hall

Your letter told me all I hoped it might. Now, if my case is to progress, I fear there is no alternative to a meeting between us. Would you be so kind as to call upon me on Friday afternoon at four? If a visit here is not convenient, then please suggest another place where we might meet.

Your servant

Sherlock Holmes

There were no letters of importance the next day, but the morning after that, the Friday Holmes had suggested for the meeting, the early post brought the following extraordinary communication.

My Dear Mr Holmes

I have seen something which has made me very much afraid. Last evening, as I looked out of my bedroom window before retiring, I saw a man in the garden. At first I could scarcely believe my eyes. It was dark, the only light coming from a nearby streetlamp, and I thought I must be looking at a shadow or a curiously grown shrub. But no, it was a man, and such a man. Mr Holmes, I swear to you he was the very tallest, thinnest man I have ever seen. He stood beside a clump of wisteria which grows to nearly six feet, and yet his head and shoulders were above the topmost branch. I know that you are a tall man, but this fellow is a positive giant. His head was bare, and I could see he had a high, shining forehead and long, dark hair, though his features were hidden. He appeared to be looking directly up at my window. I called to my mother, but before she could come the man inclined his head, almost as if nodding to me, and I caught a glint from his eyes which could only have been caused by the streetlight catching the lenses of spectacles. Then he put on a tall hat which increased his height still further and walked quickly to the garden gate and out into the street.

I have never seen this man before. Could he be my persecutor? What motive has he, Mr Holmes, in this pursuit of me? I beg you to help me.

Yours very sincerely

Rose Welch-Hall

When he had read the letter Holmes passed it across to me and descended for a while into thought. 'You will notice,' he said at length, 'several interesting features. Leaving aside the point that she does not address my request for a meeting – is it possible she wrote this before receiving my last letter? – I am most intrigued by her knowledge of my height. She clearly knows something of my appearance. Is it possible that she has been watching me? And this story, with its nightmare setting and almost superhuman figure of menace, does it not strike you as pure fiction, the creation of an imagination suckled on the bloods and dreadfuls of the station booksellers?'

'I think that a little unchivalrous, Holmes,' said I. 'The lady is in difficulty, and I find her story both believable and troubling. Should we not try our utmost to protect her from what ever horror follows her, be it real or imagined?'

'No doubt you are right, Watson,' he replied casually. 'In which case I can do no better than repeat my plea for a meeting.'

He wrote a short note to this effect, suggesting that Miss Welch-Hall visit our rooms on Monday morning. Since Wiggins could not be found, Holmes entrusted the note to another of the Irregulars, apparently without any qualms about its safe delivery.

Before the day was out we had our reply in the form of a telegram. Miss Welch-Hall wrote: 'I will be there. I hope you will not take it amiss if I wear a veil.'

'Why should I object to one more veil,' asked Holmes, 'when the lady is already concealed by so many?'

On Monday morning Holmes was more light-hearted than I had seen him in months. I delighted to see the improvement written in his face and figure during that week. His appetite had improved too, and he ate a good breakfast before summoning Mrs Hudson.

'You may take away the breakfast things now,' he said. 'And by the way, I am expecting a lady at ten. When she arrives, I would be much obliged if you would do the following. Ask her, please, for a calling card. If, as I expect, she does not possess one, then give her this pen and ask her to write her name on this blank card.' He placed the pen and card on the breakfast tray. 'Then bring the card up to me. Is that clear?'

'Quite clear,' said Mrs Hudson.

'Thank you.'

At a few minutes before ten we heard the jingle of the door-bell and Holmes took up position beside the fireplace, motioning me to remain in my chair. I could see that he was, for all his show of nonchalance as he leant against the mantel, deeply excited. After a minute Mrs Hudson knocked and came in with the lady's card upon a salver. Holmes picked it up, and a cloud passed across his face as he read it. He threw it across to me, and I was much astonished to read not the name of Rose Welch-Hall but that of 'Miss Lucy Lennox'. It was clear too that the handwriting was quite different from that we had grown used to from our correspondent.

'Ask her to join us, please,' said Holmes.

Thirty seconds later the lady was standing in our presence. She was tall and fashionably dressed, though it was clear her clothes were not of high quality. Her face was thickly veiled, revealing only a shapely mouth and firm chin, a little chalky with face-powder.

'Mr Holmes,' she said, holding out a gloved hand. 'I am very pleased to meet you.'

'And I you. But what name am I to use? I was expecting Miss Rose Welch-Hall this morning.'

'I am she,' replied the lady. 'I am also Lucy Lennox. But, as you may guess, neither name is that I was given at birth. May I sit? Thank you. I was christened Edith Jones, but I am an actress and use the stage name Lucy Lennox. You may call me by that name.'

'Thank you,' said Holmes. 'But pray tell me, where does Rose Welch-Hall come from?'

'Why from this gentleman,' she said, indicating me. It was clear that the game was, for some as yet unknown reason, up. I smiled a little sheepishly at Holmes.

'Watson, you old deceiver,' he said, chuckling. 'Who would have thought it? And yet, I had my suspicions. It was very well done. The story was just right to catch my interest – the name being an anagram, the mystery upon a mystery, the ebb and flow of data, none of it leading to a firm conclusion. When I spotted the error in the chronology of the cards, the answer from the lady was so perfectly what was needed that I wondered then if we might not have a spy in our rooms. I suspected you, Watson. There was something, well, Watsonian about those letters. You dictated them, I suppose, to your most obliging lady-friend, whose handwriting, and indeed face, I have never seen?' I nodded. 'You have gone to great lengths, old friend, and I perceive your motives. They were of the best. You went so far as to hire the services of this lady to act the part of your persecuted heroine. No doubt you schooled her over these last few days, while I thought you were attending to your patients and your latest romantic conquest. Well, Watson, I thank you, and I applaud you. But this lady has let you down and, I'll wager, she has a very good reason for doing so.'

I looked across at Lucy with some hostility. I had, as Holmes suggested, spent some hours, not to mention five guineas, preparing her for this interview, and could not imagine why she had immediately abandoned our agreed plan. I should add that she had been recommended to me by a friend of Charlotte Carwitham, whom I had first asked to play the role. But Charlotte is no actress and, though willing, in a good cause, to write letters in the person of another and collect replies from a tobacconist near her home, she declined to appear before Sherlock Holmes as Rose Welch-Hall. She had a friend in Camden, however, who was also interested in the theatre, and that friend gave me the name of Lucy Lennox, swearing that she was both reliable and discreet. Lucy was a married lady, so there could be no suggestion of impropriety in our dealings, and she was not, I regret to say, a great success on the stage, so that she was both glad of the work I had given her and not likely to be recognized by Holmes, even without her veil.

Lucy smiled back at me, with something of the same embarrassment with which I had recently regarded Holmes. She raised her veil and said, 'I am sorry Doctor. I must return these.' She held out a small white envelope which I took. It was heavy and I guessed, correctly, that it contained my five guineas. 'Mr Holmes is quite right. I could not continue our game of charades while more weighty matters lay upon my mind. The truth is that my husband is missing, and I fear he may have done himself harm. I know a good deal of your powers, Mr Holmes, from what Doctor Watson here has told me, and I entreat you to help me find him before it is too late.'

'Well, well,' said Holmes. 'One mystery is scarcely cleared up before another presents itself. Tell me everything, and I will see what may be done.'

Lucy Lennox (as we must now call her) regarded Holmes earnestly for a moment and then said, 'I believe you are a man who values the truth, and will only be obstructed in your work by any small deceptions which I may, for the best of reasons, attempt.' Holmes nodded assent. 'I will tell you, therefore, that I do not love my husband. Indeed, I love another and have been, for some weeks now, planning to end my marriage and throw in my lot with Bobbie, that is to say Robert Corrall, the man I love. My great fear, Mr Holmes, is that Tom has learned of my plans before I was quite ready to impart them, and has taken some drastic action as a result.'

'Let us be quite clear,' said Holmes. 'Do you believe your husband has taken his own life?'

'I fear as much. Though I do not love him, sir, I still recall the happier days of our marriage, and have a warm regard for him, in spite of everything, so that my heart fairly breaks at the idea that he might, for love of me, have harmed himself.'

'The loss of love, then, is all on your side?'

'Most certainly. It is the one reason I have found it so hard to tell Tom of my own changed heart. I know how deeply this will wound him.'

'What reason do you have to think he now knows of your liaison with Mr Corrall?'

'None save his absence, and the fact that theatre-folk are talkative. My meetings with Bobbie have not gone unobserved, and the tongues of actors and actresses will wag. Tom must have found out about us, somehow.'

'When did you last see the gentleman?'

'On Saturday morning. He has a leading part in *What Shall We Call Her?* at Pye's Theatre and is also rehearsing a new role for Mr Millan. On Saturday he was due to perform in a matinée, but could not be found. His cigar-case and other personal items were in his dressing-room, as was his costume, but he was quite vanished. A search was made of the theatre and of all the nearby public houses, for it is no secret that Tom has in the past been inclined to drink to excess when in both high and low spirits, but there was no trace of him. When the curtain went up, Tom's understudy, Mr Abraham Roach, took the part and, by all accounts, acquitted himself admirably. I did not learn of this until tea-time when Tom failed to return from the theatre. I sent round an enquiry, and was told of his absence. He missed that evening's performance too, and I have had no word of him since. Can you help me, Mr Holmes?'

'I will try,' said Holmes. 'I wonder if you would answer a few simple questions, please? Thank you. What is your husband's name?'

'He is Thomas Gold. It is his real name, unlike mine, and he uses it also upon the stage.'

'Would you describe him, please?'

'I can do better. I have a photograph.'

Lucy opened her reticule and took out a small portrait printed on card, of the sort used by theatre-folk to present to their admirers. It showed a handsome man in his mid-thirties, with slightly curly black hair and a dark complexion. He was dressed in an old-fashioned frock-coat and printed beneath the photograph were the words 'Mr Thomas Gold in the role of Robert Audley'.

'That was in seventy-nine,' Lucy added, 'and gives a good idea of his appearance.'

'May I retain this for a while?' asked Holmes.

'Anything, if it will help you to find him.'

'Thank you. You have been admirably frank. I wonder how you came to meet Mr Robert Corrall?'

'He too is on the stage, and we acted together at the Gaiety only last year. It was one of those instant attractions, Mr Holmes. We fell into one another's arms and I knew I had found my true love. He is a little younger than myself, but that is of no matter when two people are destined for one another.'

'I see,' said Holmes. 'Does your husband know Mr Corrall?'

'Why yes, they have acted together in the past and are to play brothers in the play I mentioned, which Tom is now rehearsing for Mr Millan.'

'Has Mr Gold shown any sign of hostility to Mr Corrall, or *vice versa*?'

'I believe not. Bobbie has, of course, feelings of his own about Tom, but I have told him of the sad state of our marriage and he quite understands, and has promised to do nothing to make his own feelings plain.'

'And what, pray, is the sad state of your marriage?'

'I mentioned that Tom has, in the past, been too fond of the bottle, and it is that which has chiefly driven away those tender feelings I once had for him. He has shown me no actual violence, but when in drink he was often very angry and said such foul things that I could never have forgiven him, though he seemed to have forgotten his words when he was sober again, and was perfectly loving towards me. He made a pledge, however, to abjure drink in 1880 and, so far as I know, has not had more than a glass of beer with dinner since that time. Yet, he has not been the same carefree, happy Thomas I married. His brow has often been dark, and he has been prey to fears and nervousness about his work on the stage which is quite unlike him. Indeed, his whole character has changed, though, as I have already re-marked, I believe his love for me remains constant. It would have been better, perhaps, if that too had altered.'

'Thank you. Just one more question. I happen to know there have been a number of petty thefts from actors and actresses in recent weeks. Have you lost any items of value?'

Lucy looked a little surprised at this question. 'No, sir,' she said. 'I have lost nothing. But Tom complained of having mislaid some gold cufflinks which he later believed had been stolen. We are not rich people, Mr Holmes, and those cufflinks were among the most valuable things my husband possessed. They had belonged to his father, and it upset him very much to lose them.'

'When did they go missing?'

'Oh, about two weeks ago, I think.'

'And has anything been stolen from Mr Corrall?'

'No. But several of my friends have lost small and valuable objects – rings, watches, purses containing money, and so forth.

Can you really imagine there is any connection between the disappearance of my husband and the work of some petty thief?'

'I think it possible, but I do not insist upon it,' said Holmes casually. 'It has been most instructive to meet you, Miss Lennox, and I shall be very glad to look into your small problem.'

'Thank you,' said Lucy with evident feeling.

'Would you be so kind as to write down your address?' asked Holmes, returning to her the card on which she had already written her name. 'And allow me to call upon you later today to report any progress?'

'Of course, Mr Holmes. Do you you have hope of finding Tom alive?'

'There is always hope,' said Holmes, 'but it is fair to warn you that I may fail to find him at all, or may discover the removal of a great impediment to your union with Mr Corrall.'

'I understand,' said the actress, looking Holmes directly in the eye.

'Well,' said my friend when Lucy Lennox had departed our rooms, 'what do you make of her story?'

'I know the lady a little better than you, Holmes, having spent some hours with her lately, and my own belief is that she is absolutely honest.'

'Despite being an actress?'

'Holmes, that is unfair.'

'Perhaps so. But the essence of theatrical performance is dissembling, is it not? And Miss Lennox was employed by a good fellow very lately for the particular purpose of deceiving me. Is she still attempting to deceive me, I wonder?'

'I should say not.'

'There are some suggestive words here,' added Holmes. 'The name of the play in which Mr Gold was acting is particularly appropriate is it not? The same is true of the role he was playing when this small photograph was taken.'

'Robert Audley. Is he not the hero of *Lady Audley's Secret*?'

'Quite so. It must have been Suter's dramatization. I wish I could recall more of the plot of that shocking work. I seem to remember it involves a handsome young woman who pretends to be named Lucy in order to marry a rich man while her former husband is still alive, a life she later extinguishes with some decisive force.'

'Are you suggesting that Miss Lennox is living out the plot of an outlandish play?'

'Not at all, old friend. That would be as meaningless as pointing out to you that no woman would, surely, wish to exchange Gold for Corrall. It is a co-incidence of words, no more. But I do wonder if Lucy Lennox is quite so frank or so solicitous for her late husband as she pretends to be.'

'Her late husband? You believe he is dead then?'

'He may have abandoned her, or have returned to the bottle and be lying drunk in some gutter. But, one way or the other, he will not be Lucy's husband for much longer, and the impediment to her marriage with Bobbie may already have been removed for once and all. That gentleman, Robert Corrall, clearly has a good deal to gain by the disappearance of Mr Gold. And we must also consider the possibility that Abraham Roach has taken some action against the man. Actors are sometimes jealous, ambitious people. How far might such a man go to ensure his promotion from invisible understudy to leading man in a popular play, I wonder?'

'It seems a pretty thin motive for murder.'

'I have known a man killed for much less. But this Roach need not murder his man to achieve his end, merely divert him from his work, or detain him against his will. The interests of these theatre-folk seem so strong against our client's husband that I cannot help but suspect the worst. But we can gain no more by theorizing. If you can spare an hour or two, we will make a few enquiries and see what may be learned among the greasepaint and limelight.'

Twenty minutes later we were at the stage-door of Pye's Theatre in Guildford Road. We had left our rooms with no idea of where to find the building, but when I mentioned this to Holmes he laughed and said, 'every jarvey knows the theatres of London as he knows his own face in the mirror. We will not find it difficult to make our way there.' And so it proved.

The theatre was not one of the more refined establishments of the type, and the board outside was plastered with gaudy posters for all manner of popular entertainments. The freshest was a brightly-printed announcement for *What Shall We Call Her?*, described as the 'Sensational new play by Mrs Cooper, with Mr Thomas Gold and Miss Fanny Fairburn'. What must have been a scene from the play in question was presented beneath these words, with a woman kneeling at the feet of a stern-looking gentleman with side-whiskers, her face upturned, her hands clasped in supplication.

Holmes sent his card in at the door, and soon a small and well-dressed Jew stood before us. He smiled and introduced himself as Jacob Pye, the proprietor and manager of the theatre. Holmes asked to see Mr Gold's dressing-room, and we were led through narrow brick-walled corridors, past a series of green-painted doors, until we came to a small room, bright with gaslight.

'I understand Mr Gold was last seen here on Saturday morning, some time before the *matinée* performance. Did you see him yourself?'

'Yes, sir,' said Pye. 'I make a point of walking round the theatre when a show is on, keeping up with my actors and making sure all is well with them. I saw Tom at a little before midday, when I called in here.'

Holmes began a careful search of the room, while he continued to hold the proprietor in conversation. I noticed the cigar-case which Lucy had mentioned lying on the actor's dressing table, and a suit of clothes, which I took to be his costume, hanging up just inside the door.

'Did Mr Gold seem in his usual temper?'

'Well, that is not easy to say, Mr Holmes. His temper has been so variable of late that I could not swear to his having a usual one. But he was in good spirits, even high spirits. He smiled and joked with me, and I remember he was playing with a cream-coloured ball, which he passed from hand to hand.'

'A ball, you say? How large?'

'About the size of a cricket ball.'

'Pray, did he mention his wife, or Mr Corrall?'

'Not that I recall, sir. I wished him well for the performance, in the curious language that actors prefer, and he said he felt sure he would be on sparkling form that afternoon. But he was gone, sir, when the call-boy came for him shortly before the show was due to start. I asked around and no one had seen him leave. The stage door is always attended, but he could easily have walked through the house and out by the front entrance without anyone noticing. Indeed, he must have done just that, for a very careful search of the building showed that he was not here.'

'Is he especially friendly with anyone in the cast of your present play?'

'Why, yes, he and Neville Thrale, who plays the manservant in *What Shall We Call Her?*, are very thick. Neville is a younger actor, and Tom has been so kind as to share some of his wisdom and experience with him.'

'Is Mr Thrale here now? I should very much like to speak with him.'

'I am afraid not. He has a part in Frederick Millan's new play, and is rehearsing at Camden. Poor Frederick will be looking to recast one of his leading men now that Tom has vanished. Unless, that is, you can trace our missing lead.'

'I have hopes,' said Holmes. 'But it will be no easy matter, and I fear that, for now at least, Mr Abraham Roach will have to do his best in your play.'

'Abraham has shown himself a very fine actor,' replied Pye. 'Much better than any of us suspected. But he is no Tom Gold,

84

and has not quite the same appeal for the ladies, who seem to find Tom very fascinating ... on the stage, I mean.'

'Thank you. One last question. There is talk of an outbreak of petty thefts from theatres in recent weeks; have you heard anything of this?'

'I have heard talk, sir,' said the proprietor. 'The actors are worried that one of their number is a thief, though no one knows who it might be. My own theory is that someone from outside has been creeping into theatres while shows are under way and raiding the dressing rooms. I cannot believe one of my actors is responsible. They have their faults, sir, but they are honest men and women. Not a thief among them.'

Holmes thanked Mr Pye warmly, and left him with a promise that we would return before the week was out to watch a performance of *What Shall We Call Her?* It was a prospect I regarded with more curiosity than pleasure.

'What now?' I asked as we walked towards the cab-rank in Russell Square.

'Now we have a bite of lunch,' said Holmes. 'And then we will visit Mr Frederick Millan's establishment to see if we cannot make friends with Neville Thrale.'

After lunch we caught a cab and, in ten minutes, found ourselves outside another theatre, on the outskirts of Camden. It looked very much like the place we had recently left, being the same class of shabby building with brightly-coloured posters on boards outside the entrance. The current production was, however, something rather more elevated – *The Tempest* with William Waterson as Prospero. We walked round to the stage-door, but, finding it unattended, entered the dark and slightly malodorous passages of the theatre unnoticed. After a few minutes we came across a boy carrying a box of artificial swords, and gained from him directions to Neville Thrale's dressing room.

Holmes knocked on the door and a thin, high voice bade us enter. Thrale was a good-looking young man of little more than twenty, with fine, yellow hair. He was dressed in a coarse shirt and trousers, like those of a workman. I was not sure whether this was a costume or his own clothes. He was tall, but rather thin and awkward in his movements as he came to greet us.

'If you are looking for Mr Gold,' said he, 'he is using the next dressing-room but one. But, I fear, you will not find him at home.'

'My name is Sherlock Holmes,' said my friend. 'This is Dr Watson, and we are, indeed, looking for Mr Gold, but not perhaps in the sense you imagine. I am a private agent, and have been retained by Miss Lucy Lennox to find her husband. May we sit down?'

Thrale nodded and we took the two plain wooden chairs that stood beside his dressing-table.

'I would be glad indeed to know what has become of Tom,' the actor said. 'He has been very good to me, and I hate to think of him suffering alone with the pain that woman has caused him.'

'He knows, then, that his wife loves another.'

'Of course. Such a ... liaison could never have been kept a secret for long. He knows she intends to leave him, and I believe it has driven him to despair. He is, perhaps, not the most perfect husband. But he is absolutely loyal to Miss Lennox. He might enjoy the favours of any young actress, or lady admirer, he chooses. Some, perhaps many, have offered themselves. I believe his current leading lady, Miss Fairburn, is quite besotted with him. But he has remained steadfast in his love for that unworthy woman.'

'Pray, when did you last see Mr Gold?'

'Last Friday, when we rehearsed together for Millan's latest. It is a good play, Mr Holmes, and will make the names Thomas Gold and Robert Corrall household words.'

'And might, perhaps, do your own career no harm?'

'That is true.'

'It remains true of you and Mr Corrall, whether or not we are able to return Thomas Gold to the company.'

86

'That is also true. Though it will be a poor show if Tom is not there at opening night.'

'Is Corrall a good hand?'

'Oh, he acts well enough, and is not a bad sort. Save that he is foolishly infatuated with another man's wife! But I cannot blame him too much for that. Lucy Lennox is strong, and Robert Corrall weak, so that she will have her way.'

'I see. When you saw Mr Gold on Friday, was he in good spirits?'

'In truth, he was in a curious mood. We sat together for a while after the rehearsal, before he left for dinner, in this very room, and his temperament veered between joy and despair. For a while he sighed over the prospect of losing Lucy, then he seemed to rally and talked, curiously, of the happiness that Mr Corrall and his wife would find together. He said a strange thing, Mr Holmes. He said, almost in a loving tone, "Soon they will lie together for ever, tangled in the roots of the Camden Rose".'

'Were those his exact words?'

'Why, yes. I can remember words, Mr Holmes, especially when they are so strange and beautiful. Tom is a man with poetry in his soul. He loves Shakespeare, and the poets of King George's reign ...'

'Pray, what did you take to be his meaning, when he spoke of the roots of the Camden Rose?'

'I could not say, sir. Indeed, I asked him to explain but he slipped into a reverie, and would say no more.'

'How very interesting. Thank you, Mr Thrale. One last question. I have heard mention of a few petty thefts among actors recently. Have you been unfortunate enough to lose anything?'

'I have, and I would not call it a petty matter. My gold watch has been taken. It was the most precious thing I had, and I was very sorry indeed to lose it. The police believe a sneak-thief is at work in theatre-land, but they seem unable to find the man or return any of the precious things he has taken.'

'It is a case which may never be solved,' said Holmes. 'But it is not impossible that your watch will be returned to you.'

'And Tom?'

'That I cannot say.'

Neville Thrale took a gold watch from his pocket and looked at it. 'I borrowed this from my father,' he said. 'It keeps good time, but is nothing near so fine as the one I have lost. Now, it is nearly three, Mr Holmes, and I must go upstairs to continue our rehearsal. If you would like to sit in the stalls for a while and watch, I am sure Mr Millan would have no objection. It is a really fine play, and you will see Mr Corrall in his element.'

'Thank you, but I have an engagement elsewhere,' said Holmes. 'I shall hope to see the play, and Mr Corrall, in performance, once the drama has been perfected.'

As we made our way towards the stage-door we heard the muffled sounds of running feet and cries from the auditorium above, suggesting that a battle scene or riot might be in rehearsal that afternoon. Once in the street I turned to Holmes and asked him what our next move would be.

'Now,' he said, 'we will pay a visit to Miss Lennox to report our progress.'

'Have we made any progress?'

'We stride forward like men in seven-league boots,' he replied, smiling.

The address Lucy had given us was in Bayham Street, and it took only a few minutes to travel there by cab. Our knock was answered by an ancient woman with straggling grey hair who peered at the card Holmes gave her so closely, and for such a long time, that I concluded she could barely see, or read, or both. At length she invited us in and took the card upstairs to the rooms occupied by Miss Lennox and Mr Gold. Two minutes later we heard a flurry on the stairs and Lucy herself burst into sight.

'Mr Holmes, Dr Watson, how very good to see you, and so soon. I do hope you have news for me. Come up, come up.'

We followed her up three flights of stairs to the top of the house, where she invited us through a low door and into a small sitting room. The walls were decorated with faded prints and posters for various theatrical performances, and the furniture was old and battered, but a good fire was burning and the room was warm and cheerful.

'Welcome to our modest home,' said Lucy. 'It is all we can afford, I am afraid. We have just four rooms, this one, which serves as dining and drawing room, my little kitchen, and our two bedrooms. We do for ourselves, of course. Can I offer you some tea?'

'Later, perhaps,' said Holmes.

'And do you have news for me?' she begged.

'Pray tell me,' said Holmes. 'Do you believe your husband is dead?'

'I fear as much. But I hope, with all my heart, that I might be wrong. Until there is proof, one way or the other, I will continue to hope.'

'Well, that, at least, is good,' said Holmes. 'You said a moment ago that you have two bedrooms. Might I ask to see your husband's room?'

'You assume, Mr Holmes, that my husband has a bedroom of his own ... and you are correct. Even before our life together was quite ruined by his drinking we each had our own bedroom; unless we were acting in the same play, which was rare, our hours would not often co-incide and it was more convenient if we could come and go without disturbing one another in the evenings. When Tom was in drink it became, as I am sure you can imagine, quite essential for me to have my own room into which I could retreat and be apart from him. I believe he also found the arrangement agreeable. But come, I will show you.'

She stood, and led us to a doorway covered with a curtain. Beyond was a short corridor with two doors to the right and a window at the end. We followed Lucy to the farther door, which she opened to admit us. The room was somewhat untidy, with a bed along one wall, a large, old-fashioned writing desk against another, and a small wardrobe directly facing us. The floor was scattered with pages from a newspaper, and books and papers were piled here and there on the floor, on the desk, on the bed and on the sill of the small window. Holmes entered slowly and began to peer at the contents of the room. His attention quickly fixed upon the desk and the piles of paper there. After a few moments he snorted, however, in a manner which suggested he had found little to interest him. He motioned to me to join him, and I crossed quickly to the desk, leaving Lucy standing in the doorway.

'Nothing here but playbills and reviews,' said he in an unexpectedly cheerful voice. Then in an undertone he added, 'You're feeling faint, Watson.'

'Am I?' I whispered.

'My dear friend,' he said more loudly, with a look of concern on his face. 'Are you feeling faint?'

I had, after a moment's confusion, grasped Holmes's intention and was quick enough to answer, with all the conviction I could, 'Why, yes. I'm terribly sorry Miss Lennox. I do feel most unsteady.'

Holmes swept some of the papers from the bed. 'Sit down, old friend,' he said. 'That's better. You have still not quite recovered, I think, from that attack of pneumonia. I blame myself for tearing round town with you at my heels and never giving a thought to ... Miss Lennox, I believe now might be the very time for that tea you mentioned.'

'Yes,' I agreed, doing my best to look like a pneumonia patient. 'A cup of tea would be just the thing.'

'Of course,' said Lucy, who had entered the room and was half way across the carpet of newspapers.

'I shall stay here and look after Watson while you make it,' said Holmes.

Lucy hesitated for a moment, then turned and left the room.

'Thank you,' I called after her, as weakly as I could.

As soon as we heard the swish of the curtain at the end of the corridor, Holmes said, 'Quick Watson. These old desks very often have a secret drawer or compartment. Help me find it!'

I leapt up and we both attacked the desk. It did not take Holmes more than ten seconds to locate the catch hidden behind one of the drawers. There was a gentle click, and the central panel between the pigeon-holes sprang open to reveal two further drawers, with handles made of pink string. Holmes quickly pulled them both out. One was empty, but the other contained a small black leather case. He opened it and showed me the contents. It was all too familiar. There was a hypodermic syringe, several bright needles and three small vials, two empty and one half full of a cloudy liquid. He sniffed at the top of the half-full vial, then pulled out its cork and poured a little of the fluid onto his finger-tip. This he also sniffed, and then tasted.

'A solution of cocaine,' he whispered. 'A little stronger, I think, than my own preferred mixture.'

Then he picked up the empty drawer and examined it. He sniffed it too, and handed it over to me.

'What does that smell of?' he asked.

'Why, cricket bats!' I said.

'Quite so. It is linseed oil, if I am not mistaken.'

There was a tiny sound from the corridor, and Holmes quickly put the syringe and bottles into their case and slipped it into his pocket. Then he returned the secret drawers to their homes and snapped the panel back into place with one hand while pushing me gently towards the bed with the other. I had sat down and was ready to resume my role as invalid in no time. Indeed, I had moved so swiftly that we had to wait for several seconds until Lucy appeared in the doorway.

'I have put the kettle on the stove,' she said, 'and it will soon be boiled.'

'Watson tells me he needs air,' said Holmes, with such anxiety in his voice that I almost believed him myself. 'I hope you will forgive us if we forego the tea, and take a turn outside.'

'Of course,' said Lucy, her face working with emotion. 'But what about my husband?'

'I am close,' said Holmes. 'I am very close. I will be back as soon as I can. Just one, very brief, question, if I may?' He helped me to my feet and we walked slowly towards the door. 'What would your husband have meant by the Camden Rose?'

'Why, that is his pet-name for Mr Millan's theatre. He has names for all the theatres he works in. Pye's he calls "Jacob's Folly" since, for all his kind heart, Mr Pye could no more tell a good play from a bad and has hits from time to time by pure luck. The best theatres, the ones Tom loves most, he names "the Rose" after Shakespeare's place in Southwark, of famous memory. Because there are several Roses, he always adds an epithet. Millan's is the "Camden Rose", the Globe is "Sefton's Rose", the Gaiety is …'.

Holmes cut her short with a wave of his hand. 'Thank you. We must make haste if my friend is not to faint quite away.'

We passed quickly out through the small drawing-room and down the three flights of stairs to the street. Once there Holmes hurried me to a cab and in a few minutes we were back at the stage-door of Millan's theatre. This time the door was guarded by a commissionaire, who took in Holmes's card. We had to wait several minutes, and I could see Holmes was bursting with impatience to be about his business. At length a short, plump man with round spectacles appeared before us.

'I am Frederick Millan,' said he, with no great show of warmth. 'We are rehearsing at the moment, sir, so I beg you to state your business briefly.'

'My name is Sherlock Holmes, and I am trying to trace Mr Thomas Gold. Is there a cellar beneath your theatre?'

At the mention of Mr Gold's name the proprietor's expression changed utterly. 'Yes, sir,' he said. 'There are old cellars under our feet, from the house that stood on this site long before the theatre was built.'

'May we see them, please? It is a matter of some urgency.'

'Of course, follow me.'

We passed the commissionaire, to whom Millan spoke a few words which I did not catch, and followed the proprietor along the same passage we had walked down barely an hour before. We came to a small door on the left, which Millan opened and bade us enter. He struck a match and lit a couple of candles which stood on a shelf inside the door, handing one to Holmes. By their light we could see an old stone staircase leading down.

'We use the cellars for storage,' said Millan as we descended. 'But they are too damp for scenery or costumes, so we use the space primarily for wine for the bar and coal for the boilers.' We came into a large, vaulted cellar with coal piled high in arched recesses to either side. Holmes took his candle to each in turn and examined what lay there. An archway at the end led into a smaller room with racks of wine bottles to one side, and a pile of old barrels to the other; at the far end was another arch, leading to a still smaller room, cluttered with various objects. I noticed several sheets of curved and rusted metal that looked as if they might have been parts of a suit of armour, and a heap of bulging sacks, covered in a bloom of greenish mould. At the narrowest end of this cellar was a heavy wooden door. Holmes stopped as soon as he saw it, and held his candle high. The floor had recently been swept clean before the door, and lying there in the pool of light, on its side, was a single black leather boot.

The door itself was ancient, but very clean and solid-looking. It had a brass handle and a large iron catch on the outside, which glistened in the candle-light as if it had been recently oiled.

'Hullo,' said Millan. 'Something has happened here. Last time I saw this door it was thick with dust, and stood open. And who's boot is that?'

'What lies beyond?' asked Holmes.

'Just a little room. It used to be a strong-room, I think, for the old house, but it has no lock now, just that catch. The hinges are very rusty. It does not move easily, and we leave it open because there is a ventilator in there. It helps with the damp.'

Holmes tried the catch and lifted it easily. He pulled at the handle, but the door appeared to be stuck. He gave it a harder tug and, with a click and a curious sucking sound it swung towards him. A blast of foul air caught in our nostrils as we peered inside.

We saw a chamber about five feet square, quite empty save for the figure of a man half crouching, half kneeling against the opposite wall, his back towards us. I made to move into the room, but Holmes held me back.

'Get one of those sacks, Watson,' he said, 'and place it against the door to keep it open.' I did as I was asked and dragged one of the mouldy sacks, which turned out to contain empty wine bottles, into position. 'And another,' said Holmes. 'We would not wish to suffer the same fate as our friend here.' I obeyed and placed a second sack against the door. Then we entered. Holmes put his candle on the floor and gently touched the man on the shoulder. He fell backwards onto the flags, his head and shoulders lying in the doorway. The sight of his face made Millan gasp. I confess, I too felt a thrill of horror at his appearance. His eyes were wild and bloodshot, and his expression one of anger and horror. His lips were black and his cheeks and brow a dark purple. It was clear, all the same, that we had found the missing actor. But for his side-whiskers he was the image of the man in the photograph Lucy had given Holmes.

'Mr Millan,' said Holmes. 'I fear it is now a case for the police. Would you be so kind as to send out for a constable? Thank you.'

With a moment's hesitation and a backward look of horror, the proprietor left us alone.

'Now, Watson,' said Holmes. 'Do you believe Lucy Lennox to be an honest woman, innocent of any part in what has happened here?'

'I do.'

94

'Very well. We will act accordingly.'

Holmes began to search the dead man's clothes. I noticed, as he did so, that Mr Gold was wearing only one boot. Holmes quickly found a leather-covered case, very similar to that he had abstracted from Gold's desk, and something small and hard wrapped in a grimy rag. He opened the case, and I saw that it too contained a syringe and bottles of cocaine. He unwrapped the rag to reveal a small oil can, of the sort used by cyclists to lubricate their machines. Holmes slipped both items into his pocket. Then he looked round the cellar. I followed his gaze, and realized I had been mistaken in my original perception that the room was empty, save for the body. In one corner lay a small sack made of some black material, perhaps satin. Holmes picked it up and carefully emptied the contents onto the breast of the dead man. There were four gold watches, three pearl or diamond necklaces, half a dozen cufflinks, as many rings, two silver cigarette cases, three small purses and a golden tie-pin in the form of a Masonic symbol.

'Quickly, Watson. We must put this treasure into our own pockets, and the bag too. Good. Now we have a moment or two to make observations before the good proprietor returns. You see that grille?' He pointed to a rusted iron grating, about eight inches square, set into the wall above the corpse. 'That is the ventilator Mr Millan mentioned. Do you see how it is half choked with a whitish material?' I nodded, and noticed shreds of the same stuff fallen on the floor round the dead man's feet. Holmes took Gold's right hand and held it up. The fingers also bore traces of the same material.

'What is it?' I asked.

'Glazier's putty,' replied Holmes, gathering the shreds from the floor and rolling them into a ball. He stood up and began to examine the door. 'Notice how this door has recently been renovated. The surface has been cleaned and any cracks sealed up with plaster. The hinges have been freshly oiled and here, round the jamb ...'

95

'More putty?'

'Yes, a line of putty has been run round the inside of the frame, on all four sides. You see what it means?'

'The room has been sealed.'

'Quite.'

'So … Thomas Gold sealed himself in here?'

'That is my belief.'

'It is a curious way to end one's own life.'

'Nevertheless, that is what we are going to tell Lucy he did. As far as she and the world are concerned, he died at his own hand, in a state of desolation at the knowledge that he had lost the love of his wife.'

'I see. But what really happened?'

'That we cannot know. But I may share a theory or two with you this evening, should we have a quiet moment at Baker Street. Now I hear the gentle footsteps of the good Mr Millan, and the heavier tread of a constable, and we must be ready with our interpretation of this melancholy evidence.' He indicated the body of Thomas Gold.

That evening we sat beside the fire at Baker Street and smoked in silence for a while.

'I can prove none of what I am about to tell you,' said Holmes at length. 'Indeed, it is little more than surmise and theory, and you may dismiss it as fancy if you choose. I believe it will be better for the friends of Mr Thomas Gold, and for the peace of mind of his widow, to believe he took his own life for love of Lucy Lennox. Indeed, love, of a sort, was his motive. But, as I read it, he made a very different plan. Consider the words reported to us by Mr Thrale. Tom Gold looked forward to the moment when his wife and Mr Corrall might "lie together for ever, tangled in the roots of the Camden Rose". Could he really have been wishing them well? I choose to put a more sinister interpretation on this curious phrase. In short, he intended them to be united only in their graves.

'Gold's nature was artistic and passionate, and was, you will admit, damaged by his use of cocaine, which I believe he chose in preference to drink after taking the blue ribbon for Lucy's sake. When he learned of her final betrayal of their marriage, he devised a plan of revenge. He came upon that small room in the cellars at Millan's theatre, and it gave him the idea for a scheme both devilish and simple. Over the course of several weeks, between rehearsals, he worked on that room to make it quite air-tight. He repaired the door and sealed its cracks, and blocked the ventilator by stuffing putty into the grille in the room, and more into the corresponding grating in the pavement outside the theatre. His intention was to lure the lovers there and seal them in. My guess is that he aimed to draw them to that cellar as the most private place in the building, where the three of them might talk without being disturbed. No doubt he would have tempted them with mention of an important, private matter he wished to discuss; perhaps he planned to hint that he was willing to facilitate a divorce from Lucy and leave the way clear for the lovers to marry. One may imagine the scene in his unhealthy mind. The appointed hour arrives and the lovers meet in the small room, whispering together. They wait, but Tom is late. Then of a sudden he emerges from some hiding place in the larger cellar and slams the door. The lovers might cry out, but the room is almost sound-proof, and certainly no one in the theatre will hear their cries. Soon the air will be exhausted and they will fall silent. Later, when they must be dead, Gold will return and remove the putty from the door and ventilator. Likewise he will expunge as much of the oil as he can from the hinges and catch of the door, and smear dirt from the floor over every part of it, to conceal his recent repairs. In due time the bodies will be found in that little room, and it will be taken for a trysting-place, the door having slammed shut by accident and sealed them in. That was Thomas Gold's plan.

'I believe he intended to spring his trap last Sunday, after the rehearsal which Millan would have held that afternoon. On

Saturday morning, before his *matinée*, he had an hour or two
to spare and crept out of Pye's theatre. He took a cab or an
omnibus to Millan's establishment and stole down to the cellar
to complete his preparations. It was probably then that he ran
a bead of putty round the inside of the door-frame, having prop-
ped the door open with his boot. Gold wanted the putty to be
fresh when he sprang his trap, and had with him a ball of the
stuff, which Jacob Pye had observed in his hands. He had kept
putty in one of the secret drawers of his desk too; that was the
source of the odour of linseed oil which you noticed. When the
door was ready he stuffed the last of the putty into the ventilator
grille. It was then that his boot fell to one side and the door, its
hinges freshly oiled, swung into place. We may imagine the man's
feelings when he understood that his carefully-prepared trap
had sprung not upon the poachers but upon the gamekeeper.
He had but a few minutes to live. He attempted to claw the
putty out of the ventilator. But it was no good. The other end
of the flue had been blocked by a most determined man, and
no air could enter. No doubt he cried out, in rage and fear. But
no one heard him, as he himself had planned.'

'Extraordinary,' I said. 'I hope you may, perhaps, take a
lesson from this, Holmes, on the dangers of cocaine.'

Holmes waved his hand in impatience. 'Gold's was a common
intellect, emotional and susceptible. Mine is altogether stronger.'

I drew in my breath, but said no more on the matter. Instead
I asked Holmes, 'What about the stolen items we found in the
cellar? Why did Gold have those?'

'It is my belief that he intended not only to kill his wife and
her lover, but to ruin their reputations too – or, at least, that of
Mr Corrall. As part of his plan he had taken precious objects
from his actor friends, being careful not to steal from Lucy or
Corrall themselves. He added his own cufflinks to the horde,
and made a point of reporting their loss to the police and talking
of the matter openly. I believe he intended those objects to be
found with Corrall's body, so that the police would conclude

he was the thief and, thus, what good name may have remained to him would have been destroyed.'

'Such malevolence,' said I.

'Born of love,' said Holmes, 'of a sort. One thought keeps returning to mind. I wonder how likely it is that a boot, used to prop a door open, might fall upon its side?'

'It is possible.'

'At the beginning of this case, Watson, I conjured an old ghost for you with the name Reginald Musgrave. You will remember that in that case too a man died in a small chamber, deprived of air, and there was some doubt about whether the slab had fallen into place by accident or the prop supporting it had been dashed aside by Rachel Howells. In this case too, there is such a doubt.'

'But who could have done such a thing?'

'Perhaps Neville Thrale understood more of what Gold had said to him than he admitted. Perhaps Robert Corrall heard, or overheard, something which gave him a clue to Gold's plans. Perhaps one of the other players in this little drama knows more than he is saying. Abraham Roach, Jacob Pye and Frederick Millan all stand in the wings. But is not the most likely hand the small, pale one of the woman who knew Tom Gold all-too-well and had much to gain by his death?'

'I cannot believe it,' said I.

'Perhaps,' said Holmes, 'we had better believe that the boot fell by accident, disturbed perhaps by a cellar rat.'

The following day Holmes showed me two short articles in the *Pall Mall Gazette*. One had the headline 'Suicide of an actor' and the other 'Recovery of stolen goods'. The former told, in outline, the circumstances of Gold's death, while the latter reported that a black bag containing precious objects reported stolen by members of the theatrical community had been found behind scenery at Pye's theatre. There was no clue to the identity of the thief and the objects were being returned to their owners.

Two days later, a letter arrived at 221B Baker Street. Enclosed in the envelope was a single gold cufflink. The letter was written on paper with a black border and ran in this way:

My Dear Mr Holmes

I write to thank you for your kind diligence in searching for my husband. It is a source of great regret to me that he took the withdrawal of my affections so to heart that it drove him to self-murder, and in such a curious manner that I cannot help but think the balance of his mind altered by the strength of his feelings. I mourn for my husband. But you are a man of the world, Mr Holmes, and will not be surprised if, after a suitable period, you read of the marriage of Miss Lucy Lennox and Mr Robert Corrall.

I hope you will come to see Robert in his new play at Millan's theatre. It is called *The Two Brothers*, and will make his name, and that of the author. Mr Millan is dedicating the production to Tom's memory and has asked Neville Thrale to play the part Tom would have taken. He is rather young, but will do it well, I think.

I enclose a small token of my gratitude. It is one of Tom's cufflinks, which the police found only recently and returned to me this morning. I shall keep the other as a memento of my late husband. It is a great pity the cufflinks had not been found sooner. Who knows but their return might have cheered Tom a little, and might, perhaps, have saved him from that last despair. On such small matters, sometimes, life or death may hang.

I remain, yours most sincerely

Edith Gold (in the theatre, Lucy Lennox)

III

The Adventure of the Scarlet Thorn

THERE ARE A GREAT MANY CASES from the years of my collaboration with Sherlock Holmes which are, for one reason or another, quite unsuitable for publication in the present age. I can foresee a time, however, when all objections to the dissemination of the details may be lifted. Even the case of the Scarlet Thorn, which I think too tainted with brutality for contemporary taste, may, with the passage of time, lose something of its horror and be of interest to the general reader. I shall endeavour, therefore, to write it down plainly, though parts of the story are quite repulsive even to an old soldier and medical man like myself.

The adventure began one Tuesday in February of the year 1884. Holmes had been working on the Rookmont diamond mystery for five days, having been consulted by Inspector Lestrade upon the matter almost as soon as the theft was reported. The case had caused considerable public interest but had so far proved impenetrable even to the great mind of Holmes. The diamonds were not large, but numerous and very fine, and had been torn from the tiara of the Duchess of Rookmont while she was staying at Brown's Hotel in Dover Street. The circumstances of the loss were not broadcast at the time, but there can be no objection to my revealing them now.

The Duchess was a firm believer in spiritualism, and on the evening of the theft she and three friends had gathered after dinner to hold a *séance* in her sitting-room at the Hotel. A medium had been engaged, an elderly lady known as Madam Spinarossa, and the avowed purpose of the evening was to contact the spirit of the Duke, who had died some four years previously. The drapes were drawn and the doors locked. Madam Spinarossa arranged the participants – two ladies and two gentlemen, all of unimpeachable character – round a card table and turned out the gas. In the darkness she resumed her seat, asked the group to join hands and then began her attempt to reach the realm of the dead. At first there was no result, but then, with a sigh and a groan from the medium, contact was made and after a few moments everyone present heard the voice of a man, coming not from the medium but from elsewhere in the room. The Duchess later swore that the voice was that of her late husband. He spoke for some minutes, although at times contact was lost and the air was filled with gasps and groans, while the table was felt to shudder and rise up slightly. At last there was a sound of choking and a hoarse scream from Spinarossa and she cried out that the spirit of the Duke had departed and they must break the circle. This they did, and one of the men, Colonel James Hind, lit the gas. The first thing the friends noticed was that the medium's black dress was soiled with white matter, which she later claimed to be 'ectoplasm', and she appeared to have sunk into unconsciousness with her head upon her breast. The gentlemen began to attempt to revive her, when the air was riven by another scream, this time from the other lady present, Matilda Grayson, the niece of the Duchess. She was pointing in stark horror at her Grace's head. The Duchess was too shocked to react, and at first the men could perceive nothing wrong, until they looked closely at the tiara she was wearing and found that every single diamond had been extracted from it.

After a few minutes the Duchess recovered from the shock of this discovery, and stated to the amazement of all that she believed the spirit of her late husband to have taken the jewels with him to the nether-world. He had given her the tiara on their wedding day more than forty years previously, and she professed herself convinced that he had taken back the stones as a punishment for some sin which she had committed against him. When pressed on the matter she declined to say more, but spoke so fervently that it was clear she believed this explanation for the disappearance of the diamonds. Colonel Hind and the other gentleman, Lord Vincent Carleston, were of a different opinion however, and unlocked the door at once to call for the police. A constable was found in Dover Street, and he was quickly joined by three others and the tenacious Lestrade. The room and its occupants were searched thoroughly, but nothing was found and the medium, who seemed to be suffering greatly from the effects of her trance, was allowed to depart.

The sitting-room had been locked throughout the *séance*, and the occupants were certain that no one could have got in or out while the room was dark. Subsequent inquiries failed to trace Madam Spinarossa, and suspicion naturally fell upon her, despite her age and infirmity. But of the diamonds, or the means of their abstraction, there was no clue. This was the problem with which Holmes had been struggling for five days when an unwelcome interruption came in the person of Mr William Everson Hartshorne. Mrs Hudson delivered his card late one evening, and I could see from Holmes's expression that he did not relish this distraction from the Rookmont case. However, when he looked at the man's card, his attitude changed.

'Take a look at this, Watson,' he said, handing me the calling-card. 'I think Mr Hartshorne may prove after all a most interesting visitor. Show him up, Mrs Hudson.'

I examined the card. It seemed unremarkable, bearing the engraved name of our visitor and his address at 9B Bruton Street, London W. In a few moments William Hartshorne himself stood before us. He was a young man, not yet thirty, but with an air of success and confidence. He had fairish hair and wore a small neat moustache and a look of perplexity. Holmes asked him to be seated and tell us his story.

'Well, Mr Holmes, I hesitate to trouble you with something so commonplace. But, I confess, I was deeply disturbed by the whole business, and can find no explanation, unless it were some sort of prank or joke.'

'The smallest mysteries are often the most intractable and the most fascinating,' said Holmes. 'Pray tell us the whole story, and omit nothing, even those details which may seem incidental.'

'I am,' said our visitor, 'in business on my own account in Great Portland Street, and was returning from work yesterday evening, having stayed very late in the office to deal with certain papers. It was a pleasant evening so I decided to walk home, as I often do. It was quite dark, of course, but the streets are well lit in the area, and as I turned into Bruton Street I noticed something lying on the pavement under one of the streetlamps. The road was deserted and a cold wind was blowing from the river. As I drew nearer to the object I perceived that it was large and flat, like a piece of panelling, and was somewhat surprised on coming closer to recognise it as a door. I could clearly see the brazen handle projecting, and the hinges. You will imagine my consternation upon coming into the circle of light to find that this was nothing more or less than my own front door. There was the familiar letterbox, the damage where a beggar had once struck the panels with his stick, and the brass number 9B. I was still twenty yards or so from the point where my door should have been, and my heart was in my mouth as I ran towards my rooms. The doorway was dark and I hesitated to enter. But I am no coward, Mr Holmes, and I steeled myself to go inside. In the hall I felt my way to the stand and took up a heavy stick, fearing that my open, indeed absent, door might signify burglary. I went into every room and lit the gas, all the while fearing to find a scene of ruin. But my apartments appeared to be untouched. I could find not a book, not a toothbrush, out of place. I was somewhat upset and perplexed by this business, as you might imagine, and sleep was out of the question. So, having made sure there was no one in my rooms, I lit the gas in the hall and took up a sentry position with my stick, hoping I would not have to fight to defend my open doorway. It was an uncomfortable night, but a quiet one. In the early morning I attracted the attention of a passing boy, and persuaded him to fetch a carpenter and his mate, who retrieved my door for me, and screwed it back into its original position. Then I went to work. My business affairs could not be postponed, and I was again obliged to work late. When I returned home I half expected to find the door again missing. But this was not the case and, having checked that my rooms were thoroughly secure, I came straight here. Well, Mr Holmes, that is my story. Could it have been a joke, do you think?'

'I very much doubt it. Tell me, was there any sign of damage to the lock or other parts of the door?'

'That is another curious thing. The door was quite unmarked. The carpenter who refitted it disbelieved my story, I think, and suspected me of having removed the thing myself. The lock had not been broken, and the hinges were still screwed to the door; all that was missing was the eight brass screws which had held the hinges to the door-frame, and they could not have been removed until the door was open.'

'Is it possible that you accidentally left the door unlocked when you departed for work that morning.'

'Impossible, I think. I am not a rich man, Mr Holmes, but I have some precious books and a collection of coins which I am concerned to keep safe, so I am assiduous about seeing to the locks and windows.'

'And may I see your front door key?'

Hartshorne handed over a small bunch, indicating a brass key of medium size. Holmes squinted at it, then handed back the bunch.

'Thank you. I think, Mr Hartshorne, that you are in no great danger. However, until I have made further enquiries I would not be happy to return you to your rooms, and hope you might accept the rather rough hospitality which the Doctor and I can offer you. It will only be the divan, I fear, but I venture to suggest that you will be safer here than anywhere else in London.'

Hartshorne readily accepted this offer and in the morning, after Mrs Hudson had supplied us with a good breakfast, Holmes suggested we pay a visit to 9B Bruton Street. It was a relatively short walk from Baker Street, and we soon arrived at the solid blue-painted front door which had so recently been found upon the pavement. Holmes examined it with his glass for some minutes, then asked Hartshorne to open the door, which he did with the key he had shown us the previous evening. In the hall Holmes scrutinised the lock and the hinges and then, to my surprise, announced that he was satisfied and that our friend would not need to spend another night on the couch at Baker Street. He bade Hartshorne farewell, with a promise to return presently with the solution to the mystery.

I followed him across the street where he walked slowly past the houses there before turning into Barlow Place. From here we passed down a nameless alley into Grafton Street, where we turned right, then left into Dover Street, and immediately found ourselves before Brown's Hotel. I had not realised how very close we were.

'I suppose we might as well take a look at the Duchess's rooms, while we are here,' said my friend casually. I suspected this had been his intention all along, and that he had dismissed Hartshorne so readily in order to get back on the scent of the Rookmont diamonds. Having sent his card up to the Duchess's rooms, we were soon admitted to the scene of the crime. The Duchess greeted us herself with great courtesy, though she clearly had no idea of who Holmes was and seemed somewhat amused by the notion of a consulting detective assisting the police. She was a lively woman of six and sixty, whose face gave more than a hint of the great beauty for which she had once been famed. She appeared to have no servants in her entourage and, as we entered her sitting-room, I noticed a half-eaten packet of Huntley and Palmer's biscuits on the mantel-shelf, which I thought a little curious. Having indulged Holmes's desire to see her bedroom and to examine the ruined tiara, we returned to the sitting-room and sat down at the same card table where the *séance* had been held six days previously.

'Your Grace,' said Holmes, 'is most kind to accommodate us. I wonder if you could give us your account of the disappearance of your diamonds?'

'I told everything to the police inspector who came in answer to James's summons, but I have no objection to repeating myself. I have wanted to contact my dear husband for some months now, and have made several attempts to do so, using different mediums. Last Thursday night was the first time I had success, and I bless Madam Spinarossa for her very special powers. George, my husband, came through quite clearly. I swear it was him, Mr Holmes, and he spoke to me so kindly of our life together and his happiness in paradise. But during the *séance*, he took a small revenge upon me by removing all the diamonds from my tiara. He had a perfect right. He gave them to me with his own hand, and with the same hand took them back.'

'Then you are not of the opinion that the diamonds were stolen?'

'Indeed no. I am quite sure that I will never see them again in this world. I have forfeited the right to them.'

'When you heard the voice of the Duke, was it possible to say where in the room it appeared to emanate from?'

'Oh, from the air, Mr Holmes, from the air.'

'But did it seem to come from one particular direction more than another?'

'I suppose it came from over there.' She indicated the curtained window. Holmes inspected the casement and the small table which stood beside it, picking up with his finger-tip and sniffing at a little dust which he found there.

While he worked, he asked the Duchess, 'Did you converse with the Duke?'

'Oh yes, I asked him several questions, which he answered greatly to my satisfaction and pleasure.'

'While you spoke with him did his voice appear to move about the room?'

'No, it came always from the air around the window. But the voice of Madam Spinarossa came from elsewhere, of course, from beside me where she was seated.'

'Throughout the *séance* you and she held hands?'

'Quite so. And I held dear James's hand upon the other side.'

'And did you feel or hear any disturbance about your head when the late Duke removed the diamonds?'

'None. But the fingers of a ghost are as gossamer, Mr Holmes, and I would hardly expect to have felt anything.'

'Indeed. I understand there was some shaking of the table once the *séance* had begun.'

'Poor Madam Spinarossa knocked against it in the dark before she had even sat down, but after that it was still until my husband appeared. Then there were some tremblings of the board, mostly I think when Spinarossa was having trouble maintaining contact with George.'

'Once the *séance* was over, and the disappearance of the diamonds was noticed, how did Madam Spinarossa seem?'

'Much shaken, I fear. She had generated ectoplasm during her trance, and seemed barely alive when James relit the gas. When the police arrived she recovered a little, but I was much concerned for her. James and Vincent both insisted upon being searched for the diamonds, and so did dear Mattie; I too offered to allow the policemen to search my person, and they did so in a most respectful manner. Madam Spinarossa was treated shamefully, however, and searched while unfit to understand what had happened, let alone give her consent. Of course, the police found nothing. How could they? At length they allowed my friends, and the medium, to leave.'

Holmes mused for a moment. 'I believe your Grace may be mistaken in your interpretation of what took place that evening.'

'How so, Mr Holmes?'

'It may be true that your late husband's spirit abstracted the stones, and that they will never again be seen by mortal eyes.

But, I ask you to reconsider your belief that their removal was a punishment or revenge upon you. True, your husband took back the jewels he had once given you. But were they not insured?'

The Duchess nodded. I confess I was taken aback by my friend's words, as I knew what little respect he had for the deceit of mediums and the popular belief in spiritualism. But I knew Holmes well enough to hold my tongue, and smiled indulgently at the Duchess.

'Perhaps,' said my friend, 'the late Duke took the diamonds as a kindness to you, rather than a punishment.'

She flushed and raised a hand to her mouth. Holmes nodded kindly. They understood one another, although I confess I was baffled.

Holmes bade the Duchess farewell and we left the hotel, catching a hansom in Dover Street. When we were on our way I asked Holmes what he meant by encouraging the foolishness of an old lady.

'Sometimes,' he replied, 'it is kinder to compound a deception, and her Grace is right on one point, I am sure. She will never see her diamonds again. We, on the other hand, may be more fortunate. Now my friend, I must ask you to wait for me at Baker Street while I pursue certain enquiries which I must make alone.'

I spent the remainder of the day in our rooms trying to write a coherent account of all that had occurred, and reviewing the evidence we had so far gathered. I formed for myself a small theory which accounted for some, at least, of the curious features of the case. I reasoned that Madam Spinarossa must have been responsible for the theft of the diamonds, and that she had achieved it by the use of an ingenious device consisting of two false hands, made perhaps of india rubber, separated by a stiff rod, perhaps of telescopic construction. This she had concealed beneath her robes until the lights were doused, when she took out her device and laid it upon the table between the Duchess and Matilda Grayson, each of whom took one of the false hands in her own, believing it to be that of the medium. This left Spinarossa's own hands free to remove the tiara and prise out the diamonds, covering the noise with groans and sighs, while a confederate hidden behind the window curtain spoke with the voice of the Duke.

Although I could see some flaws in this theory, and it did not cover all the facts, yet I felt sure Holmes would be impressed by my deductions when he returned. When he finally appeared, at a little after eight, however, my suggestions caused him some amusement.

'I congratulate you, Watson. You have hit upon the answer!' said he. 'The medium must have owned a set of rubber hands. But wait! What became of those hands? How did she conceal them from a police search? And how did her confederate at the window gain entry and exit without being seen, when the window had clearly not been opened for many years? No, I fear we must seek both a simpler and a more radical explanation for what occurred in that small dark room. You are, however, quite right in your basic deduction that the medium took the diamonds. But the story does not end there and, I fear, we will uncover further crimes committed in pursuit of those stones. Even now friend Lestrade is waiting for us in Bruton Street to take the matter to its conclusion. I should be most grateful for your help in that conclusion. Will you join me?'

I smiled and nodded, though felt a little crushed by Holmes's summary rejection of my theory.

'Good man. You have your revolver? Excellent.'

We caught another cab and made the short journey to the end of Bruton Street where we alighted beside Lestrade and four constables. Holmes had obviously indicated to the Inspector that something was afoot, for Lestrade's face was grimmer than usual as we set off along the pavement.

As we walked I whispered to Holmes 'Is this the solution to the diamond theft, or to the mystery of Hartshorne's front door?'

'Why to both, old friend, to both.'

We stopped before a dark house bearing the number 38A. Holmes raised a hand for us to wait, and approached the door. He produced a dark lantern and by the narrowest blade of light examined the entrance. Then he put out a hand and tried the handle. The door opened and I heard his intake of breath. He beckoned us to follow, and we entered a dark hall. There was a slaughterhouse smell in the air, and I prepared myself for the worst. Holmes led the way, cutting through the blackness with a thin beam from his lantern. At the end of the passage were two doors, both standing open. Holmes illuminated the space beyond first one, then the other.

'Lestrade,' he said. 'Please keep your men back until I have examined this room.' The Inspector sighed and accompanied Holmes and myself through the door. 'No need for silence now,' said Holmes. 'We are too late to change the course of events.'

He lit the gas, and a ghastly scene met our eyes. The room was unfurnished save for two chairs, a small table and two make-shift beds upon the floor. Lying beside them, upon the bare boards, were two bodies. They were both young men with dark hair and complexions, and both had gaping wounds in their throats. A dark brown puddle surrounded the two figures, whose limbs were contorted and faces racked with exertion and fear. They had clearly fallen while fighting for their lives. Holmes asked us to remain by the door while he examined the bodies and the contents of the room. Some objects on the table caught his particular interest and he inspected them with his glass for some minutes. Then he gestured for us to join him. I quickly examined the bodies, though there was clearly nothing that could be done for them. Then I joined Holmes at the table.

Laid out there was a singular array of objects. There were the separate parts of a large old fashioned door-lock with a brass façade, a pile of brass screws, a leather bag containing tools, a small metal lantern, a pile of grey powder, an unfamiliar-looking revolver, and the remains of a simple meal. But what held our attention was a range of human body pieces, laid out neatly like specimens in a museum; there were eight fingers, two toes, an ear, a fleshy lump which was probably a nose, and several other pieces which propriety prevents me from naming. These grim trophies were not bloody, but as clean and presentable as it was possible for them to be, which somehow made their appearance still more horrific. I glanced over at the two bodies. Clearly the parts on the table had not originated there, but from some other man, or men.

'What is all this, Holmes?' I asked.

The great detective said nothing, but pointed to the wall beside the door. Here a large mark or cipher had been drawn in blood upon the bare plaster. At first I thought it was a cross, but the lower tip was pointed and I realised that it represented a sword or dagger.

'What is it?' said Lestrade.

'That,' said Holmes, 'Is the Scarlet Thorn.'

We were, I think, too affected by the contents of that room to discuss the matter there. Lestrade left his constables to record the details and remove the bodies while he and I returned with Holmes to Baker Street, where a full explanation was promised. Once settled in familiar surroundings my good spirits returned somewhat and, having lit my pipe, I pressed Holmes to explain the case.

'First of all,' said he, 'I must tell you that a very great man has recently died. Indeed, he has been murdered, and in the most unpleasant circumstances. But I am getting ahead of my story. What we have just witnessed was the final scene of what began as a much simpler drama, planned by a criminal group as a means of raising money. I am speaking of a brutal Italian secret society known as the Spina Rossa, or Scarlet Thorn, which hired a clever thief to abstract the valuable diamonds of the Duchess of Rookmont. Some of the details of the case remain obscure, but I suspect they anticipated a burglary, or some other simple robbery. However, the man they had hired was none other than Salvatore Barozzi, who had perhaps the third or fourth most subtle criminal mind I have ever encountered. I came across him many years ago, when I was myself considering a career on the stage. He was an actor, and an uncommonly talented one. But his talents were put to evil ends, and latterly he made his living by assuming the character of some pious, trustworthy or harmless individual and tricking his way into the confidence of his victim, who was quickly robbed, or worse. Then the disguise was shed and the actor moved on. He was that most dangerous specimen, the criminal who loves his crime, the impostor who relishes each new imposture. When the Spina Rossa commissioned him to seize the Rookmont diamonds he began to research the life and mind of the Duchess, and conceived a meticulous plan based upon her natural weaknesses. He assumed the character of an elderly medium.'

'You mean Madam Spinarossa was a man?' I asked.

'Precisely. I would give twenty pounds to have seen him play the part. He must have acted quite brilliantly. Having convinced the Duchess that he was a spiritualist and could contact her late husband, he arranged a *séance* in the lady's sitting-room, carefully positioning the participants round a small table before turning out the lights. Then he knocked against the table and repositioned it in the dark, to confuse the geography of the situation, before asking everyone to hold hands. You may imagine how each groped for the nearest hand and, taking it, assumed they were holding onto the person next to them. And so they were. But Barozzi had silently removed himself and his chair from the circle, so that the Duchess held her niece's hand, and *vice versa*, while each believed herself linked to the medium. Thus, Doctor, the possession of additional rubber hands was quite unnecessary round such a small table.'

I smiled as warmly as I could and looked into the fire.

'The actor made appropriate noises with his head placed between that of the Duchess and her niece – just where they

THE REMAINS OF SHERLOCK HOLMES

would expect such noises to emanate from. Then he fell silent, lifted the tiara from the Duchess's head and moved to the table by the window.'

'But would the Duchess not have felt the removal of her tiara?' I asked.

'No. For two reasons. Firstly, she was concentrating upon the *séance* and anticipating, no doubt with suppressed excitement, communication with her late husband. Secondly, her very splendid head of silver hair is, in fact, entirely false. I observed this during our interview, and Barozzi must have made the same discovery while researching his subject. It was a simple matter for him to unclip the tiara from her Grace's hairpiece without detection. Once at the side table by the window he made further sounds and began to impersonate the Duke. This was, perhaps, the cleverest part of his deception, since he had evidently discovered something of the manner of his Grace's speech and the tone of his voice, probably through contact with one or more of the Duke's former servants. In any case, the Duchess was all too ready to believe that the voice was that of her beloved George. While he spoke, Barozzi prised the diamonds from the tiara and, I deduce, placed them in a small pocket specially sewn into the front of his gown. At several points during the *séance*, to maintain the illusion, and no doubt to increase his pleasure at the deception, he returned to the table, shook it about, and again assumed the person of the medium. When all the diamonds were safe in his pocket he once more returned to the table, clipped the tiara back into her Grace's false hair, and made further groaning and gasping noises, finally inducing himself to vomit, probably by the simple expedient of inserting a finger into his oesophagus. He had previously consumed a large meal of some whitish substance, perhaps tapioca or porridge, in order to give an impressive appearance to the result. This regurgitation had a very explicit purpose, which I will shortly come to. Then Barozzi took up his chair, screamed and, in the voice of Madam Spinarossa, demanded that the circle be broken. Everyone released the hands they were holding and, after a few moments, Colonel Hind stood up and lit the gas. While he did so, Barozzi replaced his chair where it had formerly been and sat down upon it, assuming the appearance of one in a swoon. The rest of that scene you know. The police were called and you, Lestrade, arrived to question those present. No doubt you suspected Madam Spinarossa, but a search of her seemingly unconscious body produced no results. I suggest, Lestrade, that your constable was a little less thorough than he might have been. He naturally did not wish to touch the ejecta which covered the front of the old lady's dress, so missed the special pocket which was concealed there and where Barozzi had, as it were, aimed his regurgitation.

'After a while Barozzi feigned a small recovery, and mumbled something about ectoplasm. Believing him to be a sick, perhaps deranged, old woman, he was released into the care of a constable. Tell me Lestrade, what became of that constable.'

'Well, Mr Holmes, he claims that when he and the old lady got down into the hotel lobby she seemed much recovered and asked him to leave her there, saying she would request the manager to call her a cab. He was, I imagine, rather keener to be back on the case with me than to play nursemaid to a filthy old woman.'

'That was just as Barozzi planned. What he had not reckoned on, however, was the involvement of a second gang. Somehow his plan had become known to a rival Italian secret society, known as the Fratelli; this was probably an unwanted effect of the meticulous research which Barozzi had undertaken, and which had aroused the curiosity of someone connected with the Fratelli. Perhaps Barozzi saw someone he recognised as he left the Hotel, or perhaps he did not know precisely who was following him; but it seems clear that he knew he was pursued as he fled into Grafton Street and thence into the alley which leads to Barlow Place. He did not wish to be found in possession of the diamonds, so cast round for somewhere to hide them.

He had only a minute. But at that moment a brilliant inspiration struck him. He ran to the nearest door and fed the diamonds into the keyhole, where they fell down inside the mechanism of the large lock. Then he ran on, knowing at least that if he was overhauled he could claim innocence; perhaps, in this event, he intended to assume some other character. We shall never know, for he seems to have got clean away. However, his good fortune was spent and, despite his great talent for changing his face and voice, the Fratelli hunted him down.

'What happened next was, I am afraid, most uncivilised. The agents who had found Barozzi forced him to reveal what he had done with the precious stones. We may assume that he resisted them as best he could, but the gradual removal of certain extremities from his body was, no doubt, sufficient inducement for him to admit the truth.'

'You mean those fingers and other pieces we found in Bruton Street belonged to this Barozzi?'

'I believe so. His torturers took them away as trophies, and as proof for their criminal masters that they had done their duty by the brotherhood.'

'But where is Barozzi? Is he still alive?'

'I regret, Watson, that I can not yet answer your first question. As for your second, I believe that no man could survive the torment Barozzi suffered and, in any case, the agents of the Fratelli would hardly have considered their duty done if they had allowed him to live. It was his death, the death of a great actor, which I lamented when I began my tale.'

'I see ... Do please continue.'

'The agents travelled to Bruton Street where they rented an empty apartment at number 38A. I learned this today when I visited the local letting agents to inquire if anyone of Italian appearance had rented property in or near Bruton Street within the last few days.'

'But how did you know they were Italians?' I asked. 'And why should they be based near Bruton Street?'

'The use of the name "Spinarossa" by the fake medium betrayed the origins of the crime. And Bruton Street was obvious from the testimony of our friend Hartshorne. The two agents waited in their rooms for nightfall, then went out, armed with suitable tools, to find number 98 Bruton Street, which was the address given to them by Barozzi. You will have noticed, Watson, that Bruton Street is unusual for having consecutive numbering along each side, so that number 1 is next to 2, and so on. It seems that our Italian friends assumed the usual arrangement of even numbers on one side of the street and odd on the other. Barozzi had told them that number 98 was at the end of the street, so I believe they walked to the end before looking closely at any house numbers. The first they chanced to look at was probably 97 or 99, so they crossed the road to find 98, and there believed they had found the right house, conveniently far from a streetlamp. By the light of a small lantern they examined the door with its large Chubb's lever lock, of a sort manufactured some twenty years ago. Now this lock has the peculiar distinction of being relatively simple for an expert to pick, but unusually difficult to remove. So the Italians set to work to unlock the door and, when they had done so, the quickest method of removing the lock was to unscrew the entire door and carry it away. They held it between them, and hurried along the pavement, back towards their rented rooms. It was this peculiar behaviour that led me to the knowledge that they had some bolt-hole nearby. Why else carry the door along the street? Had they possessed a carriage or some other vehicle they would surely have brought it up to receive the door, and they would hardly have risked carrying their prize any great distance. I reasoned that they must have a den in the same street, or very nearby, which could be reached on foot in a matter of minutes. However, when they passed under a streetlamp one of the robbers glanced at the door and realised they had made an unfortunate error. It bore not the number 98 but 9B. Immediately they dropped their prize, and hurried back to the end of the street to seek out the right door, which you may be sure they were very careful to identify correctly. They were fortunate too in finding there a very different lock. It was an old Bramah design, much less secure, which could easily be parted from the door by a combination of crude force and the removal of four screws. I noticed as we passed along that side of Bruton Street this morning that the door of number 98 showed signs of recent damage and wore a shining new lock. It was not necessary for our agents to pick the lock or open the door, they simply removed the mechanism and returned with it to their rooms. There they took the lock to pieces and extracted the Rookmont diamonds.

'Very soon, however, the business took another unexpected turn. Perhaps one of the Italians was an expert in precious stones, and saw something in one of the diamonds to arouse his suspicion. He took out his revolver, a particularly fine piece of Italian workmanship, and struck one of the diamonds with the butt. It crumbled into dust. He struck another stone, and another, and found that every one of the Rookmont diamonds was fake.

'We may imagine the scene, the consternation of the Italians, their oaths and suspicions that Barozzi had, by some obscure means, managed to deceive them and had hidden the real diamonds elsewhere. But, in truth, Barozzi had himself been deceived. He had removed the diamonds from the tiara in the dark, remember, and any skill he may have possessed to detect their true composition was blind-folded; indeed, he crushed one of the stones in removing it – I noted the powder on the side-table in her Grace's room – but no doubt dismissed the sensation of dust in his hands as due to the crumbling of the mounting paste used to assemble the tiara. Had he been working with any light he would no doubt have perceived the truth about the diamonds.'

'I don't understand this, Mr Holmes,' said Lestrade. 'If neither this Barozzi nor his murderers got their hands on the diamonds, then who did?'

'Between ourselves, I think we may assume they have been sold secretly to some dealer and very probably dispersed beyond these shores.'

'But who sold them?'

'Why the Duchess, of course. She did her best to conceal from us the unfortunate state of her finances. But a noblewoman who keeps no personal servants and is reduced to dining upon Huntley and Palmer's biscuits in her hotel room must be very seriously embarrassed. It is no secret that the Duke left considerable debts, and I believe his widow has been impelled to sell her most precious asset, the diamonds which her late husband gave her as a wedding gift. The Duchess had her tiara rigged with false stones, but felt such shame that when they disappeared during a *séance* she assumed the knowing spectre of the Duke to have punished her for disposing of his gift. If you remember Watson, I suggested that she might view his ghostly actions in a different light. After all, the stones were insured and, if stolen – as has now been reported in all the papers – the Duchess could in due course expect to receive their value from the underwriters. Only she, and no doubt a trusted friend or two, and we three, know the truth.'

'But that is a kind of fraud, Mr Holmes.'

'You are perfectly correct, Lestrade. But I suggest that, in this case, you withdraw your long arm. Who would not feel pity for an elderly noblewoman brought so low through the ill-fortune and misjudgments of her husband? And can we not be satisfied that, through the actions of the Duchess, the Fratelli and the Spina Rossa have both been denied the benefit of her diamonds?'

'It is a pretty point,' said Lestrade, 'and one on which I should be a poor policeman if I agreed. But perhaps I should be a poor Englishman if I did not.'

Holmes bowed to the Inspector, who smiled proudly.

'But Holmes,' I said. 'You have explained the loss of the diamonds, and how they came into the hands of the Fratelli. But who were those two dead men, and how did they meet their end?'

'They were the agents of the Fratelli, Watson. It seems the Spina Rossa quickly learned what had befallen Barozzi, and guessed that he had betrayed the hiding place of the diamonds to another society. It was a simple matter for me to locate the hideout of Barozzi's murderers, and the agents of the Scarlet Thorn followed a similar procedure and sent assassins to despatch their rivals and retrieve the diamonds. They succeeded in the first task, but of the stones the only traces were a broken lock and a pile of grey powder. Whether they understood what had become of the stones I know not, but they left with empty hands, having drawn their symbol upon the wall in the blood of their rivals.'

In due course we heard from Lestrade that the Duchess of Rookmont had been compensated for the theft of her diamonds. William Everson Hartshorne was told as much of the story as Holmes thought fit and, no doubt, slept a good deal more soundly in his bed thereafter. Of the agents of the Scarlet Thorn no trace was ever found, but the body of Barozzi was at length discovered in a garret in Seven Dials. He was horribly mutilated and Holmes identified him by his injuries, by the curiously-stained female dress and box of make-up which were found in his possession, and by the presence, in a secret pocket in that dress, of a single artificial diamond.

IV

The Mystery of Dorian Gray

FOR SEVERAL YEARS AFTER MY MARRIAGE IN 1887, and my departure from the rooms of Sherlock Holmes in Baker Street, I saw my old friend only intermittently, being much occupied with the novelties of married life, the material concerns of buying and equipping a new home and the demands of my medical practice. From time to time I accompanied Holmes in one of his cases, or had from him a fascinating report of an adventure which he had successfully concluded. Some of these have already been presented to the public under such titles as 'The Adventure of the Red-Headed League' and 'The Engineer's Thumb', while others remain unpublished for a variety of reasons. The stories of the Scarlet Thorn, the Professor's Assistant, and the Giant Rat of Sumatra[1] are, perhaps, a little too *outré* for contemporary taste, while the Adventure of the Silent Valet, the Killing of Lady Grace Everley and the story I am about to tell, the Mystery of Dorian Gray involved individuals whose social or political positions imposed a duty of secrecy. In due time, however, when a century and more has passed, these tales may be told.

It was a warm and drowsy afternoon in the summer of 1890, a little more than two years after my marriage, when I received a note from Holmes inviting me to accompany him to the Albert Hall, where Patti was giving one of her regular performances. Knowing my friend's keen appreciation of the soprano, and delighted by the unexpected invitation, I accepted without hesitation and met Holmes as agreed at Hyde Park Corner. He

---

1. Of all the stories mentioned, only this one, concerning the 'Giant Rat of Sumatra' remains undiscovered.

seemed, if anything, to have grown a little thinner, his cheeks a little more sallow in the months since I had seen him last, but his eyes were bright with expectation and, I suspected, the mental stimulation of an engaging problem. The music was exquisite, despite the notorious echo of the Hall, and Holmes attended with that look of dreamy abstraction which, I knew, betrayed the highest level of mental activity. His eyelids drooped, his head was bent forward and a little to one side, while his thin hands moved almost imperceptibly in time to the music. When it was over, and Patti had accepted her third curtain-call, we walked in silence to the corner of Exhibition Road and caught a cab to Baker Street. Holmes was still sunk in the reverie induced by the soprano, and once we had settled ourselves in the familiar sitting room and lit our pipes, he sat for many minutes without moving or speaking. At length I asked him if he had any interesting cases on hand.

'Oh, nothing much,' he replied casually. 'Though there is one small problem which it might amuse you to hear of. Indeed, I should value your opinion upon it, as a friend and as a medical man. You have heard of the peculiar death of Dorian Gray?'

I nodded. No one living in England who read a newspaper or heard the chattering of porters and cabmen could have failed to know something of this extraordinary case. The reader may remember that Gray's body was found in a locked attic room at his house in Grosvenor Square, before a portrait of himself as a young man. He had been stabbed to the heart. The murder of so well-known a socialite would have caused comment under any circumstances, but this case was rendered more remarkable by certain wild conjectures and superstitious stories which had appeared in the newspapers. Although not yet forty, it was generally believed that Gray's body was horribly afflicted with age and disease, while in life he had been renowned for his beauty and vigour. It was said that he had left a journal, in which he recorded a pact with the forces of darkness which guaranteed his continued youth, while his portrait had assumed the marks of time and dissolution. In the journal Gray confessed to a life of pleasure and crime, including the murder of the artist Basil Hallward, who had painted the portrait in 1870, when Gray was eighteen. The final result of his life of excess was, it was said, an outburst of self-loathing, and the final entry in the journal recorded Gray's intention to destroy the painting with a knife and break the unholy pact. The more extravagant newspapers had made much of the fancy of a handsome youth stabbing a painting of himself as a hideous old man and, by some supernatural means, plunging the knife into his own breast and assuming all the corruption of the life he had led, while the portrait was returned to its original state. *The Times* and the *Pall Mall Gazette* had reported only that the Metropolitan Police had found a body which was believed to be Gray's and that they were attempting to establish the circumstances of his death and the whereabouts of Hallward. The body had been discovered some eight weeks before the evening on which I had joined Holmes at the Albert Hall, and even then the subject was far from dead in the pages of the popular papers.

I told Holmes what I knew of the case.

'Then you have heard,' said he 'of the journal which Gray is said to have kept?' I nodded. 'It is here.' He indicated two morocco-bound volumes which lay on the table. 'Inspector Gregson was assigned the case, but has been able to pursue it only so far.' Holmes tapped his pipe on the edge of the grate and began to refill it abstractedly from the Persian slipper. 'It is a most engaging mystery,' he continued, 'and I have already made some progress in the case. The police were first alerted by two gentlemen who were walking in Grosvenor Square shortly after midnight and heard a terrible scream. They found a constable, who knocked at Gray's door. There was no answer, however, and we have only the word of Gray's manservant, Francis Triphook, for how the body was found. Triphook says he was woken by the scream and, after some hesitation, he and two other servants tried to force the door of the attic whence the sound had apparently come. The door could not be opened. There is, however, a small balcony outside the garret and they were able to gain entry at last by climbing out of another attic window and across the roof to that balcony. Triphook was obliged to force the window there to gain admittance to the garret, which Gray had used as a schoolroom in his childhood. Upon entering, Triphook found a most curious scene. One wall was occupied by a large portrait of his master as a young man, a portrait which Triphook had never seen before. Apart from this, the chamber was meanly furnished with an old table, three kitchen chairs, a bookcase containing schoolbooks and an old painted Italian chest. The room had not been aired or cleaned for many years, and the place was hung with cobwebs and exceedingly musty. The carpet was patterned with footprints, some themselves half covered with dust – Triphook was quite certain on this point – showing that the room had not been completely deserted in recent years. What drew his attention, however, was the body of a man which lay upon the floor beneath the portrait with a knife buried in its breast.

'For a moment Triphook believed he had found his master. But when he lit a candle and examined the face, he changed his opinion. This was a much older man, lined and emaciated, with wispy grey hair and claw-like fingers. Yet he was wearing Gray's clothes and, it was discovered, his jewellery and rings. Among the latter was a gold signet ring, a gift from Lord Radley on Gray's coming of age, which, Triphook had been told, could not now be removed from his master's finger. Upon closer examination, a similarity was perceived between the features of the dead man and those of Gray, and the servants began to mutter that this was indeed their master, somehow transformed. Upon the table were the two volumes which you see here, and Triphook glanced at the text and read enough to understand that this was his master's testament and confession. The police constable was admitted at last, and he called upon Gregson to investigate the case. He read the journal and found it to be a remarkable document, written, it would seem, over the course of nearly twenty years and containing all the particulars you have mentioned, and more besides. There was talk of a pact with some unnamed power, there was the corruption of the painting while Gray himself remained young, there was the malign influence of a particular book, and there was a confession of the murder of Basil Hallward. Here, read for yourself the closing words.'

Holmes rose, gathered one of the books from the table and handed it to me. It was a small folio, the size of a ledger, but richly bound in deep red morocco and tooled with a crest which I took to be that of Gray's family. I turned the pages, which were closely covered with ink manuscript, until I reached the final entry. Here I read 'Monday, April 18th. Enough. My picture mocks me. I have a knife and will end my torment and destroy the unspeakable thing.'

'Surely,' I said, 'this is a forgery, manufactured to cover the murder of this man, whoever he is, and give the impression that he was Dorian Gray.'

'That was Gregson's first thought, and the most obvious conclusion. However, there is evidence to the contrary. Gregson brought the journal to me and I was able, through an analysis of the handwriting, ink and paper, to say with some certainty that this document was written by Gray over a period of many years. His hand changes perceptibly, as a man's will as the seasons pass, and the inks used represent perfectly the periods at which the various entries are alleged to have been made. If this is a forgery, it is an extremely clever and accomplished one. I am inclined to believe it genuine, at least as to authorship and approximate period of composition.'

'Even so, Gray could have written it over a period of years, with this deception in mind.'

'Indeed. This may yet prove to be the truth. But there is one still more compelling reason to think that the dead man was, after all, Dorian Gray. Leaving aside the question of the clothes and jewellery, and the passing resemblance of the features, a very remarkable abnormality was discovered when the body was examined. I have seen the corpse myself, in the mortuary at Saint Mary's, and can confirm that the dead man has six toes on each of his feet. After some investigation, Dorian Gray's physician, Dr Joseph Basalgette of Harley Street, was identified and confirmed that his patient had suffered from this particular malformation. I was able to obtain confirmation from a lady in Whitechapel, who had chanced to see Mr Gray in a state of undress. She remembered the business with unusual clarity, as the gentleman had attempted to conceal his feet and flew into a rage when he realised she had perceived his condition. This is one matter on which I should value your medical opinion. How common is such a deformity?'

'Extremely uncommon,' I replied. 'I have never seen a case myself, though I have read accounts of infants born with additional toes or digits. A sixth finger is generally removed by a surgeon, but toes are a different matter, and since the condition is harmless many doctors prefer to leave them intact.'

'Quite so. You see then that the case for this dead man being Gray is in fact very strong. Yet what are we to make of the physical change in his appearance? And who, or what, was responsible for his murder?' I confessed myself baffled. 'Tomorrow at nine, if you are at liberty to accompany me, we will visit Grosvenor Square and see if we cannot cast a little light into the darkness.'

'I shall be delighted.'

'In the meantime, Watson, I would ask you only to consider one page of the journal, which bears a curious anomaly.' The volume was still in my lap, and at Holmes's direction I turned to a particular page. 'Please be so kind as to read the first sentence of the second paragraph.' It ran as follows:

I procured from Paris no less than 8 large-paper copies of the first edition, and had them bound in different colours, so that they might suit my various moods and the changing fancies of a nature over which I seem, at times, to have almost entirely lost control.

'Do you notice anything unusual in the writing? Not in the words, which certainly have some grammatical peculiarities, but in the writing itself?'

'It is a refined hand,' I said. 'Educated, a little cramped, written with a fine-nibbed pen.'

'Look closely at the figure eight.'

I tilted the page to catch the light and peered at the character. 'It has been altered,' I said at last.

'Indeed. The lower left-hand curve of the figure has been added later, in blue-black ink, while the remainder of the character has a distinct brownish tint. Perhaps it is of no matter, and represents merely the correction of an error, but I choose to see more and shall be most interested to see how many copies of this unnamed book, which appears to have had such an influence upon our hero, may be found in his library.'

The next morning at the appointed hour I met Holmes at Baker Street and we made the short walk to Grosvenor Square. The houses there are, as the reader may know, of a luxurious character, and as we approached the scene of the tragedy I saw two men waiting for us on the doorstep. One I recognised as Gregson of Scotland Yard, while the other was a taller, leaner figure in a bowler hat and long brown coat, with a greying moustache and an unusually fine Roman nose. This, Holmes informed me, was the valet Triphook.

Gregson greeted us with a nod and we entered the house. The ground floor was dominated by a large drawing room or saloon which had served as Gray's library and study, and was lined with brightly-bound books. There was a large desk covered with papers, two divans, several small tables bearing statuettes and vases and, facing us, a pair of French doors giving access to a terrace where more statuary was visible. A vivid yellow tapestry depicting some classical scene covered the wall between the French doors. Holmes asked us to remain in the hall while he made his initial search of the room. He crept slowly, on all fours, across the rich carpet, examining it with his glass. At length he straightened up and beckoned us to join him. Then he began a minute study of the papers on the desk, and the books and artworks with which the room was ornamented. At one bookshelf he paused and chuckled to himself.

'Look here, Watson,' he said. 'This is evidently the poisonous work of which our Mr Gray was so fond.'

The shelf bore an array of rich volumes, including a series of eight of precisely the same proportions, bound in leather of different colours. I picked one up, read the spine and made out:

LA REGRET
N. SAURET

The title was tooled in silver[2] on the pale blue morocco, save for the letters 'E' in the second word and 'A' in the fourth, which were both in gold. I opened the volume and cast my eye over the text. It was in French, but there were etchings which gave a sense of the subject matter and suggested a tale of crime and pleasure in the Paris of the recent past.

'What do you notice, Watson, about these volumes, taken as a series?'

I considered for a moment and reported, 'There are eight identical copies, bound in scarlet, orange, green, pale blue, dark blue, violet, black and white morocco, and tooled in such a way that when placed in this sequence the gold letters on all the spines spell out the same title and author's name that appear in silver and gold on each spine.'

'Capital Watson! Now, what is missing from the sequence?'

'Well, nothing, so far as I can see.'

2. The lettering was probably, in fact, tooled in white gold or some other alloy, since silver would quickly have tarnished to black.

'What about the spaces? You see, the orange copy has the "A" of "LA" and the full stop of "N." in gold, and the green copy has the "R" and "S" of "REGRET" and "SAURET" similarly emboldened, but there is no copy to represent the spaces between the words. What colour is missing from the spectrum, at just the point where these spaces should fall?'

I looked again at the row of books. 'Yellow,' I said.

'Quite so. Where is the yellow copy?'

'Perhaps Mr Gray had an aversion to the colour,' I suggested.

'Come, come,' said Holmes. 'Look at that tapestry, and the other books here. I would say he had a positive love of that colour. When we find a yellow-bound copy of Monsieur Sauret's infamous work, bearing Dorian Gray's *ex libris*, we will be a great deal closer to solving this mystery.'

I took up the pale blue copy and opened it again, to examine Gray's curious book-plate and fix it in my mind. Holmes, reading my intention, said 'No need to memorise it, Watson. I took a few unused examples from the bureau.' He handed me a copy of the book-plate, which I placed inside my pocket-book.[3]

3. The book-plate was pinned to Watson's manuscript, and is reproduced above.

'Now, Mr Triphook,' said Holmes. 'Do you know the location of the secret press in this room, which your late master refers to in his diary?'

'Yes, sir,' replied the valet. 'I chanced to see it open once, when I thought Mr Gray absent and entered the room without knocking to search for a missing hairbrush. It is here.' He moved to the panelling beside one of the French doors and rapped upon it. A few seconds were sufficient to reveal the secret of the catch to Holmes's glass, and he had the panel open almost at once. He asked Triphook to light a lamp and bring it over, and by its light we all peered into the cavity. It was empty save for a parcel of black fabric stuffed into the bottom. This Holmes carefully extracted and unpacked on the floor. It consisted of a black cape lined with green satin, which had formed the wrapping, and several further garments within. There was an opera-hat, a rough corduroy coat and trousers, a brown cloth cap, a new and well-polished pair of boots, a green silk cravat, a dress shirt and three pairs of kid gloves. Holmes hummed to himself as he laid these garments out, examining each one with his glass before placing it on the carpet. On the collar of the cape he detected some pinkish powder, which he first sniffed and then tasted, before scraping a few grains into an envelope with his pocket-knife. At length he expressed himself satisfied, bundled the clothes up again and returned them to the press.

Next Holmes asked to see the room in which the body had been found, and Triphook led the way up two flights of stairs, along a passage past the servants' quarters, and up another staircase to the attics, where he indicated a small door, which Holmes opened. Again he asked us all to wait outside while he examined the floor. The morning light was striking in through the windows, illuminating a ragged carpet covered with dust and grimy footmarks. It was clear that some heavy object had been dragged from one corner to the doorway, pulling up the carpet in several places and exposing the bare boards beneath. In that corner where the trail began, a tall painting hung on the wall, shrouded with a purple cloth embroidered in gold. The room answered the description I had heard, being occupied only by a fireplace, a simple wooden table, three chairs, a bookcase and a painted chest. Holmes examined the floor with close attention, making all the while a sequence of joyous and despairing noises; I could guess much of what he was thinking, how he cursed the heavy-footed policemen who had thundered in and out, dragging the body away in such a manner as to obliterate any clues which lay in its path. Yet, at the same time, there was evidently something to be gathered from the seeming chaos of trails and footmarks. Twice he stopped and scratched with his pocket-knife at what looked like patches of dirt, scraping specimens into envelopes, and at one point he opened the window and examined the balcony beyond.

At last he beckoned us to join him. With a flourish he pulled the cover from the painting to reveal a full-length portrait of a remarkably handsome young man in a richly-decorated gilded frame. The canvas was damaged however, there being a short gash upon the breast of the subject's shirt. I looked more closely and saw that it was fringed with a dark brown stain of blood, or something very like it. I stood back and regarded the picture again. I am no expert on the fine arts, but the quality of the painting and the good looks of the subject were clear even to me. Gregson too seemed to regard the picture with reserved appreciation, while Triphook gazed at it with frank devotion.

'A pretty fellow, is he not?' said Holmes. Gregson and I agreed, while Triphook nodded dumbly. 'Would you say, Mr Triphook, that this is a good likeness of your master?'

'I would, sir,' he replied emphatically.

'Even now, twenty years after the portrait was painted?'

'Indeed. I can see little difference in his face and figure, though his hair and clothes are naturally those of a very young man.'

'Before you discovered the body, had you ever seen inside this room?'

'No, sir. It was always locked.'

'And when you found the body, the door was still locked?'

'Yes, from the inside.'

'You came in by the window, from the balcony? Was the window also locked?'

'Yes, sir. It was necessary for me, Hollis and Jenks to force the bolts. I do not believe anyone could have got in or out after Mr Gray entered and locked the door.'

'Then you are convinced that the body you found was that of your master?'

Triphook hesitated. 'I think, sir, that it must have been. Yet I am at a loss to explain how he died, or how he came to be so transformed.'

'You give no credit, then, to the story of a pact with the devil, or to the transformation of the portrait and a kind of suicide?'

'I confess … I am at a loss.'

'One last question. Was the key to the window found upon the body?'

'The key to this room,' he replied, 'which was found in the door, was on a ring with one other, which fitted the window.'

Holmes said nothing for some minutes. He was lost in thought, staring at the picture of Dorian Gray. At last he drew in his breath, and announced that we should leave at once. He thanked Gregson and Triphook and hurried me from the house. Outside we caught a cab, and Holmes gave the driver an address in Soho and an injunction to make haste. For some minutes we drove in silence, Holmes sitting with his head sunk forward on his breast and his eyes half-closed.

At length he spoke. 'Would that I had seen that room before the constables tramped in and out and swept the floor with the body. I might then have been sure of my conclusions.'

'You have made conclusions, then?'

'Putative conclusions, Watson.'

'And what are your putative conclusions?'

'You will admit that there are, on the face of it, four possible explanations. The first is that we take as true this story of a pact with the devil, the ageing of the portrait and the death of Dorian Gray at his own hands. Certainly it fits all the facts before us, but may be objected to because it would require the acceptance of magical, or satanic, influences of which we have no evidence. It is also, perhaps, a little too neat, in having been presented to us in the form of a written narrative which agrees with almost all the facts in our hands. The second explanation is that Gray was a clever lunatic, believing himself invulnerable to the attacks of time while he seemed to see his youthful picture age. If this were the case it would explain the journal, and some of Gray's behaviour, but it would also mean that he was deluded about his own continued beauty; we would have to conclude that he was the old and shrunken man who died in that attic room, at his own hand. We know, however, that he was not deceived about his appearance, as an examination of the columns of any newspaper will show. I have myself seen Mr Gray within the last year, and Triphook has confirmed his youthful looks. Nevertheless, we cannot be certain that Gray was sane, and that he was not deluded about the changes in the portrait and the reasons for them. The third possible explanation is that he was being deceived by someone else into believing the portrait to be changing to reflect his dissolution, while he retained his good looks. This seems, at first, rather unlikely. However, I found some suggestive evidence. Before the painting I discovered spots of what looked to be oil paint, in at least two different shades. Someone could have entered the attic unknown to Gray and cleverly altered the painting, adding lines, grey hair, and later a red stain to his hand. It would have taken a skilled artist, one who knew his subject well and had been following the course of his life. This would explain the journal, and Gray's declining mastery over his will. But the apparent transformation of a living young man into a dead old one remains unexplained, as do the motives for such an elaborate deception. The fourth solution is that the journal is, as you suggested, a clever construction, designed to lead us away from the truth. In this case, the dead man found in the attic cannot be Gray, who is living now under an assumed identity. I found some evidence to support this theory too. In the attic, despite the best efforts of her Majesty's constables, there were footprints to suggest that two men had entered that room eight weeks ago, and that one had killed the other before departing by the balcony. If only I could be sure of those footprints.'

'But the window was locked, with the key in the inner door.'

'Easily dealt with. A duplicate key could have been used to lock the window from the outside – you will have noticed that the lock has keyholes both within and without.'

I had not noticed this, but nodded in agreement. As I did so, Holmes rapped with his cane on the hatch above us and shouted 'Can you go no faster, man?' The driver grunted and whipped up his horse. In a few minutes we arrived in a narrow street and jumped out before a small barber's shop. The name 'P I R A N E S I' appeared above the window, but the glass was dark and a notice hanging inside read:

Mr Piranesi begs to inform his friends and customers that he is in holiday in Roma and his shop is in charge of only a watchman

Holmes drew in his breath and his brow darkened. 'I very much fear we are too late,' said he. 'It was a long shot, Watson, but we might have saved him.'

'Who?'

'Piranesi, of course. A descendant of the famous engraver and, in his own field, an equally brilliant artist.'

'I take it you are not referring to his skill as a barber?'

'No, indeed.'

Holmes produced a bunch of skeleton keys and soon opened the shop door. Inside we passed through the dusty barber's shop and into an inner room. Here Holmes lit a candle and opened another door which led to a flight of cellar stairs. As soon as he did so a horrible odour rose towards us, and I began to understand what we might find in the room beneath. We descended the stairs into a large cellar where a barber's chair occupied the centre of the floor. Seated in it, facing us, was the body of a man, in a state of early decomposition, exacerbated by the recent hot weather. I came forward and examined the corpse by the light of the candle which Holmes held up. He was a small man in late middle age, with dark hair flecked with grey and an unnaturally black moustache. His throat had been cut, and the front of his barber's pinafore was black with dried blood. Holmes began to search the room. There were several small side tables, piled with bottles, vials, cardboard boxes and tubes of what looked like paint. When I moved to examine them, Holmes waved me away and pointed to a door on the far side of the cellar.

'Have a look in there, would you,' he said. 'It is something in your line, and I should be glad to know what you make of it.' I lit another candle and opened the door upon a familiar scene. It was a small operating-theatre, neat and clean, with an array of twinkling instruments laid out beside a modern cutting-table and chloroform equipment.

'We are dealing with a very ruthless and cunning criminal,' said Holmes from the doorway. 'I knew Piranesi, and guessed at once he was not the author of that notice in the window. It was a clever attempt to imitate the English of an Italian-speaker, using "in holiday" to suggest "*in vacanza*" and the Italian form of Rome, but Piranesi had thoroughly mastered the English tongue and would not have made such an error. How long would you say he has been dead, Watson?'

'Some weeks,' I replied. 'What did he do, this great artist?'

'He transformed men, Watson, and women too on occasion. He was the greatest master I have ever known of the art of make-up. He could make a common porter pass for a Persian Prince, or a Chinaman for a Portuguese. I have consulted Piranesi myself, and have bought some of the best theatrical paints the world has to offer through him. It was the paint that led me here. That powder on Gray's collar was supplied by our late friend; it has a most distinctive composition and can only be acquired from one place in London.'

'But what of all this medical equipment?'

'His work sometimes went beyond the superficial, Watson. He was experimenting with certain surgical techniques to alter the physical characteristics of his clients. These, combined with a careful use of paint and costume, could alter the appearance of an individual utterly.'

'I see. And did he use these skills to help criminals?'

'Anyone who would pay. I am sure the Police will say there were a great many who would wish to silence him. But I believe I know the name of his murderer. Come, Piranesi cannot help us, nor we him. Let us visit someone who may be more forth-coming about Mr Dorian Gray. We can call in at Scotland Yard on the way and inform Gregson of the Italian's passing.'

We took another cab and, having done our duty by London's official force, Holmes instructed the driver to take us to Hanover Square. We drew up at one of the many imposing houses there. But this one was decked out in funeral colours. Black crêpe upon the front door and black hangings at the windows informed us that the household was in mourning. Our knock was answered by a liveried footman who glanced at my friend's card without betraying emotion and presently informed us that her Grace would meet us in the yellow drawing room. We were shown into a spacious chamber decorated with unforced elegance, in a style I took to be the latest fashion, though Holmes, who fancied himself an expert in such matters, whispered 'Very 1870s!' as we entered.

'Let me express my condolences on the loss of your late hus-band, the Duke,' he said to the widow who greeted us. She was a dainty woman of middle years with remarkably fine features and, despite her sombre dress, a cheerful and vigorous appearance. Holmes took her hand and introduced me to the Duchess of Monmouth. I knew, of course, of the elderly Duke's passing and also of the renowned youth and beauty of his widow.

After those pleasantries which Holmes could conjure with extraordinary ease when the situation required them, the Duchess said, 'I suppose you have come to ask me about my poor friend Mr Gray?' Holmes nodded. 'A Police Inspector was here only yesterday, and asked me many questions. But he refused to tell me anything. Can you tell me what has become of Dorian? I have been in turmoil since the news of his disappearance reached me. I suppose you will not mind if I speak plainly?' Again my friend nodded. 'Is he dead, Mr Holmes, is he dead?'

'I fear so, your Grace.'

'Then it is true?' She raised a handkerchief to her face and her voice wavered. 'I heard they had found a body in his house. Poor Dorian. And is it true also that he was ... transformed?'

'I regret I am not at liberty to say.'

'I understand. I have suffered much lately; first my dear husband, and now Mr Gray. It is too much to bear.' She covered her eyes with her handkerchief. I found myself affected by her display of feminine feeling and wished to say something comforting, yet was at a loss to find the right words.

'Take comfort,' said Holmes. 'A lady in your position has many good friends, and, at such times, good friends count for a good deal. Young Lord Reekie is a most upright man on whom you can lean, and I gather you are close to that remarkable nobleman the Graf von Schön-Graustein.'

She shot him a glance of surprise, perhaps of anger, but said in a perfectly level tone, 'You are right, Mr Holmes, and most kind, most kind. But please, ask me your questions. I am not strong at present.'

'I have but two questions, your Grace. Perhaps, in the first instance, you might describe for me the Police Inspector you spoke to yesterday?'

She frowned and said 'I did not pay much attention to such a person, Mr Holmes. But I recall that he was tall with greying hair, and looked rather pale and ill.'

'Very good. And my second question is to ask where the Graf von Schön-Graustein may be found?'

Her frown deepened. 'Why, at Mr D'Oyly Carte's hotel at the Savoy Theatre. But do you not wish to ask me about Mr Gray?'

'You have already been most helpful on that score, and we will detain you no longer at this difficult time.'

With a curious glance at my friend she bade us farewell. As the footman showed us out, I noticed another servant hurrying into the drawing room in answer to the bell which we could just hear ringing furiously in the servants' quarters below. Holmes had asked our cabman to wait and now promised him a guinea if he would convey us to the Savoy in less than ten minutes.

'I fear I may have overplayed my hand,' he said when we were settled in the cab, 'but I could not resist.'

'What do you mean?'

'It was a good performance, but not good enough to deceive me, not by a long measure, and I am afraid I let her know that I had seen through her deception. She is even now sending a message to the Count to warn him of my understanding of the case. It is vitally important that we arrive before the messenger.'

The Graf von Schön-Graustein was a figure known to me from the newspaper columns. He had recently arrived from Prussia and made an impact in society. He was said to be a small man with fierce, ugly features and an unruly moustache, but a soldier of considerable bravery and a frequent dualist who had been wounded more than once while protecting the honour of a lady. The cabman, keen to earn his screw, made the wheels of the hansom sing and the brake squeal as we pulled up at the Savoy well within the stipulated time. Holmes threw him a sovereign before we hurried into the foyer and asked to be announced to the Count. The name of Sherlock Holmes had a pleasing effect on the hotel manager, who took us to the room himself and knocked upon the door. There was silence. After a second knock he took out a bunch of keys and opened the door before us.

Not for the first time that day I was confronted by a corpse. Lying just inside the door, his feet towards us, was the body of a small man in late middle age, his face contorted with astonishment and pain, and a red-brown stain upon the bib of his dress-shirt. I examined the body. If this was indeed the Graf von Schön-Graustein, the papers had been merciful when describing him. His face was that of a wild boar, with thick reddish side-whiskers and moustache. His bared teeth were yellow and black and his cheeks and brow were marked with scars, some clearly of recent date. A deep sword-wound in his breast was the cause of his death.

'Again we are too late,' said Holmes. 'But this time, I confess, my remorse is tempered by the knowledge that before us lie the ruins of one of the most hated and dishonourable men in London.'

'Surely,' said the hotel manager, his face dead white, 'we must afford the dead some respect, sir. He was, after all, a man of noble blood and a soldier of honour.'

'Of noble blood,' said Holmes. 'But far from noble of heart and certainly not a man of honour.'

'But he is the Graf von Schön-Graustein!' said the manager.

'No,' said Holmes. 'He is Dorian Gray.'

'Good Lord,' I said. 'Are you sure?'

'Quite. Doctor, if you would oblige me by removing one of his boots – yes, and the sock also – and tell me what you see.'

'There is a fresh scar here, beside the smallest toe.'

'Indeed. Where the tell-tale extra toe has been removed. You will find the same is true of the other foot.' He walked to the nightstand and picked up a book which lay there. 'And here is the missing yellow copy of that curious French work which meant so much to our late friend.' He flapped the volume open and shut, then handed it to me as I rose. It was a copy of M. Sauret's *La Regret*, richly bound in crushed yellow morocco and titled in silver. I opened the front cover, looking for Gray's book-plate, and found a rectangular scar where something had been scraped away from the leather doublure. I took out the plate which Holmes had given me and held it against the scar. The two were precisely the same shape and size.

Inspector Gregson was summoned and Holmes gave him the outline of our morning's adventure. Once the body of the Count, or Gray as we should properly call him, had been removed from the scene, Holmes pocketed the yellow-bound book and invited Gregson to return with us to Baker Street where he promised luncheon and a full explanation. On the way we stopped at a telegraph office and Gregson and I waited in the cab while Holmes sent several telegrams. By this stage I was fairly itching for an explanation but, knowing my friend's inclinations of old, forbore to press him on the matter until we were comfortably seated at Baker Street, smoking after the excellent meal which Mrs Hudson had prepared for us. At last Holmes refilled his pipe and assumed the familiar bearing of the storyteller who knows he has an eager audience and a leading part in the story he is about to tell.

'You are insufferable, Holmes,' I said. 'We have been waiting long enough. Tell us what you know.'

'I dare say I am a little irritating at times, old friend, and for that I am sorry. But I needed time to think and, even now, though I have the threads in my hands I cannot see all their knots and convolutions clearly. But I will lay before you what I know. You will remember, Watson, my four potential explanations for the story of Gray and his ageing portrait. You will admit that all had possibilities, and problems, but as I thought the matter over I grew convinced that the body found before the painting could not be that of Mr Gray, and that his diary and the pattern of the last twenty years of his life had been, at least in part, a subtle preparation. Our discovery of the unfortunate Piranesi tended to confirm me in this opinion.

'Let me say that I knew Gray personally, not well, but more than by reputation alone, and he was the most ruthless and amoral pleasure-seeker in London. Indeed, he was more than a pleasure-seeker. He was hungry for experience, for personal indulgence and experiment, and sought to satisfy these desires in high and low society without the least trace of conscience. I have seen him myself, thinly disguised, in some opium den or other ill-favoured house. The diary is accurate in this respect, as it is in many others, though it mentions but a fraction of his crimes. In the course of twenty years of licentious living he succeeded in outraging almost every friend he had known. He disgraced and ruined more than one lady and several gentlemen also. I knew Sir Henry Ashton slightly, before he came under Gray's influence and fell from his high place. I have spoken with the father of young Adrian Singleton, who has very good cause to blame Gray for the destruction of his son. Even Gray's closest friend and partner in hedonism, Lord Henry Wotton, whose love survived even the ruin of his sister, became a bitter enemy when he discovered that the failure of his marriage was the direct result of Gray's interference with Lady Wotton's feelings.

'Our friend knew that he could sustain such a life of ruthless pleasure only for a limited period, and so prepared, almost from the first, an extremely ingenious means to escape the growing multitude of his enemies. He wrote a personal diary in which he recorded some of the truths of his debauchery, along with the untruth of a pact with dark forces and the changing of Basil Hallward's portrait. Then, when he felt his life threatened on all sides, he executed his stratagem. He found a man who had some passing resemblance to himself, but an older man with a corrupt appearance, and he murdered him. He dressed the corpse in his own clothes ...'

'But wait, Holmes,' I said. 'What about the man's deformed feet?'

My friend smiled ruefully. 'That skein is still tangled in this mystery, I fear. But I will unpick it, Watson, I will. In the mean time, be so good as to allow me to continue. Gray dressed the corpse in his own evening clothes and jewels and laid it before the painting. Then he took up the knife he had used upon his victim and stabbed the heart of his painted self with it, before returning the blade to the wound in the corpse's breast. Grey had already completed his diary in such a way as to suggest he had himself died and been stricken with all the corruption which he claimed had formerly afflicted his picture. He let out a power-ful scream and left via the balcony, locking the window behind him. He crossed the roofs and escaped into the city. I do not know precisely how he climbed down from the roof, but it would have been easy enough to use a rope – either carried with him or left in place beforehand – to lower himself into the mews behind the house. Gregson, I suggest you might look for such a rope, if you find yourself with a minute or two to spare tomorrow.

'Gray then made his way to Piranesi's shop where he had ar-ranged to be transformed. This would be no common disguise, but the Italian's masterpiece. Gray was a customer of long-standing, having used Piranesi's skill to preserve his youthful appearance since the early 1870s, and Gray had no doubt promised a very large sum for the final transformation. Piranesi operated upon his face to turn him from the handsome English gentleman we all knew into his opposite, a coarse-featured, war-scarred Prussian. The extra toes were also carefully removed by Piranesi, who was rewarded not with gold but with a mortal wound be-neath his chin.

'I deduced, as the case progressed, that Gray could not have worked entirely alone. He must have needed shelter during the healing of his surgery and help to procure food, medicines and an *entrée* into Society for his new character. There was, so far as I knew, but one person whose proximity to our quarry had not proved destructive, and that was Gladys, the Duchess of Monmouth. Her love for Gray was undimmed and when her husband died she was in the perfect position to shelter her old friend in his new guise. I had read in the newspapers of the recent arrival in London of a scarred Prussian nobleman, and of his immediate friendship with the Duchess. It was elementary to conclude that the so-called Graf von Schön-Graustein was, in fact, Dorian Gray. You will observe that his name might be translated as the Count of Beau Graystone – a most suggestive, vain and foolish invention on Gray's part.'

Holmes's pipe had gone out while he was talking, and he paused to relight it with a coal from the fire. 'We must now,' he said, sending up a plume of blue-grey smoke, 'address a greater question. Who killed Dorian Gray? As soon as I began to study his life I detected another hand at the same task, another foot pursuing the same quarry. You will remember, Watson, the tall Police Inspector her Grace described – certainly not our friend Gregson here. Indeed, if he will forgive me, I doubted at once that this visitor was a genuine policeman since he seemed to be so very close upon the scent.' Gregson made a face but said nothing. 'He might have been any one of Gray's enemies, of course, but I deduced that he was probably someone whom Gray did not fear. My reasoning was that Gray would have covered his tracks very carefully, and have been convinced that his complex ploy would shake off all those enemies he believed he had reason to flee. Otherwise, why engage in such a complicated and costly charade? I deduced that – well, you shall see for yourselves. Unless I am much mistaken, one who can answer these questions better than I is at the door.'

There was a faint noise in the hall and then a sharp knock. Mrs Hudson entered, followed by a tall gentleman in a long black coat and muffler who aroused my immediate concern. He had the dead white skin and hollow cheeks of a very sick man, yet his expression was one of calm amusement.

Holmes extended his hand. 'Mr Basil Hallward?' he said. The sick man nodded, and lowered himself into the chair which I indicated.

'But surely, Holmes, Dorian Gray confessed to murdering Mr Hallward?'

'Indeed he did. He believed he had done so. But, happily, in this one venture, he failed. Perhaps, if he feels equal to the task, we might ask Mr Hallward to tell his own story.'

I poured our guest a large brandy and, after tossing it off, he began. 'You seem to know all, Mr Holmes. I came in answer to the telegram which you contrived to send to my mother, the only living soul who knew where to find me. To my shame I once loved Dorian Gray, and painted a portrait of him; it was a remarkable likeness and the greatest work of my life, but he hid it away and would not let me see it for twenty years. As time passed, I became aware of Dorian's nature, and I sought at first to save him and then to keep myself completely apart from him. Last autumn, however, he summoned me, with a promise of renewed friendship and a sight of the portrait. I was tempted, and fancied I might, perhaps, still bring some good influence to bear upon him. But I was mistaken. With little show of politeness he took me to an attic room where he unveiled the picture. I confess I was delighted to see it. I knew I would never paint such a portrait again and, while I admired it by the light of a lamp, Dorian locked the door and said quite calmly that he intended to kill me. At first I though this a joke, but quickly learned that he was in earnest. I asked him why, and he said he was curious to know what it would be like to take a life, whether he might enjoy the act, how he might feel during the killing and afterwards. I asked why he had chosen me, and again he had his reasons. I had failed as an artist. I had painted a portrait of him as a saint, which mocked his true nature. I had patronised and tried to change him, when his nature was infinitely superior to mine. And I had once broken a marble statuette of a faun which had been very dear to him. This last astonished me, for I hardly recalled the incident. But to Dorian it was most significant. I had clumsily destroyed a thing of beauty, an exquisite possession and a symbol of his own youth and loveliness, and so my life was forfeit. This seemed to be his chief reason for choosing me. I was so astonished that I hardly resisted when he drew a knife and struck at my neck.

'I remember no more until I woke in great pain to see a man's face before me. It was not a face I knew, but he whispered that he was a medical man and would save me if he could. His name was Alan Campbell and Gray had engaged him, under considerable duress, to dispose of my corpse. However, when he had entered the attic with a chest of chemicals and apparatus he had found not a dead man but one on the threshold of death. He injected me with morphine and then with some rapid and, I dare say, rather makeshift surgery repaired my wounds. By this stage I was again unconscious, but he later told me how he had crept onto the balcony and climbed across to the next house, and the next. There he found the equivalent attic occupied by a young man, a student, whom he easily induced to help him. Between them they carried me across the balconies, into the student's room and down to the street, where the student accompanied me to Campbell's house. Campbell then returned to the attic and tried to erase all signs that I had been there. He scrubbed the table and floor, and burned chemicals in the grate to give the impression that my remains had been destroyed with acid. Gray was very ignorant of chemistry and biology, so it was not difficult to fool him, and Campbell felt he had done well by saving me under the nose of the man who had intended me such evil. Indeed, he had done very well, and he nursed me over the following weeks, until I was well enough to visit my mother and find new lodgings. Everyone believed I was in Paris, and later I was spoken of as having disappeared. Only Campbell, the student who had aided us and my mother knew the truth.'

The artist paused and I poured him another brandy which he drank, more slowly this time. He was sweating profusely. 'I regret to say that Campbell too is dead. It was generally held to be suicide, for he was found in his laboratory with his own revolver at his side. But I believe Gray murdered him, to silence him about my fate. When I learned this, I determined to pursue Gray to his end. I was in the fortunate position of being dead, in his eyes, so could follow him as only a ghost may. I planned my revenge – not just for his murderous assault on me, but for Campbell and all the others whom Gray had destroyed. I quickly realised that my victim was working towards some imminent end. I witnessed his visits to Piranesi and his preparations for departure. I learned that he had transferred a great sum of money to a bank account in the name of a Prussian nobleman. Then suddenly the papers were full of the story of his death. I had not foreseen this, but guessed what was afoot and continued my pursuit. At last it occurred to me that the Duchess of Monmouth might know the truth and, assuming the guise of a Scotland Yard detective, I visited and questioned her closely. She gave little away, but at one moment during our interview her valet arrived with a letter; she read it at once, in my presence, and her face betrayed something of pleasure, perhaps even love. I contrived to see the letter and noted that it was written on the paper of the Savoy Hotel and signed "Schön-Graustein". I guessed immediately the significance of the name and, excusing myself from the Duchess, hurried to the Savoy.

'You may imagine the surprise on the face of the Count when he saw me. It gives me pleasure still to think of it. The man he thought he had murdered was returned as a ghost to take revenge. I allowed him half a minute to consider this, before I drew my sword-stick and ran him through. There is no more to add.'

'You realise,' said Gregson, 'that you have just confessed to murder, and I am duty-bound to arrest you.'

'I think it highly unlikely,' said Holmes, 'that Mr Hallward will see trial.'

'You are right, I fear,' said the artist. 'But I am content all the same.'

'Would you be so kind, Watson, as to examine the gentleman?'

Hallward peeled away the muffler he wore and I saw at once that his throat was not only horribly scarred with several knife-wounds but was swollen and purplish, with the distinctive odour of gangrene.

'You may arrest him if you wish,' said Holmes to Gregson. 'But a greater judge has already decreed his fate. I suggest it would be a kindness to a man who has suffered much to allow him to spend his last days in the care of his mother. He will hardly commit another crime.'

'But the law, Mr Holmes.'

'Law be hanged – consider *justice*, Gregson. Almost everyone who came close to Mr Dorian Gray has suffered. Many have died. This man's death will be, it must be hoped, the last we can blame upon that singular monster.'

'For myself, I do not care,' said Hallward. 'Since 1870 I have struggled to recapture the skill I had when I painted Dorian. But I knew, even then, that I would never paint another picture half so fine.'

Gregson, to his credit, saw the force of Holmes's words and left us that night without reporting the matter to his superiors. Holmes took up one of the volumes of Gray's diary and leafed through it. 'It is a remarkable work of fiction,' he said. 'Perhaps it should be published as such – with suitable editorial inter-vention – and attributed to some literary lion. But there is, I fear, no one whose imagination is half so fervid, half so out-landish, as that of the late Mr Gray.'

That was not quite the end of the mystery of Dorian Gray. The following day Gregson found a rope tied, as Holmes had pre-dicted, to one of the chimneys of Gray's house and depending into the mews beneath. In due time there came an answer too to the questions of the identity of the man found dead in the attic at Grosvenor Square, and of his close resemblance to Gray, even to the possession of an extra toe on each foot. The poor man's name is not important, but Holmes established that he was the illegitimate son of Lord Kelso, Gray's grandfather, and therefore his blood-relation. Kelso had been a rough, brutish man who had frequented low places and consorted with drabs. It was rumoured that more than one child had been born in Soho with his fiery temper and the familial trait of an extra toe on each foot. Gray may have known of the existence of these relatives and sought one out to meet his ends. Or perhaps he chanced upon his unfortunate kinsman in some house of sin, and seized the terrible opportunity.

V

The Adventure of the Professor's Assistant

IN CHRONICLING THE CASES undertaken by my friend Sherlock Holmes I have attempted to choose examples which demonstrate his particular system of observation and reasoning, and to avoid, so far as possible, the merely sensational. I have been aware, however, that any adventures made public must have some narrative sense to them, as well as elements of mystery and drama. I have naturally kept the most delicate and disturbing cases from the press, as well as avoiding those which did not afford Holmes any real opportunity to employ his powers. The success or failure of the case has been a less important factor, though my readers will admit that the most effective stories have generally been those in which Holmes was able to uncover the truth through pure deduction. Sometimes, however, the situation was such that time or circumstances did not allow for a full analysis of the problem on hand, and events conspired to bring about an end to the affair before Holmes could deduce the whole truth. One such case was that of Professor Beaumont and his extraordinary assistant. It is among the more shocking stories in my notebooks, and, like those of the Scarlet Thorn and of the Red Leech discovered at Camberwell, must await publication until the world is quite ready.[1]

'Have you heard of Professor Beaumont, the anthropologist?' asked Holmes. It was the late autumn of 1898, when my friend's career was at its zenith and every post brought applications for his assistance in this affair or that. He was obliged to decline

1. Both the stories mentioned are among the papers discovered in 2010.

many cases altogether, and to pass others over to the police. This morning had been no exception and his question was provoked by a letter drawn, apparently at random, from the pile awaiting attention on his desk. I admitted that the name meant nothing to me.

'His assistant, a man named Hallam Parfitt, has asked me to look into the murder of the Professor's wife. I am inclined to take the case, Watson, and not only for the erudition of his appeal and the fact that Mr Parfitt is due at any moment. There is something about the letter, or, more particularly, the envelope, that strikes me as singular. Perhaps you would glance over them and tell me what you think.'

He passed the envelope and letter to me.

'The hand is that of a young man, I should say. He has written both the letter and the envelope himself. The writing paper is a good quality laid, and the envelope likewise. The writing is neat, and the paper is folded carefully, yet Mr Parfitt has left a dirty thumb-print on the back of the envelope, no doubt when he sealed it.'

'Quite so. And yet, was it Mr Parfitt's thumb that made that mark? Look again, Watson.'

'Well, it is a distorted print, longer and narrower than usual, but I suppose it must have been smudged when he pressed down the flap.'

'No. It is a perfectly clear print. I believe it was not made by Mr Parfitt at all.'

'A servant, then, when posting the letter?'

'Perhaps. If so, the maid or valet in question must have curiously deformed hands. But here is the gentleman himself, only a few minutes early, and we shall soon know all. When the boy shows him in, Watson, have a good look at the fellow's thumbs!'

Hallam Parfitt was announced and soon stood before us. He was soberly dressed in a black suit and tie and, although he could not have been older than thirty, he was almost completely bald. He had a slight stoop and bright eyes, but, so far as I could see, his thumbs were perfectly unremarkable.

'Mr Parfitt,' said Holmes. 'I have your letter, but I regret to say that I am very busy at present and may not be able to take your case. However, since you are here, I shall listen to your story, though I perceive that you do not consider the matter an urgent one.'

'Why do you say so, Mr Holmes?'

'Many desperate men and women have stood upon that hearth rug, their clothing awry and their bootlaces half tied, testimony to the speed with which they dressed and the urgency of their petitions. You, however, have dressed most fastidiously. Your pin and watch chain are perfectly positioned, your shoes neatly tied, the handkerchief in your breast pocket carefully arranged. You are here after long, slow consideration and not in the heat of passion.'

'You are right, sir. I am a man who likes to meditate upon a problem. Perhaps it is my scientific training. I do not care to act in haste and have been considering what to do for some weeks.'

'Weeks?'

'Yes. Professor Beaumont's wife was killed five weeks ago. It was only last Thursday that I determined to speak to the detective in charge of the case and express my anxieties. He advised me, half in jest I think, to consult with you if I did not feel the official force were taking the matter seriously enough. I have been considering his proposal since that time, and decided last night to take his advice.'

'Who was this humorous policeman?'

'Tobias Gregson.'

'I am honoured indeed,' said Holmes, smiling. 'Now tell us your tale, Mr Parfitt, and bring your scientific mind to bear upon the story so that nothing of importance be omitted.'

'Thank you, sir. I have been assistant to Professor Edward Beaumont since leaving Cambridge three years ago. The Professor is one of the greatest men living in England today. His work is extraordinary, sir, and I am privileged to be numbered among those who have helped him along his path. Although he worked and taught for some years at London University, he now conducts most of his research in the laboratory at his house in Pinner, where he keeps all the specimens he needs for his studies. It was a small household. Apart from myself, the professor and his wife, there were only three servants, a butler, cook and maid. We lived quietly enough throughout the time I was there, until five weeks ago when, quite unexpectedly, the Professor's wife was murdered.

'It must have happened during the night, for when the maid came to Mrs Beaumont's bedroom at seven, she found her mistress lying dead upon the carpet. There was a wound in her head which had bled copiously and beside her lay a bronze statuette of Venus, which was also covered with blood. There could be little doubt that she had been struck with the statue. You may imagine how distressed we all were. Distress turned to a deeper shock when it was discovered that the lady had been – how shall I put it? – molested. The police were called and Inspector Gregson examined the scene. The window stood open. No one knew whether Mrs Beaumont had opened it, but it seemed clear that someone had scaled the porch, which stands directly beneath the window, and climbed into her bedroom. Perhaps they were intent upon robbing the house. Perhaps they had darker motives. In any case, the police began to search for clues and to question those who lived nearby, but found nothing to help them. There were some coarse grey-brown hairs on the carpet near Mrs Beaumont's body, but these were quickly identified as belonging to the Professor's assistant.'

Holmes held up his hand to stop our visitor. 'Are *you* not the Professor's assistant?' he said.

'I am,' replied Parfitt. 'I should have said the Professor's *other* assistant. His name is Silas.'

'You did not mention him when you listed the occupants of the house. Does Silas live elsewhere?'

'No, no. He lives in the house. But I omitted him because, well, sir, because he is not human.'

'Not human, indeed?' said Holmes, smiling.

'My master has certain very advanced theories, sir. Silas is a monkey, an eight-year-old Congo mandrill, which the Professor has brought to the most remarkable level of civilisation.'

'Male mandrills are large, powerful creatures, with a reputation for savagery,' said Holmes. 'Did the police not suspect Silas of the crime?'

'At first they did, especially when the hairs were found. But they were soon convinced that Silas is the most placid, harmless creature, and so refined by his training that he could never harm his benefactors. He is also absolutely under the Professor's control. He has the freedom of the house and had been in Mrs Beaumont's room the day before the murder, helping the butler move a cabinet from the bedroom into the corridor. This explained the presence of his hairs upon the carpet.'

'I see. Does Silas take your letters to the post box?'

'No, sir. He is not allowed outside the house. Why should you think he posts our letters?'

'The envelope of the letter you sent to me bears an inhuman thumb-print.'

'Of course. Silas sealed the envelope for me. He is an uncommonly useful helper in such small tasks, and I think it gives him genuine pleasure to perform them. I always let Silas seal my envelopes. He can do it by licking or gluing the flap and pressing it down, as he did with my letter, or even using sealing wax. It is remarkable to observe.'

'I see. You mentioned that Mrs Beaumont was found in her bedroom. Is that not also the Professor's bedroom?'

'No. They had separate rooms. The Professor often works through the night in his laboratory and did not wish to disturb his wife by his irregular habits. He was at his work the night of the murder, and did not repair to his own room until nearly dawn. Had the Professor retired earlier, he might perhaps have saved her, for their bedrooms are next to one another and he would surely have heard something of the attack. My own room, and those of the servants, are at the back of the house and we naturally heard nothing.'

'Naturally.'

'Later that day the police took away the lady's body, and the problem has lain ever since without a solution. Inspector Gregson soon dismissed the crime as the work of some local vagrant who had tried to burgle the house and killed Mrs Beaumont in panic. He has given up hope of catching the man, saying that such vagabonds have their own code of silence and will not give one another away to the police, while the murderer is probably half way to Scotland by now. However, it is not merely the sudden and quite inexplicable attack upon Mrs Beaumont, nor indeed the lack of official progress with the case, that has brought me here. It is also the Professor's reaction. Although he appears stricken with grief, as one would expect of a devoted husband, he has expressed no frustration with the slow progress of the police, no anger towards the perpetrator of the crime, nor indeed any interest in seeing the case solved. To anyone who knows the Professor, his keen mind, sometimes violent temper and unwillingness to accept less than perfect rigour in the work of others, as in his own work, this reaction is quite uncharacteristic. He has simply hung his head in sorrow and immersed himself in his research.'

'Grief and shock can cause the strangest of reactions,' I said. 'His unusual fatalism might pass at any time, and be replaced by other emotions.'

'At first I thought the same. For some weeks I expected an explosion from the Professor. But as time passed he seemed to grow more resigned and introspective. I asked several times after his well being, only to be told that all was well and advised to forget the past and devote myself to work, as he had done. I began to suspect, sir – it gives me pain to say it – that he knew more about his wife's death than he was willing or able to tell.'

'Do you think him capable of murder?' asked Holmes.

'Had the victim been some ill-mannered tradesman or missionary who had called at the house, I would have said yes. At times Professor Beaumont's anger can be quite terrifying. I believe it is a manifestation of his genius. But I do not think he could have harmed his wife, whom he loved tenderly and to whom I never knew him raise his voice, let alone his hand.'

'Did the Professor and his wife have no children?'

'They had one son who died of pertussis[2] when he was six. That was long before I came to the house, of course, and I only found out about it from the butler. Neither Professor Beaumont nor his wife ever mentioned the matter. In truth I sometimes feel I have myself become something like a son to the Professor, for he shows me great kindness and affection, as well as occasional outbursts of temper. Silas too is, in some ways, an honorary child to the family.'

'How very remarkable,' said Holmes. 'Are there any other animals in the house? Does the Professor keep a dog, for example?'

'No dog, sir. A dog might attack Silas. But there are always monkeys in the Professor's menagerie, a separate building attached to his laboratory, where they live in cages.'

'But none has the run of the house, as Silas has?'

'No, indeed. The animals are well cared for, but they have not been civilised like Silas and are always caged. I believe this is chiefly to prevent their making mischief or escaping, however, for they are guenons mostly, and none is large enough to be dangerous.'

'The Professor keeps no other Congo mandrills, then?'

'No. Silas is his only experiment in that direction.'

'I see.' Holmes was silent for a moment. 'As I have mentioned, I am very pressed at present. However, I will undertake to look into the problem. I might wish you had come to me

2. Commonly known as 'whooping cough'. Parfitt may have used the medical name knowing it would be understood by Watson, if not by Holmes.

sooner. After five weeks the scent will be faint indeed. But I will see what may be done. I am concerned, however, about the reaction of Professor Beaumont when he learns that I am involved with the case. Will he not be very displeased with you for engaging me?'

'Perhaps so, Mr Holmes,' said Parfitt. 'That was another reason for my delay in approaching you. But I am quite decided that the matter must be investigated, whatever the consequences. I felt a keen affection for Mrs Beaumont, and I am a scientist and must know the truth, even if there is difficulty, or pain, in that knowledge.'

'Very well. Is there a time when we might call at Pinner and see the house without encountering the Professor?'

'The best time would be now. He is lecturing at the University and will be busy there until late afternoon. Indeed, it was only his rare absence from Pinner today that allowed me to visit you without having to invent a pretext for leaving the house.'

'Capital. Watson, can you spare a few hours for a visit to Pinner? Good. Now, Mr Parfitt, will you go down into the street and engage a cab for us? Thank you. We will join you very shortly.'

When our visitor had left the room, Holmes smiled and rubbed his hands together gleefully. 'I believe we may be in for a very interesting excursion,' he said. 'Although I did not say as much to our friend, I think it likely we will spend a night or two under Professor Beaumont's roof, so you might pack a few things for the stay.' I made to leave for the bedroom. 'And Watson,' he added. 'Bring your revolver too.'

Little more than an hour later we alighted from the Extension Line train at Pinner station, and walked the short distance to the Professor's house. It was not a large building, but neat and elegant in the Georgian style, though much overgrown with ivy. To the right a single-storey annexe had been added in more recent years. The building stood in modest grounds and was shielded on three sides by tall trees. Thick woodland bordered the road so that, apart from the road itself, the house seemed beset by greenery and bathed in shadow, though it was now past midday and the sun was shining brightly. Despite this isolated appearance, the nearest house was only a hundred yards along the road, and a little further away was a cluster of small houses and cottages which we passed on the way from the station.

Parfitt led us through the gate and up to a side door. 'Let us not disturb the butler,' he said, producing a key. Once inside the house I was aware of a faint and slightly unpleasant odour, reminiscent of the zoological gardens. The interior was clean and furnished with modest good taste. We entered the small hall and left our coats and bags in a side room.

'Perhaps, first of all,' said Holmes, 'we could see the room where the tragedy occurred?'

'Certainly.'

Our host led us along a corridor and up a back staircase to the main landing. Here were a number of bedroom doors, and Parfitt indicated the second on the left. Before we could advance, however, Holmes caught both our sleeves and begged us to remain still while he examined the landing carpet. He spent ten minutes crawling on his hands and knees over the floor, examining it with his glass and now and then picking up some seemingly invisible fibre or fragment and holding it up to the light.

'As I feared,' he said at last. 'The passage of five weeks, and of so many boots and shoes, has destroyed any signs which might have been here. Let us try the bedroom.'

He beckoned us forward and opened the door which our host had indicated. The room within was gloomy in the extreme, the shutters being half closed and the sunlight filtered by the trees opposite. We could see at once, however, that the room was not deserted. A man in a white shirt, dark trousers and waistcoat, stood by one of the windows, looking out into the road. As we opened the door he turned towards us.

'Silas!' cried Parfitt. I perceived that this was no man. 'Why are you here?'

The great monkey approached slowly and stood before us. He was a magnificent creature, standing almost as tall as myself, though it was clear now that his legs were a good deal shorter than those of a man and his torso both more elongated and more muscular. He held his hands clasped together before him. His face was heavy and dog-like, with raised, blueish ridges on either side of his muzzle. Yet his expression was remarkably human, and his eyes seemed full of emotion. He opened his mouth, revealing ferocious white teeth, and, to my astonishment, spoke. Of course, he did not use words, but he made sounds that were a close imitation of human speech, rising and falling as if he were speaking some unfamiliar language. I remembered a tale by Poe in which an ape had committed a dreadful crime and had been heard crying out above the voice of his victim, making sounds which listeners had mistaken for some foreign tongue. Parfitt seemed to understand something of what the monkey had been trying to impart and said reassuringly, 'We all miss the lady, Silas, though you know the Professor would not be happy to see you moping in this manner. Now, please, go about your duties.'

The monkey's face assumed a look of humility and he strolled past us, out onto the landing and away down the main staircase. It was an extraordinary encounter. The seeming humanity of the creature in his actions and utterances, combined with his bestial form, was most unsettling. His attempts at speech had reminded me of the noises of certain patients I had attended, the victims of strokes, who fought to regain the power of language.

When Silas had departed, Holmes entered the room and again spent some minutes in a close examination of the carpet. He also studied the window and bed before inviting us into the room.

'I need not ask where the tragedy occurred,' said he, indicating the carpet beneath his feet, where a large brown stain of dried blood was evident.

'The maid tried to clean it up,' said Parfitt. 'Blood stains cannot easily be removed once they have dried, however, and she was so upset that I suspect she shrank from her task.'

'I see. I doubt there is more to be learned here. But I should very much like to see the Professor's laboratory, if you have access to it.'

'Indeed. Professor Beaumont trusts me in all things and I have a key to his work-room.'

We passed down the main stairs and through the house to a heavy oak door which Parfitt unlocked with a key from his chain. As he opened it, the animal smell, which I had now grown quite used to, struck me again. Inside it was very dark and Parfitt had to light the gas before we could see the place properly. The room was long and narrow, with benches along both sides, piled up with scientific apparatus. To one side were a great many glass jars containing ape and monkey heads, hands, feet and internal organs. There were several dozen brains, of various sizes, some bisected to show the complex convolutions of their inner parts. The largest jar, some three feet tall, contained the pale and shrunken body of an adult chimpanzee, crumpled into the posture of a foetus. Towards the end of the room was a door to the left, and a large desk at which the Professor evidently worked. It was piled high with papers and documents and, in a space in the centre, the corpse of a small brown monkey lay, pinned to a board, its torso cut open and the skin folded back to reveal the organs. The smell I had detected was coming, at least in part, from this grisly example of the Professor's dissections.

Holmes spent a few minutes looking over Beaumont's papers. 'What is through there?' he asked, indicating the door to the left.

'That is the menagerie,' said Parfitt, 'where the Professor keeps his live specimens. Would you care to see inside?'

Holmes nodded and the assistant unlocked the door with another key from his chain. Once again, the foul odour intensified as the door swung open. This time it was accompanied by a high, chattering sound. Parfitt preceded us and lit the gas. This room was the same shape as the Professor's laboratory, but the wall facing us was occupied with metal cages, piled one upon the other, and filled with small, brown prisoners. They stared at us and bared their yellow teeth, or howled with their heads thrown back, or paced back and forth, or slept curled like cats in the corners of their cages. The smell was now quite overwhelming but Holmes did not seem to notice as he walked slowly down the room, examining the cages and their occupants. At the far end were four larger cages, or cells, built into the fabric of the building and fronted with strong bars. Each might easily have held a man, but they were quite empty, and clean in a way the rest of the enclosures were not.

'I think I have seen all I need to,' said Holmes. 'Let us return to the sweeter air of the house.'

Parfitt extinguished the gas and led us back through the laboratory and into the hall.

'I am afraid it will be quite necessary for me to meet and speak with Professor Beaumont,' said Holmes.

'I had expected as much,' said Parfitt. 'Perhaps you will do us the honour of dining here this evening, as my guests. In the meantime, I can ask cook to prepare something cold for lunch.'

I expected Holmes to reject this offer and to suggest that we return to town to spend the afternoon pursuing other cases. But, to my surprise, he readily agreed and we spent a leisurely lunch talking with Parfitt over various scientific matters. The conversation turned to horticulture, and thence to apiculture; then Holmes and the assistant engaged for some time in a discussion of Mr Darwin's theories, and the various interpretations which Professor Beaumont had placed upon them. When we had eaten, Holmes asked if we might take a turn round the grounds.

'Of course,' said Parfitt. 'But I hope you will excuse me if I do not accompany you. The Professor will expect me to have made some progress with writing up his notes by the time he returns.'

While Parfitt returned to the laboratory, Holmes and I walked for a while in the gloomy gardens, my friend deep in thought, his hands thrust into the pockets of his overcoat. At the porch we stopped for several minutes while Holmes examined the structure and the thick ivy which clung to it and covered much of the house's façade. The window by which Mrs Beaumont's murderer had entered the house was directly above, and easily accessible to an agile man. I fancied I could have gained an entry there myself, had I been called upon to attempt the feat. We walked on and found, near the front hedge of the garden, a clump of greenery that caught Holmes's attention. It appeared at first to be the stump of a dead tree covered over with ivy and creepers. Holmes gently drew back some of the foliage and found white marble beneath. A little work with his stick soon revealed a fine gravestone or monument in the shape of an obelisk. When Holmes had drawn aside the creepers that covered the plinth we read the simple inscription:

CHARLES

'A monument to the Professor's late son?' I suggested.

'Perhaps so,' said Holmes. 'I wonder why the boy's parents went to the evident expense and trouble of erecting this elegant needle only to allow it to become so overgrown and neglected?'

'Grief may take many forms. The passion for remembrance can be overcome by a desire to forget.'

Holmes nodded but said no more, descending again into deep contemplation until we returned to the house. Parfitt met us at the door and informed us that the Professor was due home from the University at any moment. He asked us to wait in the drawing room while he broached the subject of our presence with his master. We waited in silence for a few minutes, then heard the creaking of the great front door followed by the high voice of Parfitt and the low rumbling tones of the Professor. We could make out little of what was being said, but I clearly heard the words 'interfering' and 'unwelcome' from the Professor, though it was unclear whether Parfitt or Holmes was the object of the speaker's criticism. A moment later the door flew open and Professor Beaumont stood before us.

He was a large man of about sixty, tall and heavily-built, with a mass of ill-kempt white hair and a pale, heavily-jowled face. His skin showed evidence of poor health, being both pitted and marked with liver-spots. He wore a dark suit and a black cape with a purple lining. His expression was a mixture of irritation and weariness, but he spoke with perfect calm.

'My assistant tells me that he has engaged you, Mr Holmes, to look into the matter of my wife's death. I tell you, frankly, sir, that such an investigation will prove entirely fruitless and will serve only to wake thoughts and feelings that would better have been left to sleep. The police have reached their conclusions and no action of theirs, or yours, could serve to bring my beloved Emilia back to me. Nevertheless, Mr Parfitt has seen fit to engage you and to invite you to dine with us, and good manners therefore dictate that I accept your company this evening.'

Holmes bowed slightly. At dinner we were joined by Silas and the five of us sat down in silence. A dark mood seemed to settle on the table. But Holmes can be wonderfully garrulous and uplifting when it suits his purpose, and he began a campaign to raise the spirits of the company with talk of science, the one subject which held the Professor's attention. By the time the meat was served, I believe Holmes had quite broken through the Professor's defences and they were talking together like old friends. For my part I kept casting sideways glances at Silas, who was seated to my left. He sat perfectly upright in his chair, and used a knife and fork to eat his meal, albeit holding both a little awkwardly. He also drank wine from a glass and even used the cellar to salt his meat before devouring it. His one failing in manners, so far as I could see, was a certain tendency to eat with his mouth open.

'It must be painful to speak of your late wife,' said Holmes, when the conversation flagged for a moment, 'but if I am to find out what befell her then I must ask you a few questions.'

'You are, in your own way, a scientist,' said Beaumont, 'and your method, like mine, is to question. So you must question.'

'Thank you. Will you tell me how you met?'

'I have no objection. It is a happy memory. Emilia was the daughter of one of my colleagues at the University, and some twenty years younger than myself. I had always believed I would die a bachelor, and that pursuit of the fair sex would prove a distraction from my work, though I longed to have a son to carry on that work. But when I met Emilia my mind was quite changed and I recognised a familiar spirit. She had her father's wisdom, and her mother's beauty, and she understood my work – not its details, perhaps, but its spirit, its meaning, its import. We were married within six months, in the summer of 'eighty-one, and I pursued my research with renewed vigour for the knowledge that I had such a woman at the back of me. For the next seventeen years I carried on my great experiment with the man of the Congo.' He nodded at Silas, who copied the gesture. 'While Emilia kept my house and undertook charitable works. We were very happy in every respect.'

'Perhaps not quite every respect,' said Holmes. 'You did not have the son you craved.'

'On the contrary. My boy was born after a year of marriage, and I could not have been happier. But you are right, of course, for our son only lived for six years and the doctors warned Emilia that she was not fit to carry another child. But still we had one another, and I my work.'

'You say your wife, sir, had an enquiring mind, and beauty. Was she content always to be the wife of an older man so devoted to his calling?'

I thought I detected a flash of anger in the old man's eyes and, indeed, it seemed to me a very impertinent question. But after a moment the Professor replied quite calmly.

'She was happy. Her mind was occupied with charitable works, and with literature, and as for her beauty – that was all mine, just as I was hers. We are ... we were a most devoted couple and wanted nothing else, I assure you.'

Holmes appeared to have asked all his questions, for he quickly turned the conversation back to natural science. He and the Professor talked on through dinner and, once we had withdrawn, through most of that evening, Parfitt and I attempting to make intelligent interjections from time to time. Silas was the first to retire, a little before midnight. He had been seated for some time in a specially-made armchair beside the fire, and made a curious low chattering sound that was evidently the signal that he was tired. Beaumont responded at once by wishing the monkey goodnight, and the extraordinary creature stood, bowed to each of us in turn, and left the room.

Holmes glanced at his watch, then said 'I fear we have missed the last train to Baker Street.'

'Then you must stay here as my guests,' said Beaumont with evident warmth.

'Most kind.'

It was clear that Holmes had planned this from the first, though I could not at that time imagine why he wished to stay the night. Beds were made up for us in two of the spare rooms, and we said our goodnights on the first floor landing, outside the room in which Mrs Beaumont had been killed. My room was next to this, on the other side from the Professor's, while Holmes had been given a bedroom on the other side of the corridor. Mrs Beaumont's room remained untenanted.

As we made our goodnights a curious incident occurred. The Professor said to Holmes, in a low voice, 'You are a good man, Mr Holmes, but you will find nothing here. There is no mystery to my wife's passing, any more than there was to my William's.'

'To whom do you refer?' said Holmes.

'Why to my late son, William.'

'Of course. Forgive me.'

'Now, goodnight, sir.'

When the Professor and Parfitt had retired to their rooms, Holmes took my arm. 'If the son was William,' he whispered, 'who then was Charles? These are deep waters, Watson. I believe the murderer of Mrs Beaumont is within a few yards of us now.'

'Was it the Professor, then?'

'Or Parfitt,' replied Holmes, with an infuriating smile. 'Or perhaps Silas. But these polite and intellectual proceedings mask, I fancy, a very brutal killer, driven by love and desire for Mrs Beaumont. Remain alert tonight. Keep your revolver close. I believe the murderer may show his hand before the morning.'

With these words we parted. I locked my bedroom door and made a careful examination of the room. All seemed to be in order. There was only one door, and one window, the latter looking out onto the front garden, the road and the dark wood opposite. The moon was almost full and high enough in the sky to show the details of the garden, its tangled pathways and overgrown beds, and the white needle of the curious memorial to Charles, newly exposed beside the front hedge.

I began to prepare for bed, thinking over the events of the day. However, I had barely started to undress when I heard a small noise from the window and looked round. I was astonished to see a hideous shape beyond the pane, silhouetted against the moonlight. There could be no mistake. It was Silas. He turned his head and I clearly saw his dog-like profile as he bared his teeth. He was no longer dressed in human clothes, for I could see the bristling hair upon his back and shoulders as he turned again to peer in at the pane. I was struck dumb with surprise and horror, for his shadow, huge and black and shaggy, had a most savage appearance. Before I could recover myself, however, the animal was gone. I rushed to the window and threw it open. A few streamers of ivy hung down from above and, as

I looked up, I saw a dark body climb swiftly over the gutter and out of sight.

I closed the window once more, drew the curtains and returned to my preparations for bed. As I checked my revolver and placed it beneath my pillow, I tried to tell myself that nothing could be more natural than for Silas to be allowed out at night, to play in the treetops, as he must have done in his native Congo. But the incident had left a very unpleasant impression on my mind, and it was some time before my thoughts grew still enough for sleep to overcome me.

I must have slept for several hours when I was woken by a noise from within the house. It was a loud thump, followed by a cry. For a moment I wondered if I had been dreaming. But then there came another sound, a scream of such fear and loathing as I have heard only thrice in my life. Instantly I was awake and drew my revolver from its resting place. In a second I had lit a candle and thrown open the door to the corridor, whence the cry had emanated. At almost the same moment the door to the Professor's room burst open and Beaumont rushed out, still in his nightgown, with a look of abject terror on his face. A moment later he was followed by the galloping form of Silas. The monkey's eyes were wild, he seemed to have grown to twice his former size, and his lips were drawn back in a brutish leer as he screamed and yelped in pursuit of his master.

At the head of the staircase the mandrill caught the man and the two fell to the ground, clasped together. With a terrible cry Beaumont struggled to his feet, but Silas clung to his chest, his shaggy arms wrapped round his neck, his teeth sunk into the man's face and his feet clawing viciously at his stomach. I raised the revolver and aimed it at the mandrill's head. Silas must have seen the movement of my arm, however, for he released his jaws from the Professor's cheek and turned his gaze on me. In an instant he had comprehended his danger and threw himself towards me, knocking the pistol from my grasp and my body against the doorpost. With extraordinary speed and intelligence he moved not to attack me, but towards the revolver, which he kicked so hard that it sped past the Professor and bumped away down the stairs. In a moment Silas had renewed his assault upon Beaumont, who still stood at the stair-head, his face and nightgown streaked with blood.

I shall never forget what happened in the next few moments. The seconds seemed to pass with unbearable slowness and in complete silence, though I know full well that both the mandrill and his victim were screaming loudly. Holmes had emerged from his room, still fully dressed and bearing a candle. Then, from the staircase, a fourth joined our party. I saw, to my astonishment, that it was Silas. He walked slowly – or so it seemed – up the stairs, dressed in a pale green nightshirt and a dark green dressing-gown and holding my revolver in his right paw. He looked calmly round, then raised the pistol, aimed carefully, and fired at the other mandrill, which still clung fiercely to the Professor. Without uttering another sound the creature fell to the floor, quite dead, and the Professor dropped to his knees beside it.

He subsided onto his back and, after a moment, I rushed forward to examine him. His stomach had been lacerated by the monkey's claws and there were two deep bites in his cheeks, but his injuries were not so serious as I had at first feared. He would live. Indeed, he was still conscious and groaned aloud, saying something I could not understand.

Holmes joined me.

'What is he saying?' I asked.

'I believe he is speaking the language of the Congo, and he is probably addressing Charles.'

'Charles?'

Holmes indicated the dead mandrill. I looked at the creature closely for the first time. I could see now that this was an older, larger specimen than Silas. His face was wrinkled and there were grey hairs around his ears and muzzle. Silas had shot him cleanly through the skull.

'So, this is Charles?'

'Yes,' said the Professor in a strangled voice. 'Help me up for god's sake. I had hoped I was wrong. But I guessed, I feared, that Charles was returned.'

We helped Beaumont to his feet and back into his bedroom, where he lay down on a sofa. I returned to my room for my medical bag, then began treating his wounds. Silas joined us and looked on, seemingly very concerned about his master. He still held my revolver in his paw and I turned to him and said, 'Silas, please give me my pistol'. He handed it over at once.

'How did you know about Charles?' whispered the Professor.

'I had guessed,' said Holmes, 'that Silas was not your first experiment of the sort. The fact that you had larger cages in your laboratory than were needed for the small simians you currently study suggested a former interest in greater species, and your mention of seventeen years pursuing your experiment with mandrills must have included at least one other individual, for Silas is, as your assistant told us, only eight years old.'

'It is true. I have never told Parfitt about Charles and have destroyed all my notes on the case. I did so for shame, both at the failure of my experiment and at my treatment of the brute.' He cast a glance through the open door, to where Charles's dark body lay upon the carpet. 'I had such hopes, gentlemen, such hopes. Seventeen years ago I found an infant mandrill which showed signs of intelligence and began to raise him in accordance with my theories on the brotherhood which exists between the great apes and monkeys and ourselves. I named the mandrill Charles, and he became, in time, like my own child. Indeed, my son, who was born in the same year as Charles, would often play together with the infant mandrill and they regarded one another as brothers. But as Charles reached maturity a great change came over him. He grew melancholy and aggressive and increasingly difficult to control. Though I still had some power over him, the servants found him extremely disagreeable and it became impossible to retain them. Worst of all, Charles, who now thought of himself as a man, began to show an unspeakable interest in my wife. By this stage he had grown to such a size and developed such physical strength that it was very difficult to restrain him. It became clear that he would, he must, soon commit some outrage. I pleaded with him. But to no avail.

'At that time, Charles had the run of the garden and was allowed out into woods and down into the centre of Pinner, as befits any free being. But his violent behaviour and savage appearance induced such terror in the local people that I feared for his life, and for my own reputation in the town. Something had to be done. At this time I had in my menagerie another large Congo mandrill, a dull-witted creature with none of Charles's brilliance. I am ashamed to say that one night I rendered it senseless with an injection of morphine then dressed its body in Charles's clothes and dragged it out to the road, where I beat it to death with a cricket bat.'

The Professor groaned, though it was unclear whether with the pain of his injuries or of his recollection.

'The next day I called in the police and told them that Charles had been murdered. They hardly took the matter seriously. To them, murder was the killing of a person and Charles was not a person. They knew all about my assistant and the problems he had caused in the town, and I suspect they were glad to see the death of him. In any case, they did nothing to investigate the crime and everyone assumed a group of local men had caught Charles and killed him in fear and anger. The body was left to lie in the street for a day. Many of the local people came and stared at it. Some kicked or spat upon the corpse. Then I dragged it back into the garden and buried it near the front hedge, for all to see. Shortly afterwards I had a marble tombstone erected over the grave. As far as the world knew, Charles was dead and could do no harm. But in truth he lived still, locked in one of the cages of my menagerie. He was furiously angry. Had he been able to escape then, I am sure he would have done me harm. But still I could not bear to kill him. For all his faults he had been like a son to me. So I drugged his food and, when he was unconscious, dragged his body into a separate cage which I placed inside a crate. I had been to the Congo several times, gathering specimens, and the man who organized my expeditions was a trusted friend. I paid him a very large sum to travel with the crate back to the Congo, seeing to the comforts of the prisoner all the while. The journey took many weeks and, when they arrived, the crate was driven into the heart of the country and Charles released. At first he would not leave the company of the men who had brought him there. But they had guns, and Charles knew what guns could do – he had accompanied me on hunting trips, just as Silas has, and understood how rifles and pistols operated and what damage they could do. The men had to threaten Charles with their guns, and to fire a few shots above his head, before he ran screaming into the jungle.

'I can only guess how unhappy, confused and angry he must have felt. I suppose he swore vengeance upon me and determined to return to England to pay me back. It took him twelve years to find his way. But he did it. It is extraordinary how clever, and malevolent, Charles had become. In the mean time I had lost my son and found another Congo mandrill who showed, if anything, even greater intelligence than Charles. I had learned from my mistakes and began my experiment afresh with Silas. I never let him out of the house, and made certain his animal desires would not develop. The results, gentlemen, you see before you.'

Silas, who had been standing attentively at his master's side all the while, made a small chattering noise, almost like a laugh of modesty.

'It must have been five or six weeks ago that Charles finally returned to the house. Or it might have been longer. Perhaps he watched us for some little while from the woods. When my dear wife was killed so viciously, and her body desecrated, my first and only thought was that Charles had returned. Who else would wish harm to her, or me? And yet it seemed insane. I could hardly have told the police my suspicions. I feared to confess my shameful deception about Charles's death. And had I tried to convince the constables that a wild creature had travelled half way across the world to find a small house in a rural corner of England in order to exact revenge upon an elderly scientist, they would not have believed me. I could hardly believe it myself, and hoped I might be wrong.

'After killing Emilia, Charles must have returned to the woods. Perhaps it took him time to recover from his crime, for he was not totally without conscience. Or perhaps, more likely, he waited simply in order to observe my suffering. Tonight he struck and, thanks to your presence, gentlemen, and the timely intervention of Silas, I have survived, while Charles lies dead.'

Again the Professor looked towards the corpse of the mandrill and groaned. 'I cannot help but pity him,' said he. 'His pain, his anger, must have been immense. He had good cause to hate me for I had betrayed him utterly.' Silas laid a paw upon the Professor's arm.

The next morning the family physician called upon the Professor and a nurse was engaged to care for him while he recovered from his injuries. Holmes and I returned to Baker Street. He was in a morose mood and said nothing of the matter for several days. At last, at breakfast, I asked him whether he had known of the existence of Charles before we had encountered him.

'Had I been the perfect reasoner you are so fond of depicting in your stories, Watson, I would have deduced it all,' said he. 'But I was too slow and had only begun to approach the truth when Charles appeared and brought the matter to a swift conclusion. Indeed, I had suspected Silas of the crime, and saw him as a creature forced to live against his nature so that his brutality must, from time to time, have torn through the veil of apparent civilization. But I was wrong. Yet, even now, I do not trust that monkey.'

'Silas, you mean?'

'Yes, Silas. The Professor may live to regret his great experiment, for men are men and monkeys merely brutes. The beast forced to rise above its nature is no less to be pitied and feared than the man who falls below his.'

Holmes's conjectures were never to be tested, however. As the reader may recall, Professor Edward Beaumont died the following year in a fire which also destroyed his house and all his notes and specimens. It was reported that no one else had died in the fire, which was thought to have been caused by an overturned spirit-burner in the laboratory. The servants had all been dismissed shortly after the incidents I have just described, and Beaumont was said to have been living alone at Pinner at the time of the fire. He was not quite alone, however, for what the newspapers did not report was that his companion, Silas, also perished in the fire. Indeed, when the ruin of the house was first examined by the police, the two bodies were found clasped together in the laboratory. The remains were too gravely burned for anyone to say whether they had been fighting at the time of the fire, or comforting one another, or whether, perhaps, one had attempted to drag the body of the other to safety.

VI

The Adventure of the Silent Valet

THE NUMEROUS CASES UNDERTAKEN by my friend Sherlock Holmes for members of the nobility gave him a distinctly mixed impression of that class. Very often the details could not be made public at the time, in order to protect the reputations of some of the oldest families of Europe. But in due course such restrictions may be lifted. In time the public will have forgotten the celebrated personalities involved, but may nevertheless be interested in those problems which afforded Holmes an opportunity to exercise his singular powers. One such was the mystery of Henry Middleton, the silent valet.

It was a most unfortunate case and one which marked a juncture in Holmes's career. On referring to my notes I see it began on the twenty-third day of May in the year 1901. Holmes and I had spent the morning with a wealthy gentleman in Bloomsbury who had attempted to engage my friend to solve the mystery of a lost wedding ring. Holmes declined the case but, as we were about to leave, produced the missing ring from inside one of a pair of fencing gauntlets which lay on a side-table in the hall. Holmes would accept no payment, but our client insisted that we lunch with him before we departed.

Returning to Baker Street, we found a young man waiting in our sitting room. He was tall and lean-faced, with dark hair and Piccadilly weepers, a style very much out of fashion by that date among younger men. He introduced himself as Inspector Francis Allardyce of Scotland Yard.

'I hope you will not mind my coming to you unannounced,' he said. 'Chief Inspector Gregson suggested I might call, as I have a hard case which I feel quite unable to penetrate, and he remarked that you had assisted him more than once in similar circumstances.'

Holmes greeted the young Inspector warmly and, when we were comfortably seated with our cigars, invited him to tell us of his problem.

'Well, sir,' said he. 'You know the name of Lord Mallerby, of course?' Holmes nodded. 'I regret to say that he has been murdered. It happened last night, sir, at his Lordship's house in Twickenham and the circumstances are most unusual. The Earl had been away on business and, upon returning at a quarter past nine, went straight into his study and locked the door. The study is part of a private suite of rooms on the ground floor consisting of an antechamber, the study itself, a small dressing-room and a bedroom, which Lord Mallerby liked to keep to himself. Only he, his valet, Middleton, and one maid were ever allowed to enter, and the maid but once a day at a fixed hour to clean and make up the fire in season. On this particular night, as I say, his Lordship went straight into his suite and locked the door behind him, leaving the key in the lock. At a quarter to ten a commotion was heard by the servants, and the Earl was heard to cry out incoherently before two shots were fired. The servants tried to gain entry. But the door was locked and the only other entrance to the suite was by a garden door to the study which was also found to be locked from the inside, again with the key in the lock. Matters were made worse by the absence of Middleton, who had been sent by his master on an errand shortly before the commotion broke out. After a few minutes the butler, a big Irishman named Joyce, was able to force the door of the anteroom and rush in.

'A most unpleasant scene greeted him. The study was in dis-order, the chair and several ornaments had been broken as if by a great struggle, and his Lordship's desk had been ransacked and the papers disarranged. Joyce passed through to the dres-sing-room, and thence to the bedroom where he found his master lying upon the carpet. He had been shot at close quarters, the bullet passing through the palm of his hand and into his heart. The weapon lay nearby, still warm, so there could be no doubt about the matter. It was a service revolver of the sort commonly found among old soldiers. But here is where the business becomes extremely queer. His Lordship was not alone in the room. His valet, Middleton, whom the other servants had thought elsewhere, was crouching on the floor by his master's side.

'The butler sent for the local police, who in turn called on Scotland Yard, and I arrived to find the scene just as I have described – the Earl lying dead of a bullet wound, and his valet crouching still beside him. I addressed Middleton, but he seemed to have been struck dumb, sir. He said not a word, only gazed into his master's white face. After making a careful examination of the room, I was obliged to arrest the valet and remove him to the cells. There seemed little alternative but to assume that, for some unfathomable reason, Middleton had taken it upon himself to return to the house before completing his errand and to take the life of his employer. Yet it seemed against all reason. The servants swore that Middleton was utterly devoted to Lord Mallerby, and would have laid down his own life for that of his master. He is a queer little fellow, this Middleton. He is a hunchback with the face of an old sinner, though he is no more than fifty. He has never served his country as a soldier and, indeed, is said to have a terror of firearms so that he could not accompany his master on shooting trips. He is hardly educated, and it is remarkable that Lord Mallerby should have selected him as his valet. Joyce, who has known Middleton for nearly thirty years, tells me he was originally employed as a groom but became a favourite with his Lordship because of his honesty and devotion to duty. Could such a man shoot dead his benevolent employer?

'I looked again at the evidence, and found other indications that someone else may have fired the fatal shot. The revolver, which none of the servants recognised, had J B carved upon the butt. There is nobody in the household with those initials. In the study, where a fight had clearly taken place, we found other evidence. There was a large button with a dark red thread attached. No garment could be found in the house with buttons to match. There was also a smear of blood on the doorpost, at the head height of a tall man, while there was no equivalent wound on Lord Mallerby or on Middleton, though the latter is in any case fully eighteen inches too short. All the indications are that someone else had been in those rooms, and had fought with and killed Lord Mallerby. But both doors were locked on the inside, the windows were nailed shut, and there was no other means of entry that I could see.

'One final detail which might interest you, Mr Holmes, is something we found in Middleton's pocket. He refused, and refuses, to utter a word or make any sign and my belief is that the shock of what he saw has made him mute. We searched his clothes and possessions and found, in the pocket of the jacket he was wearing, an envelope addressed to a local clergyman, a Dr Hooper. We opened the envelope and found it to contain nothing but a blank sheet of his Lordship's writing paper. There,' he flourished an envelope, 'what do you make of that?'

Holmes took it and slowly examined the exterior. It was addressed in a slightly shaky hand to Dr Abraham Hooper, The Walnuts, Park Green Crescent, Twickenham, and was marked 'URGENT' in the same hand in the top right-hand corner. There was no postage stamp. On the reverse was the remains of a red seal, with what I took to be Lord Mallerby's signet, and inside was a folded sheet of pale blue writing paper with the Earl's crest, but otherwise quite blank. Holmes turned the paper this way and that to catch a raking light, then did the same with the envelope before sniffing cautiously at both.

'The paper has been tested for secret writing, I suppose?' he said.

'It has.'

'All the same, I should like to satisfy myself, if you will permit me.' The policeman nodded, and Holmes began to work on the paper. He first warmed it gently beside one of the gas jets, then crossed to his chemical bench where he applied first a blue powder, then a few drops of some pale yellow liquid to the paper. Again he warmed it by the gas, then smiled and returned the sheet to its envelope. 'I can find nothing,' said he, 'and neither did I expect to. But it was necessary to eliminate that factor from my calculations. Would you permit me to retain this curiosity for a time? Thank you. Now Allardyce, perhaps you would favour me with the answers to a few questions.'

'Of course.'

'You have spoken with Dr Hooper, I suppose. Was he able to cast any light on this mysterious message?'

'None. He has been a close friend to the Earl, and they often dined together, but he had no reason to expect a communication on that evening and can offer no explanation.'

'We can take it, I think, that the delivery of this blank paper was the errand upon which Middleton had been sent shortly before his employer's death. Have you questioned the servants about the matter?'

'Yes, sir, and that is another strange business. The commission was not given by his Lordship in person. That afternoon a telegram arrived, apparently from the Earl, addressed to Middleton and containing certain instructions. The Earl wrote that he would be going straight to bed when he arrived home and was not to be disturbed, but had left a letter on his desk which Middleton was to fetch at once and deliver by hand to Dr Hooper that evening. He was to leave the house at exactly half past nine and walk to Hooper's villa where he was to place the message into that gentleman's hand. He was then to leave at once and return on foot to the house. The matter was said to be most urgent and delicate, and the directions were to be followed precisely. I learned about the telegram from Joyce. Middleton had been a little surprised to receive it and disclosed the contents to the butler. The telegram itself has not been found, and I believe Middleton destroyed it.'

'How long would it take Middleton to walk to Hooper's villa?'

'One of my constables walked the route, and it took him twenty-five minutes. He was of the opinion that it could not be done in less than twenty.'

'Very good. Now, I should like to hear what you know of Lord Mallerby's family circumstances. I seem to recall he was estranged from his wife and children?'

'Yes indeed. As far as I can gather, his son James and daughter Constance were both on very poor terms with his Lordship and have not seen him for more than two years. Lady Mallerby has also forsaken him and lives now with her sister, the Duchess of Morton, in Hampshire. This estrangement also dates from some two years ago, and the cause seems to have been her daughter's choice of a husband. He is, by all accounts, a fine young man but hardly of the same station, being a poor captain of Hussars. It seems Lord Mallerby would not countenance the match, while his wife and son could see that Constance would only be happy if she married this young soldier.'

'What is his name?'

'Malcolm Bristow.'

'Then he is not the JB who evidently owned the pistol. Have you interviewed him yet?'

'I have been industrious, sir, but have not performed miracles.'

Holmes smiled. 'What can you tell me of the son? Presumably he stands to inherit.'

'We are attempting to trace the Earl's will at present, but certainly James is now the eighth Earl of Mallerby.'

'And his family name?'

'Cushing, sir, though he bore the title Viscount Dinsdale until his father's death. So he too cannot be our JB.'

'What are the daughter's circumstances? I presume the Earl has cut her off?'

'Not entirely. She has a small allowance from Lord Mallerby, but it does little to supplement her husband's pay. They do not have an easy life, especially as they now have a young son.'

'You mentioned that two shots had been heard by the servants, but that Mallerby had died of a single wound. What became of the other bullet?'

'We found it in the wall of the bedroom, near where the body lay. Indeed, both bullets were in the wall, a few feet apart, since the fatal shot had passed right through his Lordship's chest.'

'And you say it also passed through one of his hands?'

'The way I see it, sir, the first shot simply missed but the second hit its target, while Mallerby held his hands thus.' The detective raised both his open hands towards us, in the gesture of a man attempting to placate, or distance himself from, an assailant. 'The second shot was fired at close range,' he said, 'and there were distinct powder-burns on the palms of both the Earl's hands.'

'Given his unhappy family circumstances, have you considered the possibility that Mallerby took his own life?'

'I have, sir, but the evidence is all against it. The nature of the shots and wounds, the struggle in the study, the cries of the Earl, the evidence of the button and blood-smear, all tend to suggest murder rather than suicide. In any case, his Lordship was held to be a most determined and cheerful nobleman, more given to laughter than to despair.'

'There were papers on the study desk, you say. Have these been examined?'

'I venture to repeat my remark about miracles, sir. I have given the papers a preliminary examination, however, and nothing struck me as of importance.'

'Where did his Lordship go on business that day, I wonder?'

'None of the servants knows, with the possible exception of Middleton, of course.'

Holmes was silent for a moment. 'The case presents some interesting features,' he said at length, 'and I will assist you as far as I am able. If Gregson has taught you anything, you will not have disturbed the scene.'

'Indeed,' said Allardyce and smiled. 'I have removed the body, of course, and the revolver and button, but everything else is just as I found it.'

'Excellent! I believe the matter is not an urgent one, and should like to think it over for a time. I will begin tomorrow morning by visiting Twickenham. Perhaps you would be good enough to meet us at Lord Mallerby's house at nine.'

Allardyce assented and bade us farewell. After he had gone Holmes took down the blackened clay pipe which for so many years he had treasured as a token of contemplation and filled it slowly by the fireplace.

'An uncomplicated case,' said he, as his head became wreathed in blue smoke, 'and one which bears strong similarities to others I have undertaken.'

'It seems quite unique to me,' I ventured.

'There are some unusual features, certainly, but the button is almost a commonplace in such affairs. I must smoke a pipe or two, however, before my mind will be quite clear on the matter.'

After a very early breakfast the following morning we took a four-wheeler from Baker Street to Waterloo station and travelled thence by train to Twickenham. At the railway station we asked directions to Lord Mallerby's house. We were yet early, so walked slowly towards the address we had been given, enjoying the freshness of the morning. As we strolled along we were overtaken by many men, women and children, on their way, no doubt, to the amusements at Eel Pie Island. Our own destination was rather more monumental, being a fine Gothic-style mansion set in very pleasant gardens that sloped down to the riverbank. We waited at the gate for a few minutes until young Allardyce appeared with a constable at his heels.

He greeted us and led us up to the house, where the door was opened by a bearded Hercules, quickly identified as the Irish butler, Joyce. When he saw Allardyce he immediately stood aside and we followed the detective to the Earl's private suite of rooms. Here everything was as he had described. On the threshold of the study we paused while Holmes took out his glass and examined the carpet minutely. As he did so, I noticed a dark brown, jagged mark upon the white post of the doorway facing us.

'Come in now, gentlemen,' said Holmes. 'But I beg you to remain here until I have completed my examination of the dressing-room.' He sat down at the desk to work through the piles of disordered papers which lay there. He clucked and tutted from time to time and scribbled a few notes in his pocket-book, but it was clear from his expression that he was finding nothing of consequence. I looked round. The only other chair in the room had been broken and the mantel-shelf had been swept clean, ornaments and a small clock lying broken on the hearth. It was clear that some great violence had been done here. At length Holmes threw down the document he was holding and sprang from the chair.

In the dressing-room he made the same close examination of the carpet but, to my surprise, only glanced at the bloodstain on the doorpost. Soon we were allowed into the dressing-room, while Holmes gave the same attention to the bedroom. From the doorway I could see the room well. It was large and comfortable, with richly-upholstered chairs and ornamental tables spaced round a huge four-posted bed, hung with tapestries. The walls were decorated with familiar paintings, and to my immediate left I noticed a dark mark on the striped wallpaper between two portraits. This was evidently one of the bullet-holes. I looked for the other and soon found it. The second bullet had passed through the portrait of a young woman, leaving a black dot ringed with dark brown on her painted cheek. Upon the carpet beneath was a broad stain, of the same deep brown hue as the mark on the doorpost.

'Come in Allardyce,' said Holmes, 'and show me where the revolver was found.' The detective indicated a spot some six feet from the bloodstain where Holmes now crouched, much as Middleton must have done two nights before.

'Would you care to see the place in the study where the button lay?' asked Allardyce.

'No, thank you,' said Holmes. 'Regrettably, while you have been extremely careful, the carpet has been crossed and crossed again by many feet, those of the servants, I presume. All the same there are some interesting indications. Now perhaps you would ask the butler to join us for a moment.'

The constable was sent to find Joyce, who soon appeared in the doorway, seeming to fill it. He was a most impressive man, tall and muscular, with a glance that mingled intelligence with something of hostility.

'Come in,' said Holmes. 'I shall not detain you long. This unfortunate business has no doubt disturbed the household very much.' The butler nodded impassively. 'I understand Middleton received a telegram containing detailed instructions on the night of his Lordship's death. Was it usual for the Earl to direct his servants thus?'

'No, sir. I cannot remember it ever happening before.'

'Did you see the telegram?'

'I saw it, sir, in Middleton's hand.'

'Do you know what it said?'

'Yes, sir. Mr Middleton read it aloud to me, being as the content was so queer.'

'Can you remember his precise words?'

'No, sir.'

'Could you paraphrase?'

'Yes, sir.' There was a pause.

'Perhaps,' said Holmes at length, 'you would do so.'

'Certainly, sir. It was something like "Straight to bed tonight. Not to be disturbed. Letter on desk to be delivered to Hooper. Fetch immediately and leave at half-past-nine precisely. Walk to Hooper's. Deliver into his hand and return on foot. For God's sake follow these instructions. Matter most delicate. Mallerby".'

'Thank you. What became of the telegram?'

'I do not know.'

'And what did Middleton make of this curious communication?'

'He was surprised, sir. He had been expecting the master to return at his usual hour of a quarter past nine, but had anticipated no further instructions that evening.'

'When the Earl returned from the City, did he usually go straight to bed?'

'I could not say, sir. But he nearly always went straight to his rooms and shut the door. He was not to be disturbed when the door was closed, unless he rang for Middleton.'

Holmes paused. 'Did Middleton pick up the letter and leave the house as instructed?'

'Yes, sir.'

'Is this the letter?' asked Holmes, producing the envelope.

'It is, sir.'

'Please look at it closely. Is it addressed in his Lordship's hand?'

Joyce bent forward and peered at the envelope. 'I cannot say, sir.'

'Please explain that.'

'The writing is very like the master's, but more tremulous. I could not swear it was his own hand.'

'Very well. Do you know of any reason why the writing might have been tremulous?'

'Well, sir, his Lordship was not young and in recent months his hand has been a little unsteady.'

'I see.' Again Holmes paused. 'Although Middleton left with the letter, he did not follow the instructions of the telegram. Do you know why?'

'No, sir.'

'Can you guess the reason?'

It was the butler's turn to hesitate. 'Perhaps, sir.'

'Please explain.'

'Well, sir, Henry, that is Mr Middleton, had not expected to be called upon again that evening. It gives me pain to say it, sir, but in the last five years or so Mr Middleton has become intemperate. He would not allow it to interfere with his duties, but I believe his crooked back was troubling him and he would drink a little too freely sometimes to dull the pain. He is a good man, sir, and utterly loyal to his master. But on that night he was intoxicated. I saw him stumble as he left the house with his letter. Perhaps he was confused about his master's instructions. That is all I can say on the matter.'

'I see.' Holmes's eyes narrowed. 'Let me ask you bluntly, Mr Joyce. Do you think Henry Middleton murdered Lord Mallerby?'

'I do not. He hated violence and guns in particular, having had a fright with one as a child. And he loved the Earl almost as a father.'

'Who do you think shot your master?'

'I do not know, sir.'

'Can you guess?'

'No, sir.'

'Very well. Now tell me, please, as simply as possible, what happened on the night of the shooting after Middleton left the house.'

The butler repeated the details of the story which Allardyce had already told us. Holmes asked him to enlarge on several points, mentioning particularly the raised voices which had been heard from within his Lordship's rooms. 'Was there just one voice?' he asked.

'It was difficult to be certain, sir.'

'But you certainly heard the Earl shouting?' Joyce nodded. 'Could you make out any of his words?'

'Only one, sir.' Holmes asked him to repeat it and Joyce lowered his voice and uttered a coarse term of abuse, which he said the Earl had shouted several times. Holmes then asked if any of the other servants had been on hand, but Joyce said he had instructed them to return to the parlour as soon as he realised that something was amiss with the Earl.

'I have one last question for you,' said Holmes. 'Where had his Lordship been when he returned to the house that day?' Joyce opened his mouth, and Holmes added quickly, 'An opinion will serve, if you do not have a fact for us.'

'Well, sir,' said the Irishman, and I could almost have believed he hid a smile in the great bush of his beard, 'it was the Earl's habit to inform the household when he left on everyday business. When he was silent on the subject, as he was on the last occasion he departed, it meant he had personal matters to attend to. In my experience, this meant either his physician, his solicitor or his family.'

'Thank you. That will be all.'

The butler bowed and left the room.

'That man is hiding something,' said Allardyce when the door was closed. I felt obliged to agree with him.

'Perhaps,' said Holmes. 'But if so, he is doing it for the best of motives. Now, Allardyce, I have a small hint which you may perhaps find useful. The mention of the Earl's solicitor is one you might follow up, I think.'

'Thank you. I will look into it. But I have a few ideas of my own too, and will get round to the Earl's family and see what I can dig out. And we must not forget, Mr Holmes, that we have a witness who almost certainly knows how the Earl met his end.'

'The silent valet?'

'Precisely. He may have lost his wits for the present, but we have ways of restoring a man to his senses when there is the little matter of murder on hand.'

'You must follow your own course, Allardyce. But, if I read the situation aright, you will get nothing from Middleton by any normal means of persuasion. Watson and I will pursue other lines for a while, and perhaps we might meet back at Baker Street at …' he consulted his watch, 'shall we say half past nine, the same hour that Middleton set out upon his interrupted errand?' The detective nodded. 'Could I ask you to take a great risk with a dangerous criminal and bring the unfortunate Mr Middleton with you? I fancy that, if your own powers of persuasion have failed, there may be something I can say to loosen his tongue.'

'It is irregular,' said Allardyce, 'but I can see no objection, provided he is properly escorted.'

'One last question. Did the Earl have any sort of knife or blade upon him when his body was found?'

'No, sir, nothing of the sort.'

'Oh well, it is of no importance.'

We left the house and said farewell to Allardyce. Holmes was silent as we strolled along the drive towards the great gate of Mallerby's estate, evidently deep in thought. Just before we reached it he stopped and stood for a few minutes, looking back at the house. I ventured to ask whether he knew who had killed Lord Mallerby. He shook his head and said, 'I do not yet have all the data in my hands. Only let me think, and make a few discreet enquiries, and I shall surely have them all.'

'Can I be of help?'

'Most certainly. I have a mission of the greatest importance for you. Here is the name and address of the Earl's physician in Harley Street.' He handed me a page torn from his pocketbook. 'I copied it from a bill I found upon his Lordship's desk. I can think of no one more suited than yourself to charm this exalted physician into speaking of the Earl's health, and of whether it was to Harley Street that Mallerby went on his last afternoon.'

'I will do my best.'

'Capital. I may be late back to Baker Street, but I shall keep our appointment, and hope to explain everything at half past nine. My first task is to make a study of this house and its grounds, now that the determined Allardyce is no longer present to assist me.' He smiled, nodded, turned and walked slowly back along the drive for fifty yards or so, then turned to his right and disappeared behind a clump of trees.

By the time the appointed hour approached I had been back at Baker Street for several hours, having completed my charge. I flattered myself to think I had done well. The Earl's doctor turned out to be an elderly specialist I had known slightly in my college days, some twenty-five years previously, and we had soon fallen into easy conversation and talked at some length of the Earl's condition.

Allardyce appeared shortly after nine, in the company of Henry Middleton. The valet was an exceedingly small fellow with a narrow, yellow face and bald head. His back was twisted and he walked with a curious uneven lope, so that he resembled nothing so much as a great hairless ape, dressed up as a valet. Like an ape too he seemed, for all his deformities, a creature of great strength and agility. I instinctively recoiled from him, especially when I saw that he was not handcuffed and that he and Allardyce were alone.

'Is it quite safe?' I whispered to the detective, indicating the valet.

'He has been released,' came the surprising reply. 'I believe I may have called Sherlock Holmes into the case too readily, for I have solved the mystery myself and Mr Middleton is free. He accompanied me here of his own will, when I explained the situation to him.'

'Then you must both be seated and take some tea,' said I, feeling a little ashamed of my harsh judgement of the valet. I looked at him again. Though certainly an extraordinary individual, there was no savagery in his face. His eyes were wide still with the horror of what he had witnessed, but there was sadness there too, and humanity, and a look of pleading, as if he dearly wished to impart what he knew.

'Will you have tea, Mr Middleton?' I asked. He neither moved his head nor made a sound, but something shifted in his expression and, again, I suppressed a shudder at his quite inhuman reaction to my question.

'You see how it is?' said Allardyce.

I rang for Mrs Hudson. To see Middleton with the teacup in his hand again changed my impression of him. His hand shook as he held it, and he seemed now like a very old man, twisted with the years, who had lost the power of speech but still understood much of what was happening about him. I asked Allardyce for the details of his discoveries, but, despite being in a state of some excitement, he was almost as silent as his companion, promising to tell all only when Holmes had joined us.

We waited. The clock struck the half hour, then the three-quarter. It was nearly ten o'clock before we heard a foot on the stair. I was heartily relieved for Allardyce seemed ready to burst with his news and could not be induced to discuss any common subject. We were to be disappointed, however, for it was not Holmes who was shown into our room but an elderly woman of common appearance, dressed in black, with a misshapen bonnet on her head and a carpet bag in her hand. After a moment the idea struck me that this might be another of Lord Mallerby's servants, his cook, perhaps.

'Madam,' said I. 'If you are seeking Mr Sherlock Holmes, then I am afraid he is not here. But if you have information for him, you may tell me everything and I will see to it that he receives your message.'

There was a sound from the old woman. I fancied at first it was a cough, then I thought it a cackle, then I recognised it as a familiar, dry laugh. The woman grew a foot in height before our eyes and I knew, with some relief, that here after all was Sherlock Holmes. I had grown used to his male disguises, and had seen him take the parts of women several times – a celebrated Duchess on one occasion. I confess that this time he had fooled me utterly.

'I am sorry, dear fellow,' he said. 'I could not resist trying my nursemaid upon you. Apart from the height, the appearance is not so difficult, but I have struggled with the voice. To disguise one's voice from someone who knows it is a most difficult art. Indeed, I would only be confident of deceiving you, Watson, if speaking a language you did not understand, as you may remember from the time I assumed the person of an Italian priest.'

'Mr Holmes,' said Allardyce. 'You are the master of your art, and no doubt your methods have been successful. But I too have some small success to report.'

'Indeed?' said Holmes, as he removed his bonnet and grey wig.

'Yes, sir. I have arrested the murderer.'

'Have you, by Jove!' said Holmes. 'And who is this unlucky beneficiary of British justice?'

'Mr Malcolm Bristow.'

'You do not surprise me. I can guess, perhaps, at your reasons for capturing this gentleman.'

'I'll wager you cannot, sir.'

'I make it an unvarying rule never to bet on such matters, and you would be wise to do the same. Besides, it would be foolish indeed to wager on any subject with Sherlock Holmes. Would I be near the mark to suggest that Mr Bristow possesses a coat which lacks a button, formerly held in place with dark red thread?'

'Yes. But there is more than that.'

'I can imagine the scene. You arrive at Bristow's residence to find the lady of the house prostrated by news of her father's murder. Perhaps she is already in a delicate condition, and there are fears for her well-being.'

'You have been there before me!' said Allardyce. 'How else could you know that Constance Bristow is with child?'

'I admit it. I had my own reasons for suspecting as much, but went to the Bristow house this afternoon in the person of an unfortunate nursemaid in want of a position. I did not see the mistress, nor her husband, but took tea with a most sympathetic cook who told me a good deal of the family circumstances.'

'I see.'

'I think it possible,' continued Holmes, 'that you arrested Mr Bristow on sight, before a word had left his lips.'

Allardyce drew a deep breath, then smiled. 'Gregson warned me that at times you would appear to be nothing less than a magician.'

'It was the cut on his brow that gave him away, was it not?'

'Quite so. Bristow is a tall man, as tall as you or I. As soon as I saw him, I noticed a piece of sticking plaster on his forehead, in just the place where a wound would have left that smear on the Earl's doorpost.'

'The unfortunate Bristow has no *alibi*, I suppose.'

'Only one in which he is supported by his wife. Both swear they were at home all night when the murder took place, Bristow being on leave and eager to spend as much time with his wife as possible. No one else can confirm their story, there being but two servants and they do not sleep in the house.'

'Capital! Now all that remains is your explanation of a few trifling points. No doubt the motive, and the revolver with J B upon the butt, can be quickly dealt with. Come, come, give us your explanation.'

'On the motive I am ahead of you, Mr Holmes. As you suggested, I called upon the Earl's solicitor, and learned that his Lordship had visited the office on the very afternoon of his murder, with the express purpose of altering his will. A new document was drawn up, signed and witnessed that day, disinheriting his Lordship's wife and daughter, and her husband, and leaving his entire estate to his son, James. The Earl left with the new will, saying he would place it with his private papers in his study. We have searched again, and the new will is not to be found anywhere in the house. It is my belief that young Bristow got wind of his father-in-law's intentions and came to the house that night to have it out with the old man. They argued, then fought, and Bristow drew a pistol. The Earl fled into the bedroom where his pursuer fired twice, missing the first time, but making good with the second bullet. Then Bristow left, taking with him the new will, which he no doubt quickly destroyed.'

'Splendid. And the revolver?'

'Bristow must have brought it with him and dropped it after firing the fatal shot, but the initials are still a mystery.'

'I believe I can help you there,' said Holmes. 'You will find that the weapon belonged to Mr Bristow's late father, Josiah, also an officer of Hussars. No doubt you might conclude that Bristow had decided to use his father's weapon because, in the unlikely event of his losing it, it would not so readily be connected with him, and so that he could show an inquiring policeman his own revolver, which had clearly not been fired for some time.'

'Thank you, Mr Holmes. That fairly paints the final stroke of the picture.'

'Not quite. You have yet to explain how Bristow succeeded in shooting his father-in-law within a locked suite of rooms and escaping without unlocking either door, or forcing a window. As I understand it, both doors were locked from the inside when Joyce gained access.'

'Well, that is true enough. Though it strikes me now that Middleton may have played his part.' He looked suddenly at the cowering valet. 'Perhaps he was in league with Bristow, let him in, then out again by the garden door, locking it immediately afterwards.'

The valet's face was very pale, his brow spotted with droplets of perspiration. There was a movement of his head which suggested a shake from side to side, but was suppressed, as if Middleton were struggling against a paralysis.

'That is extremely unlikely in itself,' said Holmes, 'given what we know of Middleton's loyalty to his master, and becomes virtually impossible when the evidence I have to hand is taken into consideration.'

'But the evidence against Bristow is so strong.'

'I have no doubt it will grow stronger. What account does he give of the lost button and the head-wound?'

'Of the button he offered no explanation, but he admits that his injury was acquired in a struggle with his father-in-law. However, he claims that this took place on the evening previous to the killing, when the Earl came to his house and taxed him with his inability to provide for his daughter. As Bristow tells it, the Earl grew violent and thrashed at him with his cane, which caught the young man upon the temple. However, I do not believe the story.'

Holmes was silent for a moment. Then he said, 'You have arrested an innocent man. I believe I know what happened in that room, and I can guess why our friend here, who knows the truth of the matter, has remained silent.'

The valet's eyes grew wide.

'Perhaps I have been too confident,' said Allardyce gently. 'If you can explain these matters better than I, pray do so.'

'Very well. First, let us consider what *should* have happened. The Earl is heard to argue with and insult a visitor in his rooms. There is a noisy struggle followed by two shots. The household is roused and Joyce, as butler, takes charge. He tries the door to the study, but it is locked. He rushes round to the garden door, which takes no less than one minute to reach – I timed the journey myself and could do it no faster – to find the door standing open ...' Allardyce opened his mouth to interject, but Holmes silenced him with a raised hand. 'The butler runs in through the garden door to find the Earl dead. He calls the police, who examine the scene and discover a revolver and a button from a coat which do not belong to the Earl. They also find evidence of a struggle, and a smear of blood on the doorpost, at head height, while there is no corresponding injury to the Earl. Investigation shows that his Lordship had just revised his will to disinherit his daughter, and leads inexorably to the arrest of his son-in-law, Malcolm Bristow, for the murder. Bristow cannot properly account for his actions at the time of the crime, has a fresh wound on his brow and a coat which wants a button. Further inquiry reveals that the one man who might have protected the Earl, his valet, had been sent out of the house on a false errand. What could be clearer?

'The police will conclude that when Bristow learned, from the Earl himself, of the plan to alter the will, he began to plot. He prepared a decoy message addressed to Dr Hooper using paper and an envelope abstracted from his Lordship's study, writing the address with a facsimile of his father-in-law's failing hand. That evening he crept in through the open garden door and left it on Mallerby's desk, having already sent a telegram in the Earl's name. Then he slipped out again and waited in a nearby stand of elms, fingering his father's loaded revolver in his pocket until he saw his victim arrive. The mass of evidence is so strong against Bristow that any court would convict and hang him. Any small objections to this story might easily be cleared up. Doctor, can you think of any?'

'I wonder,' I said, 'how Bristow knew that the Earl would return at a quarter past nine that night.'

'A simple matter for anyone who had studied the Earl's habits and possessed a Bradshaw. Mallerby invariably travelled by train, but the journey between the City and Twickenham is neither fast nor especially easy, as we discovered when we travelled there ourselves. To catch the Twickenham train one must first go to Waterloo, and the journey thence takes an hour or so. The fastest evening train leaves at a quarter past eight and arrives at six minutes past nine. It became Mallerby's invariable habit when visiting the City to dine early and catch this train. The journey from Twickenham station to his house was made by carriage, and takes some seven or eight minutes only. Unless some accident befell the Earl, his arrival home at somewhere near a quarter past nine was inevitable. Any further objections?'

Allardyce and I both shook our heads.

'That, as I said, is what *should* have happened. Now I will tell you what actually occurred. Lord Mallerby departed for the

City that morning, having left an envelope on his desk containing a blank sheet of paper and addressed very carelessly to give the impression that the writing was a forgery. When he arrived in town he sent the telegram which Mr Joyce so carefully remembered. Then he visited his lawyer to draw up a new will. He may have made other calls. On his physician perhaps?' Holmes glanced at me and I nodded. 'He had already apprised his son-in-law of his intention to disinherit Lady Mallerby and his daughter, at a private meeting the previous evening when he had expressed anger and contrived to strike the young man on the temple with his cane.

'When the Earl returned to Twickenham that evening he passed straight into his rooms and locked the door. He had left the garden door open that morning, and it was still open. He waited until a quarter to ten, confident that Middleton would do precisely as he had been instructed and would be well on his way to Hooper's villa by this hour. Then he placed on the floor a button which he had torn from Bristow's coat, very probably during the altercation of the previous night. Bristow would hardly have noticed the loss of a button at this time, given the Earl's anger and the vicious attack upon him. He disarranged the papers on his desk, then took a paper-knife which lay there and made a small cut, almost certainly on the palm of his left hand. You will remember, Allardyce, that I enquired whether the Earl had a blade in his possession. Learning that he had none, I deduced that the paper-knife must have been used. Mallerby wiped the blade carefully on his shirt-front then smeared the blood from his palm on the door post, at head-height. The Earl then shouted incoherently and swore loudly, as if in argument with some scoundrel, struck a chair against the wall and swept the ornaments from the mantel. He took up the pistol which he had abstracted from Bristow's house some weeks previously – this I determined from the friendly cook, who recalled Bristow's mentioning the disappearance of the revolver – and rushed through the dressing-room to the bedroom, where he fired one shot into the wall. Then, with his back to that wall and holding the pistol at arm's length in his right hand, operating the trigger with his thumb, he turned the revolver upon himself. He fired once, the bullet passing through his left hand which he had carefully positioned over his heart. The recoil of the pistol sent it flying from the body. Thus, with one shot, he had ended his own life and obliterated both the gash in his palm and the blood-stains on his shirt.

'It was at this point that the Earl discovered his meticulous plan had gone awry. Middleton appeared. We can but imagine the looks that passed between them. Why was the valet there, rather than approaching Dr Hooper's villa? I found the answer to that question in the stand of elms which lies between the footpath the valet must have taken and the lawn leading up to the garden door of the study.' Holmes looked at Middleton, whose face was still impassive, though his eyes spoke of inward struggle. 'You were a great deal more intoxicated than even Joyce had realised, were you not? Believing that your master would not need you again until the morning you had been drinking freely since his departure.' There was no reaction from the valet. 'I shall not be indelicate. But you may imagine the valet's indisposition on that evening, and the evidence I found of it among the elms. He must have staggered into the trees as the nausea came upon him, and remained there for some time, in a pitiable condition. Then he heard, from across the lawn, the raised voice of his master and the crash of breaking furniture. He gathered his remaining strength and ran to the Earl's aid, believing him to be assaulted. He rushed through the garden door and, as an instinct of protection, perhaps with the thought of capturing his master's attacker, closed and locked that door behind him. As he crossed the study he heard the first shot, and arrived in the bedroom in time to witness the second. The Earl fell to the ground and Middleton rushed forward and knelt beside him. Lord Mallerby had but a second or two to live, and feared that his game was up. It is my judgement that, with his last breath, he enjoined his servant in the strongest imaginable terms never to speak a word, never to tell anything.'

We all looked at Middleton. He blinked and there was a sorry light in his eyes suggestive of grief, or remorse, but his face was a white mask. We were all as silent for a moment. Then Allardyce spoke.

'So you believe there has been no murder at all,' he said, 'except for self-murder'.

'Quite so. But there has been a very serious attempt at murder, committed by the seventh Earl of Mallerby upon his unfortunate son-in-law. The intended weapon was the law.'

'Did Mallerby hate young Bristow so deeply?' I asked.

'It was his one blind spot,' replied Holmes. 'I discovered as much at Twickenham this afternoon in my female disguise. The servants knew a good deal more than our friend Mr Joyce imparted, and were happy to share their knowledge with a harmless old nursemaid.'

'All the same,' said Allardyce. 'Shooting yourself in the heart seems a rough method of disposing of your own son-in-law.'

'His Lordship truly believed his daughter would be happier, and better placed in society, as a widow. It was no very great personal sacrifice, if I am not mistaken.' Holmes looked at me.

'You are right, Holmes,' said I. 'Mallerby's doctor told me that the Earl was a dying man. He had no more than six months to live.'

'What became of the will?' asked Allardyce.

'The Earl probably destroyed it on the train, before he arrived at Twickenham, to give the impression that his fictional visitor had taken it. I think that is everything. Lord Mallerby might well have succeeded in his plan, were it not for the unexpected weakness of his valet. But ...' Holmes lapsed into meditation for a minute or two, then looked up. 'Had I been brought into the case, I think it likely that I could have solved it anyway, without the accident of Middleton's appearance at the Earl's deathbed. It was the button, you see. The rest of the plot was sound. The Earl had a stroke of luck when he discovered and was able to abstract Bristow's father's pistol, and the smudge of blood and Bristow's corresponding wound were brilliant strokes, but with the button Lord Mallerby went too far. I seem to recall a somewhat similar case in Paris in 'eighty-one. There, too, a button was the chief evidence against the intended victim of the crime.'

'Well,' said Allardyce, 'for my own part I believe you have hit upon the truth. But there is no proof, Mr Holmes, nothing to convince a jury.'

'There is one man who knows the truth. If he will only speak.' Holmes turned to Middleton and addressed him in his most coaxing manner. 'No honourable man,' he said, 'would expect you to hold fast to a promise made in such circumstances. When you made your oath, you did not know your master's murderous intentions. Now a man's life is at stake. You must speak the truth.' He paused, watching the man's immobile face. 'Do not speak now, but consider for a while, review the terms of your promise, and make your statement to Mr Allardyce soon.' Holmes turned to the policeman. 'I believe our friend will talk again before many days have passed, or will, at least, give a written account of the death of Lord Mallerby.'

In this belief, however, Holmes was mistaken. Henry Middleton never uttered another word, and refused to communicate by any other means. There was some argument about whether Bristow should be tried but, despite the intervention of Gregson and Allardyce, he was arraigned for murder that July. Lord Mallerby's status and influence were such that an imputation of suicide and attempted murder could not be made against him without clear proof. Holmes spoke at the trial, as did Allardyce and several of the servants to both households. But the jury was not convinced, and Bristow was convicted of the wilful murder of his father-in-law, the Earl. He was hanged at Newgate in January 1902.

Holmes was deeply depressed at this failure of British justice, and the outcome of the case was, I believe, one of the reasons for his decision to retire the following year (though he later re-marked to me that the replacement of the Bertillon system by the science of fingerprinting had made the job of the police a good deal easier after 1903, so that his services were no longer required – an opinion he subsequently had cause to revise). Holmes appealed thrice to Middleton to break his silence, but he was obdurate. The valet died in a lunatic asylum six months after Bristow's execution without speaking another word.

VII

The Remains of Sherlock Holmes

IT WAS IN THE SPRING OF THE YEAR 1929 that my friend Sherlock Holmes died. That, at least, is my belief, though his death has never been certified and his mortal remains have not been found. Rumours of his continued existence abound. Reports of secret work in Paris and Munich have reached my ears, and he is said to have been seen in India, dressed as a Yogi, sitting cross-legged in a cave in the Malabar Hills. But I alone am in a position to understand his peculiar fate. I intend to record what I know of Holmes's last days and, at the same time, to answer a number of disgraceful pronouncements that have appeared in the papers since his disappearance first came to public notice.

Sherlock Holmes spent his later years, as he had long intended, in solitary contemplation and apiculture on the South Downs. It is generally known that he retired from professional practice on attaining his fiftieth year. The rooms at Baker Street were vacated that August, and the chemical apparatus, books and paraphernalia of the life of a consulting detective, including the hundreds of volumes of his commonplace-books, were packed up and despatched to the small farmhouse he had found in Sussex. I once remarked in print that it lay five miles from Eastbourne, but this was a deception, intended to preserve the privacy he valued so highly. Mrs Hudson delayed letting out the Baker Street rooms for more than three years, believing that Holmes would change his mind and return to practice before very many months had passed. However, he settled readily into his rural retreat.

I visited him sometimes at week-ends, as far as my metropolitan practice and domestic commitments would allow. His mind was active as ever and subject to a certain restlessness, not entirely alleviated by long periods of research, the study of his beloved bees and the writing of a series of scientific monographs. He had determined to take no more cases, but it did not surprise me that he broke this resolution on several occasions. He was never tempted by the large fees offered from time to time, but took only those cases which held exceptional interest, or in which he felt he could do service to a friend. Many will have read his own account of his solution to the Fitzroy McPherson mystery of 1907. There are a dozen other cases undertaken after his retirement that deserve to be more widely known. In 1909, for example, he solved the mystery of the Blanchard abduction without leaving his rural villa, and in the following year advised the police in their successful pursuit of Allibone, the last of the resurrection men.[1] In 1912 he was persuaded, by the personal intervention of the Prime Minister, to undertake a secret commission for the government, and spent two years in America infiltrating a Fenian society in order to defeat the plans of our Nation's enemies. While this was 'His Last Bow' to the public, as I called it when I published the details of the case some years later, it was not his last case by any means. (Incidentally, I later regretted choosing that title for the story, for many at first misread the word 'bow' to mean the weapon of Cupid and Achilles, and wondered why Holmes should have possessed a final one).

After his success in frustrating the Baron Von Bork, in which I also played a very small part, Holmes returned to his Sussex farmhouse and buried himself once more in recondite studies. He spent a good deal of time with his violin and had some small success as a composer, using an assumed name to publish a number of charming trios and quartets. His character, his brilliance and acuity never varied, though his temper grew a little shorter as he aged, partly perhaps as a result of the rheumatic pains which began to trouble him. For my part, I had retired

1. Accounts of both the Blanchard and Allibone cases were among the papers discovered in 2010.

from practice in 1914 and, after my work in the Great War, moved with my wife to a small town-house in Hastings. Here I continued to act as a consulting surgeon to several hospitals, and began to lecture on medical matters and, occasionally, on the cases of Sherlock Holmes. I chose the location partly in order to be close to my old friend, and after 1919 began to visit him more often. His old housekeeper had died and he preferred to do for himself, cooking simple meals in the stone-flagged kitchen and keeping most irregular hours. During his secret war-work he had been obliged to give up his bees and let the house. But once re-established he acquired six new hives, though claimed his research into the complex lives of their inhabitants had reached a conclusion with the appearance of his *Practical Handbook of Bee-Culture* in 1913.

For some years he worked on a *Complete Guide to the Art of Detection*, but in 1922 abandoned the attempt, remarking that his singular powers were the product of his own mind and nature and could not, in the end, be taught to others. My own lack of success when trying to apply his methods could be seen, perhaps, as proof of this proposition. At the same time, and somewhat to my surprise, Holmes became a vegetarian. Apart from my visits, and the occasional appearance of a hopeful client, he shared no human company, though he could move in society as freely as ever when he chose to in the pursuance of one of his special cases. His only domestic companion was a large brindled cat which he called, for reasons best known to himself, 'Higgins'. I suggested once that 'Moriarty' would be more suitable, but he replied that the creature was far too unintelligent to bear that name.

As the years passed Holmes became a little less reserved about his people and his early life. When we talked by the fireside, smoking and reliving past adventures, I learned, for example, that he had had two brothers. I knew Mycroft, of course, and had been saddened to hear of his death during the Great War. But there had been another Holmes scion, the first-born, named

Sherrinford, who had been a minor artist and had died in mysterious circumstances in Egypt in 1885. Holmes had travelled to Cairo to reclaim his body, and had tried to determine the cause of his death, without any success. I was surprised to learn this, as we had been friends at the time, though I was in America when the tragedy took place. Holmes had spoken not a word of it on my return.

On the twenty-fifth day of June 1925, my beloved wife died. It has been my great blessing to have thrice married beautiful and intelligent women, and my great misfortune to have outlived all three. Holmes varied his usual rule of self-imposed isolation to attend the funeral, and afterwards made the suggestion that I move into his farmhouse. Weighed down as I was with grief I could hardly consider this at the time. But before the year was out I saw the sense of the idea, and moved my few important possessions into the spare bedroom of Holmes's villa.

Thus we found ourselves, a brindled cat and two elderly bachelors in robust, but slowly failing health, sharing rooms as we had done for so many years in youth. Between January 1926 and March 1929, we lived an almost ideal existence. I daresay our domestic arrangements were a little makeshift and informal, but we were comfortable enough and content with the wildness of the sea, the beauty of the countryside and our respective tasks. While Holmes worked on his private studies and chemical experiments, I attempted to bring order to my notes of his cases, and to prepare the important ones for future publication. At the same time I put the finishing touches to a basic manual of surgery on which I had been working since before the War.[2] We also had, as I have intimated, several new adventures to exercise us. I may not have held my revolver quite so steadily, and Holmes was hardly the brilliant pugilist of his youth, but we still counted ourselves formidable enemies to the criminals of England. The Curious Business of the Hollow Effigy and

2. Published as *Fundamentals of the Art of Surgery* (London: William Heinemann (Medical Books) Ltd, 1926).

the Mystery of the Black Lacquer Cabinet are cases from this late period which I hope to place among the papers to be published at a suitable interval after my death.[3] Our final adventure, that I am about to relate, is among the more extraordinary of Holmes's career. Before I begin the story, however, there are several newspaper reports, published following the news of my friend's disappearance, that demand comment. I would have replied to these stories at the time, were it not for Holmes's insistence in his later years that I refrain from publishing anything further about him until at least fifty years after his death.

In a well-known article of August 1929, a certain Colonel Harkness made the suggestion that my friend Sherlock Holmes was a homosexual. I can understand, perhaps, why such a suspicion might arise in the mind of someone who had not known Holmes well. He did not care for the company of women and, so far as I know, never formed an intimate attachment with a member of that sex. His only close friends were male and his closest friend was, of course, myself. But I can state, quite categorically, that our relationship was in no way like that suggested by Colonel Harkness. Apart from one incident in his youth, Holmes never, I am convinced, engaged in sexual intimacy of any sort. But perhaps, in truth, his inclination was in the direction suggested by the Colonel. It is to Holmes's great credit that he only once submitted to those impulses and lived thereafter the life of a scholar-monk.

More outrageous still is the claim of Herr Gottfried Drukker in a German newspaper, widely reported in England, that Holmes was, in fact, a. Drukker mentioned the cases of Hannah Snell in England and Deborah Sampson in America, and spoke of 'Pope Joan'. He cited Holmes's true gender as the cause of his hostility to women and close friendship with myself. He also claimed to have found the parish register recording Holmes's birth, where the sex was given as 'girl' and the forename was

3. These stories too are among those discovered in 2010. The 'Hollow Effigy' is one of the most surprising stories found, but will need careful editing.

unclear, suggesting that it should correctly be read as 'Shirley'. On such ridiculous speculation I need say no more than this – I have often accompanied Holmes to the Turkish bath and know that he was biologically male, and physiologically normal, in every respect.

One more published observation on the great detective deserves mention, though it appeared in a little-known medical paper some years before my friend's disappearance. In the *Journal of Psychological Pathology* for June 1923, Dr Ephraim Nunn suggested that Professor Moriarty had not existed but was merely a fantastical projection of Holmes's mind, a criminal counterpart to himself, that the great intellect had needed to create in order to defeat, thus disposing of the darker side of his own nature. At first this proposition seemed almost as ridiculous as that of Herr Drukker. But then I looked over the notes I had made in 1891, at the time I accompanied Holmes in his curious pursuit of, and flight from, Moriarty. I found that throughout that long journey, which resulted in the apparent death of both Holmes and his opponent at the Reichenbach Falls, I had laid eyes on the Professor only once, as he pursued our train along the platform at Victoria Station. A tall gentleman was pointed out to me by Holmes. Was he Moriarty, or some quite innocent traveller who had failed to catch his train?

I had never heard of the Professor before the outset of that particular case, and it resulted in his complete disappearance from the world, so that I came to doubt whether he had really existed. I did a little research, and found that James Moriarty, Professor of Mathematics, had lived and worked in Birmingham and had published treatises on the Binomial Theorem, Integral Calculus and other subjects. Yet I could find no evidence of criminal activity, and no dark rumours attaching to his name. Certainly a large criminal gang had been convicted in 1891 as a result of Holmes's labours, but there was no indication that this Professor Moriarty had been their leader. He seemed to have lived a life of quiet study. I could find no trace of him

after 1890, save that a man using the name Colonel James
Moriarty and claiming to be the Professor's brother, published
two letters in *The Times* in January 1893 describing the death of
Moriarty in most fanciful terms. It was these reports that led
me to publish my own account of what I then believed to have
been the demise of Sherlock Holmes. Could the James Moriarty
whom Holmes had defeated at Reichenbach really have had a
surviving brother with the same forename? Or did Holmes
invent the wicked Professor as an opponent on his own level,
when the real criminals of London were so very far beneath
him? Despite the confusion over his name, and the lack of
material evidence, I have concluded that Holmes did not invent
this enemy. I have never known a clearer mind than that of my
friend, and cannot believe it to have suffered from the pathology
suggested by Dr Nunn.

Now I must turn, with a heavy heart, to the painful case which
preceded my friend's disappearance from the world. It came to
our door in early March 1929, in the form of a telegram from an
acquaintance of mine. Samson Cardew was the manager of a
hotel at Hastings, and a near neighbour to my former medical
practice. His message ran in this way:

Dear Dr Watson

Most horrible incident. Calling Wednesday, eleven. Beg
you ask Holmes advise.

Cardew

I showed the telegram to Holmes, whose only comment was
that Cardew was either a poor man or a miser, since he had
paid for too few words for the message to convey anything of
his problem. For my sake, he agreed to listen to the fellow's
story and offer what advice he might.

'What do you know of this Samson Cardew?' he asked.

I told him what little I could, adding that I had met him only once or twice. 'He is a rather plump gentleman,' I added, 'and gives the appearance of being well-to-do. I believe his hotel business has been a success. His mother, Agnes, was a great friend to my late wife.'

'Is his father still alive?'

'No. I believe it was his death, and Samson's inheriting his business, that precipitated the move to Hastings after the War. I know no more.'

'Then we must possess ourselves in patience, and wait to learn what has ruffled this *hotelier*.'

We did not have long to wait. The telegram had arrived before breakfast on Wednesday morning, and well before eleven we heard the growl of an engine and looked out to see a battered Austin pull up at the gate of our farmhouse. Cardew burst from the car and hurried along the path to our door.

'My dear sir,' said Holmes, when our visitor had been admitted and was seated by the fire, wringing his driving-cap in his plump hands, 'pray take a few moments to calm yourself. Then tell us how we may assist you.' Cardew was even fatter than I remembered him and wore a thick, greying moustache in the style made popular by the late Earl Kitchener. His face was very pale, and he was sweating prodigiously. There was a piece of sticking-plaster on his chin, which bore a dark brown streak of blood.

'I see,' said Holmes, 'that you have recently been the victim of an assault by someone armed with a knife. Is this, perhaps, the horrible incident of which you speak?'

'It is, sir,' replied Cardew, raising a finger to the sticking-plaster. 'But how could you know I had not cut myself while shaving, or in some other accidental way?'

'Simply from the size and shape of the wound. The blood-stain shows it to be too long and curved to have been caused by a razor held by a careful man, which I perceive you to be. An accident is unlikely to have caused such a wound. The most probable cause is a knife, wielded by a right-handed man, standing to your right when the attack was made.'

'He *was* standing to my right and, now you come to mention it, held the knife in his right hand. But again ...'

My friend waved a thin hand. 'The angle and shape of the cut suggest just such an arrangement. Try it yourself with a letter-opener and a willing friend, and you will have the proof.'

'Remarkable.'

'Rudimentary. I wonder, Mr Cardew, whether you and I have met before?'

'It is possible, Mr Holmes, if you have spent time in Hastings. Or perhaps we met in London before the War.'

'Hmm. Possibly. Now, if you feel equal to the task, perhaps you would tell us your story?'

'Very well. I am the proprietor of Cardew's Hotel in Hastings. I acquired the business ten years ago, and I flatter myself that I have done well in it. I say that I am the proprietor, but really I am the Manager. My mother owns the Hotel, but she is pleased to leave everything to me. We were running along quite happily, until yesterday when one of our guests, a man called Bateman, asked for a private interview with me. He is, I suppose, in his middle forties, about my own age in fact, of genteel appearance, small in stature and with a bland face. He had been a guest for several days, and I had paid little heed to him. To my surprise, once we were seated in my office and the formalities were over, he told me that he was a collector of children's verse and was making a study of nursery rhymes. He asked me to repeat for him any which I remembered from my own childhood. This seemed a most unusual and slightly impertinent request, and not one that required the private interview he had demanded. I thought for a moment, and repeated for him Baa Baa Black Sheep and Twinkle Twinkle Little Star. He took out a notebook and made a few desultory pencil marks on one of the pages.

'"There must be something else?" he asked, in a most insist-ent tone. To tell the truth I had, by this stage, begun to suspect that he was, for some reason, trying to induce me to recite a particular rhyme which my father had taught me forty years ago. It is a curious piece of doggerel, but had been my father's favourite and he had taken great pains to teach it to me. I have particular reason to remember this rhyme, Mr Holmes, for my father mentioned it on his death-bed. Indeed, his final words to me were "Remember Charlie Vincent" – that was the name of the rhyme, "Charlie Vincent". Anyway, I decided to draw Mr Bateman on a little.

'"Do you have anything particular in mind?" I asked.

'"No, sir," said he. "But the rhymes you have told me so far are commonplace things. I am looking for the unusual. Surely, there is some such thing in your childhood?"

'I shook my head and said, "I cannot recall anything."

'Bateman sighed and tried again. "Something, perhaps, about a man named Vincent?" said he. Clearly I was right about his intentions, though I could not imagine what his game might be. Again I shook my head and told him I could remember no such rhyme. Then, quite suddenly, Bateman sprang from his chair and ran round the desk to my side. Before I knew it, he had me by the hair and a knife was pressed to my throat. I daresay it was unwise of me, Mr Holmes, but I tried to struggle to my feet and throw him off, and received this cut to my chin as a reward. He held me fast, and hissed, in a quite different tone from that he had used before, "Tell my the rhyme, or I'll slit you!"

'"What rhyme?" said I.

'"Don't play games with me," said he. "You know what I want. Tell me Charlie Vincent, and be quick about it!"

'I tried to think. For all it was a piece of nonsense, the last thing I wished to do was to oblige this ruffian. I reasoned that there must be something more to Charlie Vincent than I knew, and determined to keep it from him if I could. "I have forgotten it," I stammered.

'"Then my knife will help you remember!" said he, as he pressed it close against my neck.

'"I swear to you. All I can remember is the first two lines." I recited these, haltingly as if I were struggling with memory. I wondered if he would try to get the whole thing from me a couplet at a time. But I swore again that I could remember no more, and I think he believed me. There was frustration in his eyes, and fury too, and I thought for a moment he would really kill me for these few foolish words. I was on the point of telling him the whole thing, when he uttered a terrible oath and pushed me roughly away. I fell sideways from my chair, and when I drew myself together and rose from the floor Mr Bateman was gone.

'I hardly need tell you what an unpleasant impression this incident left upon my mind, to say nothing of my poor chin. I have particular reason to fear a knife-attack, for it is the way my father died. Almost as disturbing was the idea that a simple nursery rhyme which I knew could be the occasion for such violence. How did Bateman know about the rhyme? Why did he esteem it so highly? I began to ponder these questions, and it occurred to me that my mother's friend Dr Watson was intimate with the great Sherlock Holmes and, to him, such opaque matters might be transparent.'

'Did you not go to the police?' asked Holmes.

'I did. They are pursuing this Bateman, though they told me not to expect too much, as he had no particular physical features and his name was probably assumed. They checked his room and found no clues. All the door-knobs had been wiped clean of fingerprints, so they knew him to be an experienced criminal. It was a difficult business, as I wished to keep my troubles from my mother, who lives with me in the Hotel, and I had to ask the officers to do their work discreetly. I did not want to distress her and said nothing of the attack, telling her my wound was a shaving injury. As to the nursery rhyme, the police hardly took that seriously, and told me that Bateman was probably deluded. Here, Mr Holmes, I have taken the liberty of writing it out for you.'

Cardew reached into his jacket pocket and produced a folded sheet of paper which he handed to Holmes, who spread it out on the small table beside the fire. It bore the following verse:

> Charlie Vincent loved a dare
> Cheated Pete to pluck a pear
> Fleeced the fruit to fox an egg
> Stayed inside his hollow leg
> Sheeny green and shiny blue
> Sixteen faces all askew
> Kept his pear as a banana
> In the robes of Gloriana

'When I looked at it again,' said Cardew, 'I could see certain indications in the text. The reference to cheating hints at crime, and I can see that the pear mentioned could be a diamond, or some such precious stone, with its "faces all askew". But I can see nothing beyond these suggestions.'

Holmes smiled and rubbed his hands together in a familiar manner. 'I begin to see a light,' said he. 'Your late father holds the key to the mystery, I think. Please tell me a little more about him.'

'Well, Mr Holmes, it is curious that you should say he holds the key, for throughout his life he kept a small key on a chain about his neck. I have it here.'

Cardew loosened his tie and pulled at a gold chain which looped round his broad neck. At the end was a small, tarnished metal key, which he held out towards us. Holmes took up his glass and looked at it closely, turning it this way and that before letting it fall.

'No markings,' said he. 'But I recognise the sort of key. Now, please, tell me of your father.'

'His name was John Cardew and he was a pawnbroker in Conduit Street, until his passing in 1918. He was a successful man, Mr Holmes, and ultimately owned four shops in different parts of the city. I had no stomach for the business myself and, after his death, my mother and I decided to sell the shops and move to Hastings. He had not always been a pawnbroker, however. He was born of noble blood, and once told me that his grandfather had been a Duke. But he had been disowned by his family, and spent the first part of his life as a sailor; he was able to make some money in the Navy which he used to found the pawnbroking business in 1900. I have happy memories of him from my childhood, but for ten years, from when I was six to sixteen, he was constantly at sea and I saw nothing of him. My mother received occasional letters from around the world, and she would read them to me again and again, so that I came to know them by heart. Sometimes he mentioned Charlie Vincent, which he had taught me in my earliest youth, and now it seems that he was trying to keep the rhyme alive in my mind. Occasionally he spoke of presents he had bought for me in some exotic port, which he promised to deliver when he returned to England. I waited with keen anticipation for many years and, when at last he came to our house, his bag on his shoulder, I was not disappointed. There were the presents he had promised but, more importantly, there was my beloved father. My mother wept with joy, and he promised never to return to sea but to seek some inland occupation. After that he was, I believe, the ideal father. He cared for my mother and myself and built up the business. I became his apprentice but, as I say, the work of a pawnbroker did not suit me, though I did my best as long as father was alive.

'Our lives were very happy and secure for many years. The War affected us, of course, and I volunteered and served first in Belgium and then in Turkey. Many were much less fortunate than myself and lost their lives, or their reason. But I was blessed and survived the whole affair without a scratch. I flatter myself that I did my duty, and my pleasure at the Armistice would have been immense had it not co-incided with the death of my dear father. I received a wire while in transit back to England saying that he had been attacked in the street and lay near death. I feared I would be too late, but when I arrived at the hospital I found him still living. I believe he had fought hard against a grim adversary to remain alive long enough to say farewell to me. I came to his bed, and he smiled weakly and said 'Remember Charlie Vincent' before he passed over. At the time I thought it very poignant that he should mention the rhyme, which we had shared in my nursery so many years before, but now I begin to see his words in a different light.'

'I see,' said Holmes. 'Did you learn any more of the attack upon your father?'

'The police told me that two men, one young and one old, had tried to rob him. They took him into an alley near one of his shops where they threatened him with a knife. He was a brave man, Mr Holmes, and put up a fight in which he killed the older robber. But the younger gave him a mortal wound before running away.'

'Do you happen to know whether the older robber was bald?'

'Bald? – Why yes, I believe he was. The constable I spoke to mentioned it because he was a well-known criminal, famous for having no hair of his own and for disguising himself with a variety of wigs. I think his name was Dunn.'

'Archibald Dunn,' said Holmes, 'known as "Baldo", both for his Christian name and his smooth pate.' He thought for a moment, then said 'If I am not mistaken, I believe your father had a scar on his brow.'

'Quite so. A small white scar. Did you know him, Mr Holmes?'

'I came across him. Like many sailors, I imagine his ears were pierced for ear-rings?'

'They were, though I never saw him wearing ear-rings and the holes were virtually healed by the time he quitted the Navy.'

Again Holmes thought for a few moments. 'Some men,' he said at length, 'prefer not to know the truth if it will bring them pain. Are you such a man?'

Cardew hesitated. 'If you mean that my father was not all he claimed to be, then I have long known that to be true. For all I loved him as a son should, I knew from my mother that there was something shameful in his early life, something which had caused his noble family to disown him and which, I guessed, induced him to pursue the remote life of a sailor. If you know the truth, Mr Holmes, then I am ready for it, and beg you to tell me all you know.'

'Very well. I regret to say that your father was not a sailor. During those ten years when he was away from you, he was serving in one of her Majesty's prisons. I know this, for I helped to put him there. You will remember the case, Watson, of the attempted Coburg Square bank robbery of 1890?'

'Of course,' I said. 'The Red-Headed League! Do you mean to say that John Cardew was involved in that crime?'

Holmes nodded. 'He was John Clay, *alias* Charlie Marsh, *alias* Vincent Spaulding, *alias* John Cardew. The last name was, I think, adopted for the respectable side of his life. He married Agnes Cardew in 1883, and took her name in order to conceal his own.'

'Well, well,' said Cardew, 'I often wondered that my mother's maiden name was also Cardew. I was told it was a curious co-incidence that two Cardews should have met and married! But tell me, Mr Holmes, what sort of man was John Clay?'

'A very clever man. But, I regret to say, one who turned his intelligence to crime. When it came to the trial in 1890, I could prove only the attempted Saxe-Coburg Square robbery, but that was enough to get him twelve years. He was released after ten, in recognition of his good behaviour while a prisoner. His accomplice was Archibald Dunn, who was also convicted and sentenced to six years. Clay's sentence was the heavier, since the court recognised that he had planned the robbery and the clever device by which Jabez Wilson was kept from his shop while a tunnel was dug. You may care to know, Mr Cardew, that the shop in question was a pawnbroker's. What your father learned there evidently gave him the training he needed for a new profession. I was aware that Clay had been released from prison in 1900, but I found no evidence of wrong-doing after that date. So I think you may assume that, for all his earlier sins, John Clay became a better man when he became John Cardew.'

The *hotelier*'s lips quivered and he began again to wring his cap. 'Tell me, sir, did he ever hurt anyone?'

Holmes shook his head. 'He was a robber and a forger, but used his brains rather than his fists.'

'Thank God. What you have told me explains certain things that have never made sense to me before. But still there is the mystery of Mr Bateman and of Charlie Vincent.'

'Let me look at the paper again,' said Holmes. He contemplated the curious rhyme for several minutes, then took up a pencil and copied the text into his pocket-book. Once this was done he made some brief notes and scribbles on the pages. For a long while he was lost in these experiments, his brow creased and his mouth working. At length he smiled to himself, made a few more marks on the page, and stood up.

'Would you care to accompany me to London?' he asked.

'To London?' said Cardew.

'Yes. The conclusion of our mystery lies there. Will you come, and you too, Watson?'

'Gladly,' said I. Cardew nodded.

'If you would transport us in your motor-car, Mr Cardew, we can catch a train at Hastings and be at Charing Cross by two.'

When we arrived in Hastings, Holmes directed Cardew first to his hotel to collect papers that would prove his identity, though he would not explain what they were needed for. We also took the opportunity to meet his mother, who lived in a suite of rooms on the top floor. When she heard the name of Sherlock Holmes she raised her eyebrows and a cloud passed momentarily over her face. Perhaps she guessed something of our mission, though Cardew had introduced us only as friends who were to accompany him on urgent business to London. She greeted us with perfect courtesy, but our interview was short as Holmes was anxious to be on his way.

Throughout the train journey my friend was in a state of high excitement. I had seldom seen him so animated and, while we lunched in the dining car, he talked at length of his apicultural theories, his continuing researches into tobacco ash – an evolving discipline, as new tobacco blends are created almost weekly – and his doubts about recent advances in criminology. Both Cardew and I tried to draw him on to the question of our particular assignment, but he always changed the subject, talking now of the significance of the colours of the puffin's bill, now of the remarkable painting technique of Sir Joshua Reynolds. By the time we reached Charing Cross we were no wiser about our mission. Holmes hailed a taxi-cab and instructed the driver to take us to Cheyne's Bank in Black Lion Court. I expressed some little surprise that this establishment still existed.

'Happily for us, Watson, it does. It is one of the few private banks still operating in London. If I am right, we will be inquiring into an account which has been dormant for more than forty years. Had the Bank moved premises or been amalgamated with another, I would have doubted the success of our journey. But Cheyne's is a bank of the old sort, and I have no doubt that all will be well.'

It was five-and-twenty past two when we arrived at the ancient building. Holmes asked to see the Manager and we were shown into a beautiful, old-fashioned office with oak panelling and the warm scent of a century's cigar-smoke. The Manager was a young member of the Cheyne family, and greeted us with old-world civility. For a moment the intervening years vanished, as they sometimes will for old men, and I imagined Holmes and myself engaged in some gas-lit adventure of the 1880s. Then I looked at the modern telephone upon the desk before me and at my own wrinkled hands, which trembled slightly, and was drawn back to the present moment.

'This gentleman,' said Holmes, 'is Mr Samson Cardew, the only son of John Cardew of Conduit Street. He has come to examine the contents of his father's strong-box. I believe it has not been opened since 1885, but I presume that will not be a problem. Here are some papers which will prove Samson the legitimate heir of John Cardew.' He glanced at our companion who produced the documents. Cardew's face bore the same look of bewilderment it had worn since the beginning of our adventure.

Mr Cheyne examined the papers. 'Very satisfactory,' he said at length. 'You will be most welcome to have access to the box, but I fear it will take us some little time to establish the box-number.'

'It is number one-hundred-and-five,' said Holmes casually. Cardew's eyes grew wider still.

'Very well. The only remaining difficulty is the key. If you do not possess your father's original key it may be necessary to employ a lock-smith to open the box.'

Cardew's expression changed again, this time to one of pleasure. 'I have the key,' said he, withdrawing it from his shirt-front and lifting the chain over his head.

'Excellent. Then I will accompany you to the vault myself.'

Mr Cheyne led the way out of his office and down a white-washed corridor to an iron door with a combination lock. This he opened with a deft movement of his hand, and we followed him down a spiral staircase to another corridor. There was electric light here, but the place had clearly not been decorated for many decades; the old gas fittings were still in evidence, and the air was heavy with the damp of centuries. We passed through an iron grille and thence to another iron door, which led to a further staircase. We seemed to be descending into the very guts of London. At last we came to an old wooden door, studded with iron bosses and locked with a huge padlock. Beyond lay the vault. Here, once the electric light had been switched on, we could see shelf upon shelf of strong-boxes of all sizes, each painted with a white number. Cheyne took us to the shelf where Box 105 lay among the others. It was one of the smallest in the room, being little larger than a common house-brick, and was painted dark green. With ponderous slowness Holmes picked it up and walked to the small table which stood at one end of the vault. Here he placed the box so that we could all observe it. The lid was battered and beneath a layer of dust the initials J C were painted in white. Holmes took out his handkerchief and carefully dusted the box.

'Would you care to open it?' he asked Cardew.

The *hotelier* came forward and inserted his key. He struggled for some minutes to turn it in the lock.

'I cannot do it,' said he at length.

'Perhaps you would allow me,' said Holmes. 'I once had remarkable strength in my fingers, through playing the violin and performing certain exercises, and fancy I may still have more power there than the average man.'

'I should be much obliged.'

Holmes gripped the small key and almost at once there was a sharp click and the lid of the box sprang open. We all leaned forward to see what lay within.

My first reaction was, I confess, one of disappointment. This soon gave way to puzzlement. Inside the box were three objects – a manilla envelope, a small brown paper tube as long and thick as a man's finger, and a large bar of yellow Sunlight soap. Holmes seemed exceedingly pleased with this curious collection and chuckled to himself.

'But surely,' said Cardew, 'this is some joke. My late father has been playing a game with us.'

'A game, yes,' said Holmes. 'But no joke, I assure you.' He picked up the paper tube and handed it to our companion. 'Feel the weight, Mr Cardew. This little packet contains gold coins, sovereigns I would guess. No longer legal currency, but worth a good deal as precious metal.' Next he drew out the manilla envelope. It contained a dozen folded South African government bonds. 'These are harder to assess, and may turn out to be worthless. On the other hand they may be worth a great deal. And here,' he drew forth the bar of soap and tossed it to Cardew who caught it clumsily, 'here is something quite remarkable. Do not drop it, Mr Cardew, for it is the most precious object in the box. Indeed, it is, very probably, the most valuable object in this bank.'

Cardew sighed again. 'Are you making sport of me, Mr Holmes?' said he, his voice wavering pathetically.

'Bear up,' said Holmes. 'What I say is literally true. Does it not strike you as rather heavy for a bar of soap?' Cardew shrugged. 'I will show you its remarkable heart.' He took back the bar and laid it on the edge of the table. Then, with his pocket knife, he began to cleave it in two. The ancient soap was hard as oak and Holmes had to saw at it for several minutes before he had made a neat incision round its middle. Then he picked it up and lifted one end away with all the casual ease of a man raising the lid from a butter-dish at breakfast.

Cardew gasped and even Mr Cheyne, who had worn a banker's mask of polite indifference until this moment, drew in his breath. Projecting from the soap was a rough-cut gem-stone, as large as a quail's egg but narrowing at the visible end like the upper portion of a pear. It was a most beautiful and unusual shade of greenish blue.

'Is it an aquamarine?' I asked.

'No, Watson. This is the Ambrook sapphire, also known as the Pallarenda Pear. It weighs over 600 carats and was discovered in 1861 in a diamond-mine at Pallarenda, in Queensland, Australia, owned by the fifth Earl of Ambrook. It was cut, in a rather rough manner, by a colonial jeweller shortly after it was found, but in 1885 Ambrook determined to send it to Amsterdam to have the stone properly faceted. At the time it was valued at over a hundred thousand pounds. However, the stone was intercepted and never arrived in Holland. I was involved in the case, Watson, while you were pursuing other game in the United

States, but failed to recover the stone. I found evidence that Clay and Dunn had engineered the theft, but could never prove it and had at last to inform the Earl that his jewel was lost. To this day the insurance company has refused to pay out, however, and has remained upon the trail of this singular stone.'

Cardew's expression had passed from wonderment to joy and thence to disappointment as Holmes spoke these words. 'I must return the sapphire to Lord Ambrook,' he said. 'It is not mine to profit from.'

'You are quite right. You may perhaps keep the gold, for it will be impossible to return it to its proper owner, and it may, in any case, have been legitimately obtained by your father. But the bonds and the Pallarenda Pear must go to the police. Come, come, Mr Cardew, never look so gloomy. In 1885 the insurance company offered a reward of a thousand pounds and Lord Ambrook agreed to match that sum. I am sure his grandson, the present Earl, will honour that promise when the sapphire is back in his hands. Two thousand pounds, and a packet of sovereigns, is not a bad legacy, after all.'

'You are right, Mr Holmes. But I am ashamed of my father for stealing the stone. I suppose I must be content to know that I can return it to its legal home.' Holmes patted his shoulder. Cardew's face still betrayed considerable disappointment at the outcome of our adventure.

There were certain papers to sign before we could remove the contents of Box 105, but soon enough we were leaving the Manager's office and bidding farewell to the young representative of the great banking family.

'Come now, Holmes,' said I, as we left the building. 'We can wait no longer. Your taste for the dramatic has been satisfied. It is high time you explained everything.'

'I am sorry, old friend, but I must ask you to be patient a little longer, until we are sitting comfortably in the train to Hastings. For now I commend to your attention the venerable symbol of Cheyne's Bank, which represents the origins of the company in Tudor times.' We looked at the shining brass device of the bank, attached to the wall beside its great front-door. It was a head-and-shoulders portrait of Queen Elizabeth.

We took a taxi-cab to Scotland Yard, where the name of Sherlock Holmes still had a galvanising effect upon the officers. Most of his old friends on the force had retired or died – the death of Lestrade is one of those stories I hope to leave among my posthumous papers[4] – but Gregson was still to be found, risen now to the exalted rank of Chief Commissioner. He appeared delighted to see us, and greeted Holmes as a brother, saying indeed that he could never have climbed so high without the advice and encouragement of the great detective. We left the Ambrook sapphire and the South African bonds in his hands, and received his promise that he would return them to their proper owners and ensure that Samson Cardew took the credit. Gregson seemed genuinely affected when we bade him farewell.

Holmes was able to book a private compartment for the return train journey and, when we were settled, he took out the paper bearing the text of Charlie Vincent and laid it upon his knees.

'It is all here,' said he. 'If you can read it. You may remember, Mr Cardew, when we first met I had the impression I had seen you before. This was, of course, because of your resemblance to your father, the late John Clay. When I saw the nursery rhyme a memory was stirred. I am an old man, and memories come slowly from the back corners of my mind. When you mentioned that your father had been a pawnbroker of noble birth, Clay's use of the *alias* John Cardew came back to me, and I remembered the details of the Ambrook case. The nursery rhyme clearly referred to that exploit. Let me read it to you again: -

4. This story, entitled 'The Passing of the Old Detective', was indeed among the papers discovered in 2010.

Charlie Vincent loved a dare
Cheated Pete to pluck a pear
Fleeced the fruit to fox an egg
Stayed inside his hollow leg
Sheeny green and shiny blue
Sixteen faces all askew
Kept his pear as a banana
In the robes of Gloriana

'"Charlie Vincent" is, of course, a reference to Clay, these being two of the Christian names he liked to use. He was a daring fellow, and "cheated Pete to pluck a pear", indicating that he stole the Pallarenda Pear from the fifth Earl of Ambrook, whose given name was Peter. When it disappeared, the stone was in a fleece-lined shark-skin case, and I suspect Clay removed the sapphire and took the case only to his confederate, Dunn, in order to deceive him. Hence he "fleeced" his "fruit" to fool Dunn, who was called by his fellow criminals "Baldo" and also, for obvious reasons, "The Egg".

'The next line is a little more obscure. Since Clay did not himself possess an artificial leg, I suspect it means he hid the gem for a while inside the hollow leg of some piece of furniture, or perhaps of a statue. The next couplet simply describes the sapphire, and the following line indicates that Clay finally disguised the stone as some quite different object, as different as a banana is from a pear. Thus I had expected when we opened the deposit box to find the jewel dressed up as something else. The soap was a delightful touch, and its meaning was immediately obvious to me. Finally, the reference to hiding the pear "In the robes of Gloriana" is a simple code for Cheyne's Bank, which has the Tudor Queen as its emblem.'

'I see how you connected the poem to the crime,' I said, 'once the connection with John Clay was made. But the mention of Gloriana is vague enough, and how could you have known the number of the box?'

'All that can be read in the verse too, for it is an acrostic code. Not a simple one, I grant you, but not impenetrable to the active mind. Look here.' He indicated the rhyme. 'Take the first letter of the first line, the second of the second, the third of the third, and so on, ignoring spaces. What do you have, Watson?'

I took up the paper and began to examine it. 'It spells out C H E Y N E S B,' I said.

'Now, take the last letter of the last line, the second last of the second last, and so on, working upwards to the first. What does that add?'

Again I scrutinised the text. 'That makes A N K B O X C V.'

'Put them together, and you have CHEYNES BANK BOX CV. If we allow the use of roman numerals, it gives an exact location for the missing sapphire. I realised the solution when I looked closely at the fourth line of the rhyme. "Stayed" is a curious word, and many others would have made more sense, or better poetry. I perceived that it must have been necessary to use this word for some reason, and quickly thought of an acrostic. A few trials showed that the Y was the essential letter, and the rest followed easily.'

'Remarkable,' said Cardew. 'To think that I have had the solution in my head for the past forty years without knowing it.'

'Indeed,' said Holmes, and gave a curious smile. 'When we arrive at Hastings you must decide how much of this story you wish to impart to your admirable mother. I suspect she knows a good deal already, but you will have to play your hand as you think best.'

The daylight was fading as the train pulled into the terminus at Hastings. Cardew offered to drive us back to our farmhouse, but Holmes insisted on engaging a taxi-cab. Our new friend thanked us warmly, and hurried off along the platform. When he was gone from sight Holmes said, 'I fear I have misled Mr Cardew in some measure.'

'How so?'

'There was no reason to correct all his mistaken ideas about his late father, and I painted a picture that was rather more pretty than true. The man was no less than a murderer, though I could never prove it to the satisfaction of the police. I also had evidence that he was not entirely reformed after his release from prison. Stolen property was fenced through Cardew's pawnbroking shops, and I heard whispers of other dark dealings there. But why cause the man unnecessary pain?'

'Indeed,' I replied. 'Samson Cardew is clearly made of better stuff than his father.'

Holmes snorted. 'Kinder stuff, perhaps. But denser.'

I do not think I am more slow-witted than the average man, but still felt unclear on certain details of the case, and began to question my friend. 'Why,' I asked, 'did Clay trouble to conceal the location of the sapphire within a nursery rhyme? Why not simply tell his son where it was, especially when he lay on his death-bed?'

'There are several possible explanations. Clay feared that his old accomplice, whom he had cheated, might strike him down at any time, and wanted to give the infant Samson the key in such a form that he would be sure to remember it for the rest of his life. Perhaps he had intended to explain all when the time was right. However, I suspect the main reason was that Clay wanted to test his son. I imagine Samson was something of a disappointment to his father. His mind was not suited to Clay's line of work. He wanted both intelligence and ambition, and was to boot infuriatingly honest. Perhaps Clay hoped he would develop, that he would earn the Pallarenda Pear by cultivating his brains and the criminal streak which he simply did not possess.'

'I see. Now, why did it take so long for Dunn to catch up with Clay, and Bateman with Cardew?'

'Dunn was less successful, less intelligent than Clay, and spent much of his life in prison. He was a free man in 1914, however, but his plans to retrieve the sapphire and revenge himself upon his old partner were probably postponed because his younger accomplice was conscripted. It was no co-incidence that the Armistice immediately preceded the fatal attack on Clay, and his murderer was no doubt among the soldiers who returned from Europe at that time. I believe he was the same man who called himself Bateman, and behaved with such discourtesy to our friend the *hotelier*. Why it took him eleven years to trace Samson Cardew to Hastings I cannot say. Perhaps he too has been in prison, or in hiding abroad following Clay's murder.

'I used to know the criminals of London, Watson. But now I am out of range. I know not whether Bateman is Dunn's son, or merely his *protegé*, and we can only guess how he came to know that the location of the Ambrook sapphire had been concealed within the cipher of a nursery rhyme, of which he knew at least the title. Perhaps Clay let something slip to Dunn in the days before they found themselves in prison. Perhaps Clay mentioned the matter to another convict while in Pentonville. Or perhaps he was troubled by dreams and spoke in his sleep, so that his cell-mate gathered something of the story.'

'I wonder where Bateman is now,' I said.

Holmes was silent. A curious expression of concentration and pain passed over his face. He raised a hand to his breast and I though he was about to suffer a seizure. Then he looked wildly round and, gripping my arm, dragged me towards the exit of the station.

'I have been an utter fool, Watson,' he said between clenched teeth. 'How could I have been so slow-witted? My mind was engaged with the acrostic, and the solution to this age-old mystery, so that I failed to think the thing through. Come, quickly man, quickly, we must engage a cab and drive to Cardew's Hotel. If I am too late, I shall never forgive myself.'

We rushed into the street and jumped into the first of several taxi-cabs that were waiting there. So agitated was Holmes that I feared for his heart and begged him to be still, but he would not cease wringing his hands and cursing himself. In a few minutes we pulled up at the Hotel, and Holmes leapt from the car and ran towards the entrance. I paid the driver and followed him as quickly as I could. At the door we met Samson Cardew, who was moving with equal velocity in the opposite direction.

'Mr Holmes,' he cried, his face the colour of wax, 'thank God you are here! It is my mother, sir. She is dead!'

We hastened to Mrs Cardew's rooms at the top of the building, and I examined the lady. She lay upon the floor of her sitting-room, the smashed remains of several china ornaments on the carpet about her. She had been dead for some hours. Her eyes were wide, and a look of pain and terror was frozen on her face.

'This is the worst possible outcome,' said Holmes bitterly, 'and one which I could have averted, had I possessed a fraction of the mental powers with which *you*, Watson, have credited me.' He sat down upon a chair and rested his head in his hands. Cardew stared stupidly at him, then at me, then at the still, white face of his mother.

'What has happened here?' he asked.

Holmes drew himself upright with an effort. 'I believe Mr Bateman paid a visit to your mother while we were capering in London. I should have known it. By God, I should have known it! When he failed to draw the rhyme from you, he must inevitably turn to your closest relation. He came here and threatened your mother, just as he did you. No doubt he broke these ornaments to frighten her. Perhaps he did not intend to kill her, but he scared the lady so that he did for her all the same.'

'Her heart was weak,' said Cardew. 'She could not have stood his threats for long.' He came to his mother's side and took her hand.

'Did she know the nursery rhyme?' asked Holmes. Cardew nodded. 'Then we may presume she imparted it to Mr Bateman, before ...' He broke off. 'I am heartily sorry for you, Mr Cardew. I have done enough. All I can do now is save you the trouble of informing the police. Come, Watson, we have that small task to perform before this dreadful business is done.'

We left Samson Cardew to grieve for his mother and made our way on foot to the police station. Holmes was a changed man. He moved slowly, stiffly, as if his rheumatism were inhabiting every muscle in his body. He was stooping too, and I saw him clearly for the first time as an old man. At the station he gave the young sergeant at the desk the details of the crime, then wrote a private message to be sent to Gregson at Scotland Yard.

A few days later we were informed that the sapphire had been returned to the seventh Earl of Ambrook, who had immediately rewarded Cardew with the sum of two thousand pounds. In due course the insurance company also paid him its reward, though I fancy Cardew's pleasure at the outcome of our adventure was circumscribed by other emotions.

The man who called himself Bateman evidently had extracted the nursery rhyme from Mrs Cardew, for he appeared at Cheyne's Bank a week later, with forged papers of identity, and was arrested by the police who had been waiting for him on Holmes's instructions. He was quickly identified as Archibald Dunn's only son, Richard, a thief and extortioner well-known to the London police. Like his father he was bald, and had worn a wig when pretending to be Bateman. When he had returned to the Hotel to tax Cardew's mother, he had evidently taken a different disguise but was nevertheless recognised by several of the staff. He was also identified by Cardew as the man who had attacked him, and was later convicted of assault and manslaughter. That he had murdered John Clay, *alias* John Cardew, some eleven years previously could not be proven against him. However, I believe him to be guilty of that crime and also hold him responsible, at least in part, for the death of Sherlock Holmes.

For two weeks after the adventure of the Pallarenda Pear, my friend remained in the blackest depression. I had never known him so morose and so inclined to self-reproach, and grew seriously afraid for his heart and mind. Then he began to rally. It happened slowly, but by early April the spring seemed to have warmed his heart a little and he was something like his old self. He made several trips to London, about which he was unusually secretive. He also began to work again on his research papers and to sort his cuttings and mementos, though he put his chemical apparatus away and said he would not use it again. His bees had been neglected since the death of Mrs Cardew, but now he attended to the hives once more. After a week of careful attention he went out in the middle of the night and sealed the entrances to the hives. In the morning our nearest neighbour, a farmer named Beachcroft, arrived with a small lorry and took the hives away to establish them on his own land.

On the twenty-fourth of April I received a telegram saying that an old patient of mine was severely ill and was asking that I attend her at the last. I could hardly refuse but, when I arrived at the house, found my friend in remarkably good health, with no knowledge of the telegram. I knew then that something was afoot with Holmes, and returned as quickly as I could to our home. It had been a beautiful spring day, but night had fallen and the wind was cold as I approached the farmhouse. The place was in darkness. On the kitchen table I found an envelope addressed to me in Holmes's hand. It contained a short note, which read in the following way:

My Dear Watson

I trust you will forgive my subterfuge in decoying you to London. It was quite necessary that I have a few hours to myself, to prepare for a short sea voyage. Recent events have convinced me that such a journey is overdue. I am pleased to think that I have been of some small service to my fellows during my time on the earth. But that service is now at an end. All my personal property, including the farmhouse, has been legally transferred to you, my dear Watson. My literary remains are sorted and docketed, and you know my wishes on that front. You have been the very best of friends, and of companions, and I only regret that I have not proved a better friend to you. I beg you not to lament my departure. The time has come. Take special care of Higgins, and believe me to be, my dear friend,

Very sincerely yours,

Sherlock Holmes

I looked into Holmes's room to find that he had packed no clothes or supplies for his journey. He had, however, taken my old service revolver with him. This was all I had expected. Holmes may not have known how well I understood the significance of his short sea voyage. In the late summer of the year 1882 he had been deep in one of his periodic depressions. There was no work on hand, and he was in a fever of frustration and misery. As usual, his reaction was to seek escape in a seven-percent solution of cocaine. The injection of the drug usually induced a long reverie, but on this occasion the dream-state was preceded by a period of loquacity. He talked of many matters, of science and philosophy, religion and literature, ultimately fixing, as the drug-ridden mind often will, upon the morbid.

'I do not intend to die in my bed, Watson,' he said. 'If I am not lost in the struggle with evil, or cut down by accident, I shall take the matter into my own hands. I shall know when the time is right for a short sea voyage.'

'A sea voyage?'

'Yes. Even now I have a small boat moored on the coast. I can see myself going down to that boat, filling the bottom of it with stones and rowing out to sea on an ebb tide. I shall have with me a pistol and three cartridges, and, when I am a mile or so from shore, I will tie myself into the boat and discharge those three rounds. Two I shall fire through the planks, below the water-line, and the third I shall use upon myself. In a few minutes I shall rest in the bed of the sea. No one need suffer the shock of discovering my body. No one need know or notice that I am gone. But I will be gone, and my remains will never be recovered.'

What a man may say, or remember he has said, when his mind is in the grip of that drug might be utterly without consequence. He may have been raving. Yet I felt a cold sense of purpose, of logic, behind his words, despite the dreamy look in his hooded eyes. I believe Sherlock Holmes had planned his own death while still a young man.

I lit a lantern and walked down to the shore, where I knew Holmes kept a rowing boat, for sea-fishing and exercise. It was gone and the painter trailed in the water. The sea was very dark, but there was moonlight enough to see its oily undulations. There, I believe, many fathoms down, rest the mortal remains of the great detective, the great reasoner, my great friend, Mr Sherlock Holmes.

THE END